SEPARATED

JEANNETTE KRUPA

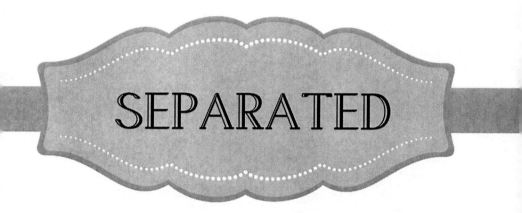

SEPARATED

TATE PUBLISHING
AND ENTERPRISES, LLC

Published by Tate Publishing & Enterprises, LLC
127 E. Trade Center Terrace | Mustang, Oklahoma 73064 USA
1.888.361.9473 | www.tatepublishing.com

Tate Publishing is committed to excellence in the publishing industry. The company reflects the philosophy established by the founders, based on Psalm 68:11,
"The Lord gave the word and great was the company of those who published it."

Book design copyright © 2014 by Tate Publishing, LLC. All rights reserved.
Cover design by Anne Gatillo
Interior design by Jimmy Sevilleno

Published in the United States of America

ISBN: 978-1-62902-449-3
1. Fiction / General
2. Fiction / Family Life
14.01.21

DEDICATION

I WANT TO THANK God for my husband, my five children, my three grandchildren, and one great-grandchild. I thank him for my writing ability, that, through my books, I can bring joy and laughter to many of my readers.

SEPARATED

THE YEAR WAS 1963. Priscilla Cole was about to give birth to her first baby at the age of twenty-five. She had always wanted a baby, but her husband, James, had always told her that they could not afford one. "Wait until I get a better job or at least get some more over time to where we can save a little money." He knew what he was asking from his wife about not having a baby was a lot to ask, but he felt that it was for the best. Although James was a hardworking man, it never seemed like they ever had enough money to care for a child. He worked as a factory worker from early morning to late in the evening, and Priscilla would have his dinner all ready for him to sit and eat when he'd come home at night. The pay he received from his job wasn't much and left them with very little to get by with.

Although it was not planned, Priscilla found out nine months ago that the two of them were going to be having a baby that they couldn't afford, and now she was in labor. She called James at work to let him know that she was about to give birth. He told her that he would leave his work right away and take her to the hospital. She had heard from her mother that having a baby wasn't what it was all cracked up to be, but now she was waiting for James to get home and she was having a hard time breathing.

She wondered if it could be because the baby was very big for her tiny-framed body. Not weighing more than 110 pounds before getting pregnant, and at her last appointment to see her doctor, she was at 170 pounds.

"Hurry, James, I can feel that the baby is ready to come, and I'm having a hard time breathing."

"I'm on my way. Just try and hold on," he said then hung up the phone to hurry home.

Priscilla lay down waiting for James to get home and take her to the hospital. *Just try and hold on—what is he thinking asking me that? Who can wait when they're in labor?* she thought to herself. Ever since she first found out that she was going to be having a baby, she could hardly wait for this day to come; even though James had told her that they couldn't afford an extra mouth to feed, she still wanted a baby. All of her friends had children by now and would ask her from time to time when she and James would be having one. Now that it was finally here, she felt scared; she never remembered anyone telling her that they had a hard time breathing before. *What if something goes wrong in the delivery room*, she thought while taking deep breaths and pushing the baby's foot down from under her rib. She and James didn't know what they were having, and to Priscilla, it didn't matter—all she cared about was that it would be a healthy baby.

"I'm here, Priscilla!" James yelled, coming in the door and looking around for her.

"James, I'm here in the bedroom," she yelled as loud as she could at the time, which wasn't too loud because of all the pain that she was in. "Come help me out to the car."

James helped her while he tried to keep her calm on their drive. "We're almost there, honey. Just hold on. Only a couple more minutes, and we'll be there."

"I think the baby is coming, James. You better pull over. I'm ready to have the baby now," she insisted.

"We're here right now," he said as he pulled right up to the entrance door. "I'm going to get someone to help us. Just a minute while I run inside to get some help."

Priscilla lay in the back of the car, trying not to push. Her back door swung open; a doctor and a lady in white jacket's came to help her on a gurney.

She cried out as she struggled to get on the bed. "Oh, hurry please. I know my baby is ready to be born," she said, gasping for breath.

"You'll be all right, ma'am," the lady reassured her as she was pushing, wheeling her as fast as she could into a room. "Sir, you'll have to wait out here in the waiting room while we take her in the delivery room. Someone will let you know as soon as your baby is born," the nurse told him as she disappeared behind closed doors.

James paced back and forth, while waiting to see what his wife would be having. As he was pacing, he thought for one brief moment that he had seen Bernadine Dell, Priscilla's mother, slip by him and go down a hallway. *How can that be? Priscilla never mentioned to me that she called her mother up, and besides that, she could never have made it here from Tennessee in time for the baby to be born.* James shook his head on the thoughts of what he thought he had seen and focused on having another mouth to feed. He knew that it didn't really matter to Priscilla what they were having, but since they were going to have a child, it should carry on the Cole name.

The nurse came out of the room from where, just more than an hour ago, they had taken his wife in. "Sir, the doctor would like to see you in the room now," she said, then led him down a hallway to where the doctor was.

James walked in the room not knowing what to expect. "Is my wife all right?" he asked, looking around the room to see where she and the baby might be at.

"Your wife is going to be fine. We have taken her to another room. I'd like to talk with you about a matter, if I may?" the doctor asked.

"What is this all about, Doc? Is my baby okay?"

The doctor was surprised by what he heard James ask about a baby. "Baby? Don't you mean 'babies'?"

"Babies? What are you talking about? Are you joking with me?" He was in complete shock.

"Are you telling me that you didn't know that your wife was having twins?"

"Twins!" James spoke louder than usual. "You have got to be kidding me! Really twins?"

"You didn't know?"

"No, this is the first that I heard of it, and my wife must not have known. Otherwise, she would have told me beforehand."

Before thinking about what he would say, the doctor began to ask questions. "Are you prepared to care for twins?"

James stood there, looking at the doctor. "Why are you asking me this?" He looked around the room for a place to sit; he felt like his knees would buckle right out from underneath him. "Twins, I just can't believe my luck. I've always said that we couldn't afford one child, but now we have two to care for," he said just above a whisper, but loud enough for the doctor to hear.

The doctor could tell that James was very surprised about the news of having twins.

"This may not be any of my business, but your wife had told me when she came in here that the two of you couldn't really afford the one that you were having. She said that you work long hours a day to make ends meet now, and she was worried what you would have to do now with an extra mouth to feed."

"Well, she's right about that. We didn't plan on this—it just happened," James said, sounding very irritated about Priscilla talking to the doctor about their business. James liked to keep things that went on in his life between his wife and himself. Now he had the doctor asking him questions about his private life. "Where is my wife at, Doc? What does she think about having two babies?"

"I don't mean to sound like I'm judging you, sir. I'm sure that you do your very best for your family. I'd like to make you a very special offer, if you would like to hear more about it." The doc went on with what he was thinking about and not even answering James's question.

James looked at the doctor, still in shock that he and his wife had two babies to care for now, instead of just the one they thought that they were having. "Offer? What kind of offer?" he asked, unsure of what the doctor was referring too, while still mumbling to himself about he and his wife having two babies to care for.

"I'm prepared to take one of your babies and give it a very nice home if the two of you thought that it might make things easier for you," the doctor said real fast to just get it out there, unsure of what kind of reaction he would receive from James.

"What!" James shouted. "You mean to tell me that you want one of my children? Have you lost your mind? Have you mentioned this to Priscilla?" James asked, rubbing the top of his head, now up from the chair he was sitting in, and pacing the floor. "Where's my wife? I want to see my wife right now."

"Please, sir, calm down. To answer your question if I have talked to your wife about this, no, I didn't. Your wife was having complications giving birth to the two, so I had to give her a shot that helped her to relax. Your wife is sleeping at the moment. I haven't had a chance to talk with her yet."

"Does she even know that she had two babies?"

"No, she is not aware of anything right now."

James sat there, thinking to himself. *How am I ever going to care for two babies? It was hard enough with just Priscilla and me. Now I will have four mouths to feed.* Then feeling under pressure, he asked the question, "What do I have?"

"Sir?" the doctor asked, not knowing what James was asking him.

"The babies, I don't even know what they are."

"You have a boy and a girl. They are both very beautiful healthy babies. I wish that you would consider hearing me out about my offer."

James looked over at the doctor. "And what might that be?" He felt very irritated.

"If you and the missus feel that you can part with one, I would be willing to pay you a great deal of money. It would be enough for you to live a good, wealthy life," the doctor said, looking at James in hopes of getting a baby.

"You would pay us for our child? Why is that? Who does that kind of thing, sell their own child?" He was beginning to wonder if he was having a bad joke played on him by a family member or a friend who knew that he wasn't prepared to care for two babies.

"First of all, I want you to know I have never asked anyone in all my years of being a doctor to sell me their child before."

"Then why me?" James asked, sounding very irritated at the doctor.

"My wife and I have wanted a child for as long as I could remember. She can't have any children, and we have been married for twenty years now, and we have both wanted a child ever since we were married. I was just hoping that if the two of you really felt that you could not afford to care for two, my wife and I would love to have one. We would love it as are very own and would give him or her the very best that life could offer. Also, you would have enough money to make some of your dreams come true too. You would never have to work those long hard hours anymore, unless you really wanted too."

James was not expecting any of what he got today, two babies, nor was he expecting a doctor to offer to buy one of his babies.

"Can I see my wife?" James asked, sounding angry with the doctor. *The nerve of him asking me to sell him one of my children, who*

----

does he think that he is? he thought to himself, but on the inside, he was screaming so loud that he thought he just might have said that out loud.

"Yes, of course, follow me." The doctor got up and walked to a door that led to where Priscilla was still asleep.

When James went in the room where they had taken his wife after giving birth, he was hoping that he would know what to do about his twins. Looking down at Priscilla as she slept, he wondered what the two of them were going to do now with the two extra mouths to feed. He kept hearing the doctor's voice in his head, *A great deal of money.* Now he felt compelled to ask the doctor how much money was he talking about. He walked away from his wife and walked over to the doctor. He didn't want to take a chance that she might hear the two of them talking. What he was about to do, he could hardly believe himself, but he felt at this time in his life, he had no other choice.

"How much money are you talking about if I was to agree with giving you one of the babies?"

He felt so ashamed even thinking about going along with what the doctor was asking him to do, that when he asked the doctor how much money he was talking about, he turned his head away so the doctor wouldn't see the tears that were forming in his eyes.

The doctor looked at James with much hope of getting a baby for him and his wife. "I am prepared to give you one hundred thousand dollars."

"One hundred thousand dollars? I have never even seen that much money before." He began to have all kinds of wild thoughts going on in his head. *I could buy my own business, and I wouldn't have to work so hard like I do now. I could make all my dreams come true for me and Priscilla.* "You know I have dreamth all my life of owning my own business." James looked at the doctor, considering his proposal, then realizing how he made himself sound. "Oh I didn't mean it like that."

The doctor acted like he didn't even noticed what James had said. He went ahead with his statement. "If we were to do this, it would have to be kept between just us. I wouldn't even want my wife to know where I got the baby from."

"Can I see the babies?"

"Yes, they are over in this room," he said as he led James into another room.

James stood there looking at both of his babies, noticing that they took on the same darker color like the French side of his wife. He took their little hands and looked at all their fingers. "They sure are small little ones, aren't they?"

"They sure are, and before long, they will need lots of clothing and all the other things that growing children need. And if you want them to have better than what you said that you been struggling with for all these years, then you will want to send them to college so they can get a good job that pays well."

James looked at the doctor, as he was talking about what the babies would be in need of now and when they are growing up. He thought how for years he has worked so hard to make ends meet; now having two more mouths to feed and to buy for, he just didn't know how he could do it. He thought about how he could own his own business and give both children a better life than he had while growing up. That would make things so much more easier to do if I had the money. "If I were to agree for you and your wife to take one of the babies, which one would you be thinking of taking?"

"It doesn't matter to me or my wife. We would be so happy to just have a baby to love and spoil."

"I know that my wife could never give up one of her children, especially knowing that she had twins. I just can't believe that we have two little ones to care for now, and I work so many long hours now and don't get much time to spend with my wife or to sleep. Now I'll have to really cut back on anything that we might have had a little extra to buy us something special, which does not come by very often," James spoke, still thinking that it will be just too much for him and his wife to care for the two little babies.

"My offer is still open. Don't you think that it will be better to have money for one child than have no money for two?"

James looked at the doctor, knowing what he was saying made perfect sense, although the very thought of him selling a baby, especially one of his own, sounded so insane. "The only way I could do this is to do it behind my wife's back." James knew that he was considering the insane thing to do. "I know that it might make me sound like a terrible person for even thinking this way. But I just don't know how we will be able to care for the both of them. Priscilla has never worked outside of the home before, and now having the babies, she never will be able too."

"I don't think that it makes you sound terrible at all. I think you sound like a man that knows when he can't care for his family the way he knows that they need caring for. If we were to do this, what would you tell your wife?"

James looked over at the doctor, with tears forming in his eyes. "I'd tell her that we have a very handsome son." He looked through a window at his wife still asleep. "Yep, that's what I'd say."

"If we are going to do this, then we don't have long to work here. Your wife will be waking up before long, and I'm sure when she wakes up, she will want to see you and her baby boy next to her bedside." The doctor knew in his heart that James had made up his mind and he had chosen to keep the boy.

"What do we need to do before my wife wakes up?" James said, placing his hands on top of his head, realizing that he was going through with the man's offer. "I will accept your offer. It's not because I don't care for my little ones. It's because I do love them that I want a better life for the both of them."

"I know that it is because you care. I can see that this is a hard decision to make. Come with me down to my office. We will write up some paperwork to make this a legal binding between the two of us."

James followed the doctor down to his office; all the while, he was trying to make his mind change about not going through with this decision behind his wife's back. But he was sure that if she knew that she had given birth to two babies, she would never let one go. James knew that it would be nearly impossible to care for the two of them on what he made for a living. He knew what he was about to do would change Priscilla and his life forever.

"Now, James, what we are about to do cannot ever be mentioned. It must never be told to another ever. We will have to work here real fast. That shot that I gave your wife will be wearing off anytime now."

"What are you suggesting that we do?" James never had any schooling after he graduated from high school, so to him, he figured that the doctor must know what formalities they needed to do to make this become legal between the two of them. "What about the nurse, what do we do about her knowing?"

"You don't have to worry about her at all," the doctor told him while filling out some paperwork.

"Why is that? We wouldn't want her to tell my wife that she has two babies, now would we?"

"No, we wouldn't want that to happen. But that nurse will never say anything about what we are planning on doing here."

"Are you sure about that?" James asked.

"I'll take a baby home to my wife today, and you and your wife will care for the one left here until he is released from the hospital. On top of the hundred thousand that I will be giving you, I will make your bill here with us disappear." The doctor was talking as if he never heard anything that James was saying to him; he was trying to get it over with before James was to change his mind or Priscilla was to wake up.

"Are you sure that the baby will be all right leaving the hospital so soon?" James questioned the doctor.

"Yes, they both are very healthy babies. I'm sure she will do fine."

"How do you know that we can trust that the nurse won't say anything to my wife or anyone else?"

"Because that nurse is my sister—she won't be telling anyone anything."

"She's your sister. I guess that does change a few things then. Why did you tell me that we couldn't tell your wife if she's behind this whole matter?"

"My wife doesn't know anything, and my sister will not reveal to her the matter of what is taking place here and now. I never told you that she was my sister before because I didn't want you to think that we planned this all along."

"Did you? After all, you are my wife's doctor?"

"No, I am not her doctor that she has been seeing. I was just on staff when she came in here. Her doctor is Dr. Ted Zimmerman. My name is Michael Freytag. I had no way of knowing that your wife was having two babies. But after your wife was telling my sister and me about how hard the two of you struggle to make ends meet, we were just hoping that this could be a chance for my wife and I to have a baby after all of these years."

"I believe you, Doc, and I am going to give you a daughter to love and raise as you're very own. What do we need to do now to make this legal?" James asked just to get this over with before he was to change his mind. He could feel that his heart was racing faster than normal and the palms of his hands held sweat to them that it felt like he had them under some water.

The doctor sat behind his desk, drawing up some paperwork, then handing them to James.

James began to read what the doctor wrote on paper. "Okay, I'll sign it. Can I hold her just once before you take her home?"

"Come with me. I can't tell you how much this means to my wife and me. I know I'm speaking for her right now, but I know that this is a dream of the both of ours."

James bent over to pick up the little girl. He held on to her so close to his chest. The doctor stood there watching as tears

----

formed on James's eyes, then he handed her over to the doctor. "She's all yours. Please love her as her mother and I would have."

"I promise you, we will love her with all of our hearts. She will have the very best that life could offer." The doctor spoke, holding the baby, with a smile written all over his face. "James, we need to go back down to my office, so you can wait there for me to go to my bank and withdraw the money from my personal account."

"Don't you think that people will wonder where I got so much money from?"

"Yes, if you let people know that you have all the money." The doctor saw how James was looking at him. "I invested a while back ago and made a nice profit on it. I'm glad that I did now so I could have me a daughter. No one in town knows that I have all that money because I didn't tell anyone. The banker isn't going to tell anyone because they want your business."

James waited for the doctor like he was instructed to do, in the meantime his sister the nurse had taken the baby girl home. James paced in the doctor's office back and forth wondering if he was doing the right thing. *Am I completely insane? Have I lost my mind? What am I doing even thinking about selling my baby girl?* He picked up his pace much faster until he felt like he was about to lose his mind. He knew that if he didn't sit down, he would fall down. He grabbed a hold of a chair and plopped on it so fast and hard that the chair tipped over on him, sending him straight to the floor, in where he was at when the doctor arrived back with the money in a big brown paper bag.

"Are you all right? Why are you sitting on the floor?" the doctor asked, helping James up from the floor.

"I tried to sit in the chair, but I somehow wound up on the floor. Look, Doc, I don't know if I can do this. What kind of a person will I be selling my little girl?"

The doctor stood there, placing the bag on his desk. "James, can I be frank with you?"

"Yes."

"You think that it will make you a bad person to be thinking about giving your child to another home. But I think that it takes love and courage to do what you have said that you would do. You see, not only will you be blessing my wife and I with a daughter, but you will be blessing your wife and son with a life that they deserve, one that will allow them to have nice things, as well as the little girl, whom, by the way, my sister has already taken her home to my wife."

"I know that you're right. I just feel like the worse person in all the world for doing this. It's going to take me some time to get over what I've done behind my wife's back. I wonder how long that it'll be before I stop feeling guilty, or if I ever will stop."

"So then we are going through with this decision I take it? Because once you have this money in your hand, there is no going back," the doctor spoke with authority.

James stood there looking at the doctor, then he reached out and took ahold of the bag. "We are going through with it, but I want you to know this isn't about the money. It's about giving both my children a better life, one that they can be proud of and not feel like they never have anything." He held the bag close to him. "Please love and care for her like her ma and I would have."

With those words spoken, he headed to the door with tears streaming down his cheeks, knowing that he would never again see his little girl. The doctor knew that James had made the right choice, but he also knew that it was hard for him to make it. James walked out to his car and put the bag of money in the trunk, then walked back into the hospital to be next to Priscilla when she woke up.

When Priscilla opened her eyes and saw that James was next to her bedside, she gave him a big smile. "What did we have?" were her first words.

James had tears come down his cheeks again, hoping that he could pull it off that they had one child. "We have a very handsome boy. I think he takes after your side of the family, having the darker skin tone like the French."

"When can I see him?"

"I'll go and see if they will bring him in your room. He may be getting a little hungry. After all, you have been asleep for a while now."

James left the room to talk with a nurse about the baby. Soon he was back with his son in whom he choose to keep.

"What do we name him?" James asked?"

"David," Priscilla said without thinking long about the name.

Days went by, and Priscilla was home with their little boy. James continued to work at the factory and waited before buying anything out of the money he had. He was trying to come up with a good enough reason to tell his wife about the money, or he could be like the doctor said and not even tell her anything about the money. He found a man who worked in the bank where he was putting his money at. The man said it was the bank's policy to never reveal to another what other bankers have inside of their accounts. Although James was a little worried about someone finding out about his money, he knew that he had to put it in the bank; he knew that he couldn't carry around that type of money with him. What if someone was to see him take some out of his car, or better yet, what if he was robbed? No it had better go into a bank where it would be safe.

After walking down the street on the main road to get himself some lunch before heading back to work, he saw the little grocery store that most the people of Port Sanilac went to do their shopping at was for sale. He had always wanted to own his own business, so he went inside to talk with someone that he knew could help him. After talking to a man at the counter, he was directed to go see the owner in the back room of the store.

"Hi, my name is James Cole." He tried to make himself look like a businessman, holding up his shoulders, where they seemed larger than usual, but forgetting that he was in his dirty factory clothes. "I was walking by the store when I noticed that you have a sign in the window saying your store is for sale."

"Yes, that's true. After fifty years, I'm selling it and moving to Florida."

"Can I ask you why you're selling it?"

"I want to retire where it's warm, and Michigan is not warm at certain times of the year. I know that you know that because I have seen you come in here in the winter months yourself to pick up some food."

"Yes, you're right about that. The winters here can be very cold at times. I thought about moving myself, but the wife wants to stay close to her family and friends. Although her parents have moved to Tennessee a few months ago." Then thinking to himself, he never did understand how she wanted to live by her folks when they never did see eye to eye.

"Are you looking on buying your own business?" the store owner asked, looking at the way James was dressed.

"Yes, as a matter of fact I am, and I was wondering how much are you asking for this place?"

"I have it listed for thirty thousand dollars. Do you think that you would be able to get a loan for that amount of money if you were interested?" he asked James in hopes of selling his store.

Before thinking what he was about to say, he blurted out something that should have been kept quiet. "I wouldn't need. a loan I have the money in the bank now if I wanted to buy it." James talked with pride to have so much in the bank, even though he knew that it came with a high price. But that was not for any other to ever know about. Then he thought to himself, *Maybe I should have never of said anything about all my money, I should have just said that I could get a loan if I was interested in buying.* James could see how the man was looking at him like he might have robbed a bank or something. "I made an investment, and it really paid off," he told the same story as the doctor did.

"Oh." The owner looked at him quite surprised. "Well, would you be interested in buying this store then? I could show you all the ropes on how things are done to keep the business going." He was hoping to talk James into it; after all he did say that he had the money, so there would be no waiting for the approval of a loan.

"I'd like to know if you make a good profit on the store?" James asked, wanting to know everything about the store.

"Well, sure I do. You can't keep a business opened up for all these years and not make a profit. I have done very well for myself owning this store, but I'm getting older, and to me, it feels like each winter is just getting colder. I need to be where the weather is much warmer. These bones of mine don't work as well as they used to back when I bought the store a number of years ago."

James looked at the short little gray-haired man, understanding about the cold winters that come every year. "I don't know anything about running a business like this," James told the man.

"If you are serious about buying a business like this one, then I will teach you all the things that are involved in running a good business. Then after I'm done, I would hope that you would take it off my hands so I can make that move to a warmer climate."

"I am very interested, and I would love for you to teach me everything that there is to know. I haven't had much schooling in my life, getting married young and all. And I've been at the same job for nine years now. I need a change, now that my wife and I have just had our first baby a few days ago."

"Congratulations with your baby! When would you like to learn how to make a business work and earn a nice profit?"

"I guess I'm ready anytime."

"Is tomorrow too soon?"

"What time do I start?" James asked with excitement.

"We open at 7:00 a.m. You can come in then. That way, you can see how we start out our day in the store."

"I'll be here. I'm sorry I didn't ask you your name."

"Sam Porter, and what is your name again?" he asked, knowing that James had given him his name when first coming in the store, but he had forgotten it.

"My name is James Cole. I live right here in town. I'll leave you to your work, but I'll be back in the morning."

The two men shook hands, then James walked out of the store, so excited about coming in the next morning and learning all that he could about running a store.

James went home trying to come up with a good reason for his wife as to why he was quitting a job of nine years. *I have to make it look like I got a new job, at least until I can come up with a good enough reason to how I got money to buy the store.* He knew in his heart that he was already planning on buying the store.

"I'm home. Honey, where's my big boy at?" James asked, coming through the door wanting to see his little baby boy.

"You're home early. Since when do you get home by five o'clock?" she asked after looking at the clock to see what time it was.

He wasn't sure on what excuse he could give her, so he just began to talk. "I quit my job."

"You quit your job? But why? What happened. We are having it hard enough to make ends meet. Why would you do something like that after we just had a baby?" she asked, surprised by what she had just heard.

"If I was ever going to see my son, then I needed something different. I couldn't go on living life and not spending time with my family. I want to be part of my son's life too, you know."

"So now what will happen to us?" She looked at him, wondering why he was sounding so upset.

"You don't need to worry about that. I got another job, one that won't keep me from my family like that factory job has done for so many years." He brought his tone of voice down a bit.

"You got another job?" she asked so surprised, knowing that he had had the same job ever since he finished high school. "What kind of job did you get?"

"I was talking with the grocery store owner, Sam Porter, about me having a new baby and how I would love to be able to see you and the baby more than I do now. So he offered me a job, and I took it." James knew what he had just told his wife a flat-out lie, but he couldn't think of what to tell her right off the top of his head.

"The grocery store? Oh, James, you have got to be kidding me! There is just no way that you will make enough money working there."

"Yes, I will, honey."

"Is the pay better than what you are getting now?"

"Yes, it is better. I will be making more a week than I do now, and I won't be away from you and David like I have been."

"How did you hear about the job? What made you go down to the store and ask about work?"

James didn't know what to say at first; he wasn't expecting her to ask him so many questions. He hadn't thought out everything that he needed to cover all the questions.

"I heard some talk at work from some of the other guys, so I wanted to get down to the store before one of them did." He didn't want her to know that he was really going to buy himself some lunch, instead of eating the same, old boring lunch that his wife had packed for him over the years.

"Then I'm very happy for you, honey. I'm happy for us. If you are getting paid more money and won't be working as many hours, that's a good thing. I know that little David and I will be happy to have you around here more."

James picked up the baby. He was so happy to be home early enough to spend time with him. But the shame that he was feeling inside for all the lies he had been telling ever since the babies were born was adding up to be so many that he wasn't sure if he was starting to believe his own lies. He tried not to think about them; he tried to convince himself that it was all done out of love for his family, so it was okay to tell a lie.

"I'm sure glad to have you home with us, honey," Priscilla said, watching James rock their baby boy. "I never thought that I would see the day where you would be home and awake enough to spend time with me and the baby."

"I feel the same way, honey. The store owner wants me there by seven in the morning. He's going to train me on how to run the store."

"Why is he going to do that?" She was surprised, first because he came home early and now he was talking about running a store. She knew he had never done that kind of work before, nor had he had any schooling in that kind of profession.

James looked at her in shock that she would question every little thing. It wasn't like Priscilla to ask so much. "Because he wants to retire, and he needs someone to take over for him. I was even talking to him about me possibly buying it from him."

As soon as he said the words *buying it from him*, he knew that he had said too much. Now he would have to work fast at coming up with excuses to whatever she might ask.

"How can you buy a store when we have no money, James? You sure are acting different for some reason today. Am I missing something? What is going on? First, you quit a job of nine years. Then you are going to run a store. Now maybe you will be buying a store. I'd love to know how you can do that when up until I got pregnant, you said that we couldn't afford a baby."

"He sounds like he would be willing to work out all those things with me." He made sure to not look at her when talking to her; he was afraid the look of guilt would be seen right through him. He continued to look at the baby as he talked.

"I hope it all goes good for you. We have had it hard enough over the years for this to go wrong when we have a little baby to care for now. Are you certain that you will be getting more money on this job?" She didn't know what else she could say to him at this point; he seemed to have all the answers to her questions.

"Yes, he and I have already talked about the money. I will be bringing home more than I did at the factory. Now, can we enjoy our first night at home together without asking so many questions?" He sounded like he was getting upset with her putting him on the spot with all the questions.

Priscilla walked over to where he was sitting holding the baby and gave him a kiss on the forehead. "I am happy that you're home with us. This is something that I have always wanted. It seemed like the only time that I really got to see you were on Sundays. And that was when there was no overtime at the factory for you."

James sat there holding the baby and thought about the one that he had given to the doctor and his wife.

If only there could have been a way to have kept both of my babies together. I wonder if they will know that one is missing. I hope and pray that one day I will get to meet the daughter that I gave up to save my family.

THE STORE

JAMES WAS UP in plenty of time to be at the store by seven. He felt that it was a change for him and he was headed in the right direction. He had high hopes for this new job. He wanted to learn everything there was to know about running a store. He tried over and over to come up with a good reason of how he could buy the store so Priscilla would never know the truth about how he got so much money. He knew that she would never believe for one minute that he saved it from working at the factory; after all, they barely got by with the little income that he had brought home. He also knew that if the truth would ever come out about him and the doctor's secret, it could end his eight-year marriage. How would he be able to let his wife know that he planned on paying cash for the store? And how could he keep a secret like this from her forever? He had thoughts racing through his mind so fast that it was hard for him to concentrate on just one thought at a time to get anything worked out.

He arrived at the store in plenty of time to start out his day of learning. Sam Porter was waiting for him when he entered the store.

"I was hoping that you were serious about coming in today and learning what it's like to be a store owner," Sam said, giving

James a handshake with a smile that made James warm up to the whole idea.

"Besides marrying my wife, I don't think that I've ever wanted anything more in all my life then to have my own business. I am very excited to learn everything that there is to know, and I'm ready anytime that you are." He could feel his heart pounding inside his chest so fast that he felt like he might die from so much excitement.

"Good. If you will come back here with me, I think that we will start by showing you how we go about ordering our products for the store."

James followed Sam and listened to everything that he had to say. He looked at all the products that they sold in the store. He listened as Sam explained to him about all the discontinued items and why they were discontinued. James took lots of notes so when he was at home, he could read up and try to memorize them. He felt confident that this was something that he could do.

"You seem to be catching on to so many things. Is this something that you really believe that you would still be interested in, even now that you got to see the ups and the downs of some of the products?" Sam asked James.

"Yes, it is," he spoke with excitement written all over his face. "Could I trouble you with something that I want to see?" James asked.

"Sure, anything that you want."

"I'd really like to see the books that show your profit and loss."

"I could show you my books, but I don't think that you could understand them."

"You said that I did well on all the other books that you showed me. What makes this one so different?"

"I would not be the one to show you them. Anyways, I have an accountant that does those books for me, and he's not in today. When you come back tomorrow, he will be here, and I will ask him to show you what the profit and loss have been lately. Trust me when I say that I have done pretty well for all these years. People have to eat, don't they?" he said with a slight grin.

"Yes, we all have to eat," James commented. "I want to thank you for taking the time to show me everything today. I'm sure that you had plenty to do, and you took the time for me. I'll be back in the morning—that is, if you don't mind showing me more about running a store?"

"Not at all. Remember I want to sell this place soon. So I welcome you to learn all that you need to know to buy the store from me."

James left the store feeling that he had just learned so much about how to run a grocery store and to run it well. He had spend all day learning and absorbing everything that he could, like a little sponge. He could feel the excitement swell up on the inside of him. Then he would remember once again what he did to get this far, then it would turn his joy into sorrow. How he wished that he could get rid of the guilt that kept rising up on the inside of him. If only he could tell his wife about what had happened when she gave birth, it would relieve so much of the guilt. But how? There was just no way he could ever come clean; he did what he felt he needed to. It was a choice that he made, and now he had to find a way to go on with his life and put the guilt behind him, in hopes of it not destroying him.

Priscilla had dinner made for him when he came home; the two talked about how his first day on the job went. James told her that he liked the job so much more than he ever liked working at the factory. He loved a challenge and the thought of one day, hopefully very soon, owning his own business.

"I thought that we could celebrate your job together," she said, walking in the dining room carrying a homemade chocolate cake that she made that afternoon while he was at work.

"That looks very nice, honey. I would love to have a piece of that."

"I thought that since we will be spending more time together, I will be able to make some things that you can now enjoy, instead of where before you would come home, eat, and go right to bed. This is going to be so much better for us that you are going to be home when it's still light out every night."

James went to work with a whole new meaning to life the following day. He was very excited to learn more about running a store. A man by the name of Greg Martin was the man he had to see when it came time to learn more about what he would make as a profit. After James and Greg met that day, they realized that they had known each other from school. They also realized that while they were in school. they never were friends there. As far as Greg was concerned, James had stolen his girlfriend and had later married her. Now James was trying to put the fact of girlfriend stealing behind him and learn from the man who had hated him for all of these years, or at least that was what he thought. He was unsure if Greg was willing to teach him what he needed to learn.

"Don't worry, James, that was a long time ago since we were kids in school. I have long gotten over the fact that you took my girl from me," he said with a chuckle. "I have been happily married for five years now. The past is what it is—the past. One can never move on in the future if you are still holding on to the past. And trust me, I would not ever want to repeat my past. It wasn't such a good one, if you know what I mean." He smiled at James.

"I'm glad to know that you don't hold it against me what I did back in school. I would really like it if we can get along now and hopefully become friends."

"Sure, that's what I'd like to. So tell me, how is Priscilla doing? I haven't seen her in years."

"She's doing very well we just had our first baby about a week ago. She's excited that I've changed jobs after working in a factory for nine years. I'll have to let her know that you are working here also."

"Have you decided to buy the store then?"

"Yes, I believe that I have." He spoke with some sort of pride that he would be the proud owner of the store.

"That's great. I know every year Mr. Porter has been talking about selling this place. Then this year, he finally decided to. He doesn't want another cold year here in Michigan. He's getting too old for it. He said his bones aren't up to another cold winter." He stopped talking then quickly changed the subject before James had the opportunity to give his reply on Mr. Porter. "I believe my wife was in the same class as Priscilla was. Let's see, you and I are twenty seven-years old, and if I'm right, Priscilla would be twenty-five, same age as my wife. Does that sound right?"

"Yeah, Priscilla is twenty-five. Who did you marry anyway?" James asked.

"Do you remember Penny Burger, the pretty little redhead?"

"I'm not sure. Is she the one who liked you when you liked Priscilla?"

"That's her. After Priscilla and I broke up, I went off to college. When I came home from school, I came here looking for a job. I ran into her here one day when she was doing some grocery shopping. She was prettier at that time, then when she was in school. We hooked up with each other, and now we've been married for five years."

"That's great. Do you have any children?"

"We have one that is about due any time now. She should be having the baby within the month."

"That's great. You'll love being a father. I can't wait to get home to see my little guy. We waited seven years before having our first one. We could never really afford one before. That's why I had to make a choice to change jobs. I was getting nowhere working at the factory."

"Do you think that you will want any more kids?" Greg looked at him, smiling ear to ear.

"After us waiting all this time on having our first one, I think that it's clear to say that we are happy with the one we have. Maybe in the future we might talk about having another one, but that won't be for a long while," James commented with laughter following.

"I think the same for us. We waited a few years before having one, and I think that if we were to want another one, it would be a few more years from now."

The two men talked about many things that took place back when they were in school. James learned that some of the people he never kept in touch with from school had died. And some of the teachers had died also. It was hard for him to believe that someone who was as young as twenty-seven had died of cancer. He never thought about the young dying of cancer before or getting killed in a car accident; he just assumed it was the old who would die of cancer.

On James's way home, he saw a sign that was posted by a mail box, advertising free dogs. Before he even realized what he was doing, he had pulled into the driveway. Before getting out of the car, he saw another sign that said Free Boxer Pups.

Well, I'm here now I might as well get out and take a look at them. What can it hurt just by looking, he told himself while getting out of the car and walking over to where the little puppies were at.

"They are eight weeks old now and ready to go to a good home," a little plump lady about the age of sixty spoke to him.

"Are they purebred boxers?"

"Yes, sir. Their mama's right over here, and the father, he's over in that cage now." She pointed in the direction of another cage. "As you can see, they are indeed purebred. I have to keep the mama and the father apart now so she doesn't go getting pregnant again."

James bent down and picked up a little puppy. It was so cute the way it was trying to chew on his ear that he just had to take it home to show his wife. "I'll take this little one here," he said as he checked it to make sure that it was a male dog. "He seems to be so playful, I like him."

"If you hear of anyone else that might want one, please send them here, will you?"

"Yes, I will, and thank you for the puppy."

When James arrived home, he was excited to show Priscilla the puppy that he had just picked up. "Look what I brought home with me, honey. I got a little puppy to grow up with David."

"Aw, he's so cute," she said, taking the puppy from James. "It is a he, isn't it?"

"Yes, it's a he. There were some girls there, but I didn't want one of them, so we don't have to worry about it having puppies.

"What made you want a puppy all of a sudden?"

"I've always wanted one, but we could never afford one before or have the time for one. So when I saw the sign that said Free Boxer Puppies, I stopped and looked at them. I wasn't sure that I would even bring one home until it started to chew on my ear. I could see how playful that he was, so I decided to bring him home then."

"Did you give him a name yet?"

"No, not yet. What do you think would be a good name to give him?"

"How about *Moe*? That's a good name for a dog, don't you think?" Priscilla stated.

"I actually had that one come to mind on my way home, so, yes, I think it is a good name for him."

James and Priscilla played with the dog and little David; they would laugh when the puppy would lick David's face.

"Honey, we shouldn't let the puppy lick the baby's face. He's way too young for that. He doesn't even understand what's going on yet," Priscilla requested even though she too was laughing.

"Okay, I'll keep it away from his face." James stopped the puppy from licking David's face.

"How did your work go for you today?"

"It went very good. Your old boyfriend is the one that's been teaching me how to keep books today."

"My old boyfriend, and who is that?" she asked out of curiosity.

James looked over at her. "Greg Martin," he said, lifting up one of his eyebrows.

"Greg Martin, he works there? It's been years since the last time that I saw him. So how is he doing?"

"Don't sound so excited, Priscilla. He's married now for five years, and they're having their first baby soon. He's the one that does the bookkeeping at the store."

Priscilla ignored his comment. "I know in school the two of you never liked each other, so how is it going for you two now?"

"People grow up and move on with their life. Do you really think he would hate me for stealing you from him so many years ago?" he said to her, knowing good and well that just earlier in the day, he thought that just maybe Greg did still hate him for stealing her away from him.

"No, not really. It's just sometimes when people don't like each other in school, when they get out of school, they usually don't care for each other, either."

"We get along just fine. I think he's gotten over what happened back in high school."

Priscilla listened as James was talking about Greg; it sounded to her that he was being a little sarcastic when saying that Greg had gotten over her.

"Why do you say it like that? It's not like I have even thought of him over the years. I'm glad that the two of you can get along now. It will make your job better for you."

James went about playing with David as if not hearing Priscilla.

"I can't believe that you can still feel threatened by me and him. It has been over for how many years now, and you still act like I'm going to jump in the car and run down to the store to go see him."

"Are you telling me that you have never thought of him over all these years?"

"That's right, I haven't. I broke up with him to be with you, so why would I spend my life thinking about being with him?"

James put the baby down and walked over to Priscilla, noticing just how foolish he was acting. "Honey, I'm sorry. Can you ever forgive me for acting like such a foolish, jealous husband? I should know better than that. It's just when I saw him today, it brought up all those old feelings about you and him."

"I do forgive you, honey, and please know that I would never want anyone else but you."

When James heard his wife of seven years say that she would never want anyone but him, he couldn't help but wonder if she would feel the same if she had known that he gave their baby girl to a doctor and his wife. Somehow, he felt that she would never feel the same way about him as she does now.

"Thank you honey for forgiving me, you are so good to me, even when I don't deserve you."

"What's this talk of 'even if you don't deserve me'? Ever since you came home and told me about Greg, you've been acting different."

"It's nothing. I have just been doing some thinking about everything, like quitting my job after nine years and having a baby boy after seven years of marriage. This is all new to me, but otherwise, I'm fine," James said as he took her in his arms and gave her a big hug and kiss.

"James, do you think that you will like this new job better than working at the factory?"

"I know that I will. I already do, even though I have been there for only two days. I'm talking with the store owner about me taking over the store for him so he can go to Florida like he wants to."

"Do you really think that you can do that?"

"He seems to think that we will be able to work out all the details between the two of us." *Be careful James*, he told himself. *Don't tell more lies to cover lies.*

"I don't know what the two of you have been talking about, but if you did take over the store for him, would you make more money than you do now?"

"Oh yes, a lot more than I do now. If what I got figured out about what I would make, it would be about one hundred and twenty dollars a week."

"Sixty dollars more a week really. Wow, that is a lot more than you have ever made before. I sure hope that everything works out for you to be able to take over the store."

"I'll find out tomorrow when I get to work. I'm going to go to bed early tonight, if that's all right with you. I have a lot of things that I need to think about before tomorrow. I'll eat then go to bed."

"Okay, honey."

Priscilla knew that a sudden change in someone's life can be stressful on them, so she wasn't going to ask him to stay up with her if he felt that he needed sleep. Although, she wondered how he would be able to fall to sleep when it was still light out. *I guess if one is tired enough, they could fall to sleep day or night.*

James ate then gave Priscilla and little David a kiss good night, and he was off to bed. All the while, Priscilla was up thinking and planning what she would do with all the extra money that would be coming into their home per week. Before she was off to bed for the night, she had a whole list of things that she wanted to buy for the baby and for the house that she was never able to buy before.

James was upstairs thinking about telling Sam that he would be buying the store from him, but there were just a few minor details that they needed to work out. He had to figure out how to buy the store with cash and not let anyone know about it but Sam; he was afraid for the truth to come out. After falling to sleep thinking about another way to lie to Priscilla, he had a dream that Priscilla found out the truth about him giving their baby away. He jumped up out of his sleep with sweat pouring from his face. Seeing that he was all alone in bed, he quickly realized that he had just been dreaming.

Oh my, I sure hope that dream never comes to pass, I don't want to lose my family. He laid his head back down, trying not to think about his dream.

BUYING THE STORE

"**M**R. PORTER, I would like to talk over some details with you when you have some time?" James asked.

"Sure, I have some time right now. If you would like to come in my office so we can talk." He gave James an ear-to-ear smile. "I'm hoping that we will be calling it *your* office here very soon."

"Yes, I do too as well." Returning a big smile, James followed close behind, his hands became sweaty from being nervous to talk with Sam about purchasing the store. James and Sam stayed in the back office for two hours before reaching an agreement on the terms of buying the store.

On James's drive home, he thought about how he would tell Priscilla about him buying the store. He took the long mile home to give him more time to come up with a plan that she would believe. Upon arriving home, he walked in the house and quickly gave her a hug. If he could only come clean and everything could be forgiven. He felt like he was walking on cloud nine now that he was the proud owner of his own grocery store. No more boss for him—he was the boss; no more over time and spending all his time making money for someone else—now it was his time to make some real money. Oh, if only he could just tell Priscilla what he did. His thoughts were interrupted when Priscilla felt the hard squeeze that he was giving her.

"Wow, what was that hug for and the big smile I don't see often enough? I take it you and your boss came to some kind of an agreement?" She looked at James in a different way than she had in a long time. Seeing the smile he was giving her sent chills up her arms. She noticed his strong, muscular built and his handsome, rugged looks that she hadn't paid any attention to in quite some time, the way his brown hair had the most perfect curls on the ends, and the way his beautiful blue eyes sparkled when he gets excited. She was remembering how she felt when, back in school, finding out that James liked her—oh, what a fine catch he was. All the girls liked her James, but yet he chose her over girls that she her self thought was much prettier than she was.

James interrupted her thoughts. "Yes, honey, we did. I am now the proud owner of the market here in town. As of today, I no longer have a boss—I am the boss."

"You have got to be kidding me! So that's why you squeezed me so hard that I felt I was about to break in two?" She looked at him, wondering how he made that happen so quickly. "How did you come to be the owner of it with no money?"

"The owner of the store knew how much that I wanted to buy it, and there was no one else looking too, so he agreed to go to the bank and let me get a loan with him as the cosigner."

He had asked the owner if he would be willing to cosign for him to get a loan so his credit could be established, and the owner agreed to help James out with that after he himself seen with his own eyes that James did indeed have the money to buy the store and then some. This way, when he was to pay for the loan, Priscilla would never have to know the truth about the money. He thought that he was being none the wiser of how he came up with covering up for himself.

"Now I just have to make a monthly payment to the bank, and the store is mine. Tomorrow, when I get to work, I will find out how to run the store like a storeowner should know."

"James, I am so happy for you. She said as she walked up behind him to give him a hug. "This is one thing that you have always said that you wanted, to be your own boss."

James felt like he was being very smart the way he handled things; the more he told lies to his wife, the easier it was for him to come up with more to cover up what he had done. He told himself that it was for the good, to save two children, and that he and his wife would finally begin to live the way life was intended to be lived. As long as the truth would never be told, James felt like life couldn't be any better.

James and Priscilla took little David for a walk in a new stroller that James had bought for the baby, never having anything new since the day they got married. James decided that if he was going to make more money than he ever had before; he might as well spend some of it. Not wanting Priscilla to know how much money he had in the bank, he would only bring enough of it home so that she would never get suspicious.

"It's a beautiful night to go walking with the warm breeze filling the air," Priscilla commented on their walk. "Thank you for buying this stroller for David. It makes things so much easier to walk the baby."

"You're welcome. I was glad to get this for him. After all, he is my baby too. And now that we have more money, I want us to be able to have and do certain things to make our life easier. I bought a collar for Moe too." He looked behind him to see if the dog was following them as they walked.

She was thinking about what he said about buying things they never could before. "That would be nice, but we need to use our head too and put some money in the bank. I think that it might be a good idea if we open up a bank account, and each week, when you get paid, we'd put some money away."

James walked thinking how to cover up what he already done by opening up a back account without his wife knowing about it. "I'll open up one."

"I would like to be on the account too, so if ever I need some money and you're not at home, I could go to the bank and take some out," Priscilla stated.

"Okay, we can do that," James spoke, knowing perfectly well that he would be opening up another account, but this time, it would have both of their names on it. He knew that he had come too far to have everything backfire on him now.

Weeks went by, and Sam was true to his word; James was getting quite the profit on the store. He was able to buy all new furniture for his home and take his wife out to eat more than she was cooking. Priscilla began to ask questions on how he was able to put so much in the bank and yet spend the way that he had been. James knew that he had allowed himself to get out of control with all of the spending that he was doing. He gave her an excuse of how he had the extra money to buy all that he did and promised that he would stop spending so much and save more.

Priscilla was happy with life. She would take David for walks to the park in his stroller and sit on the park bench, watching the birds fly high in the sky and the squirrels chase each other up and down the trees. She couldn't remember when life felt so good for her; she was finally able to have nice things, and not having to cook every time, every meal was great.

One day, as she was sitting on the bench at the park, another woman came and sat down on the same bench with her little baby.

"I love the outside when it feels warm and the sun is shining," Priscilla stated to the woman who was seated next to her.

"Yes, it is a very lovely day out. I love to take my daughter for walks when it's nice out like this."

"I've never seen you here before. Is this your first time coming here?" Priscilla asked, looking at how fancy the woman seemed to dress for coming to the park.

"No, I come here on Tuesdays and Thursdays usually. I don't get out much. I usually have a lot going on at my home," she spoke while taking the baby out of the stroller.

"You have a very pretty little girl! How old is she?" Priscilla asked.

"She's three months old. How old is your little guy?"

"He just turned three months old a couple of days ago."

"My name is Marcia, and this is my daughter, Terri."

"Nice to meet you. My name is Priscilla, and this is David.

"It's very nice to meet the two of you."

The two women talked about their baby stories and laughed over some of the things that each baby would do when taking their baths or when eating. After a few hours had passed, it was getting time for the women to go to their homes.

Priscilla looked at her watch on her wrist that James had bought for her two weeks earlier. "I better get going home. My husband will want his supper when he comes in from work. It was very nice meeting you. Maybe we will see each other again here at the park."

"It was nice to have met you too, and maybe we will run into each other here again and share more baby stories," Marcia stated.

After James came home from work, Priscilla began to tell him about her day at the park. She was all excited that she had seen the prettiest little girl that she had ever seen before in all of her life.

"You should have seen her, James. She was such a beautiful little girl she would be pretty enough to be on a cover of a magazine."

James was half listening to what she was talking about; he was into playing with David now, and the rest of the world would just have to wait.

"James, did you hear me at all?"

"Sure I did, honey. I was just playing with the baby is all. Don't you think that little David would be cute on the front cover? After all, he's the cutest little boy I have ever seen before," he stated while holding the baby high in the air and watching Moe trying to get his attention.

"Yes, he is just like his daddy, and, honey, you're the best-looking man to me that I have ever seen. You better not forget Moe. He's looking at you, wagging his tail, waiting for you to play with him too."

James stood up after placing David in his swing. "That is the nicest thing that you have ever said to me before. Thank you for that, and that is one of the reasons that I love you so very much," James said as he put his arms around his wife and gave her a big squeeze. "I think that you're pretty great too, and you are one of the finest hot chicks that I have ever met. Come on, Moe, I can play with you too." He watched Moe bite on his pant leg.

"Aw, really that is so nice for you to say that. I haven't heard you talk like that to me in a long time." Priscilla said as she stood there watching James play with both dog and baby again.

"I'm sorry that I haven't said anything like that to you in quite some time. I promise to let you hear and know that more often. I think that when I was working at the factory, I got so depressed because it seemed like that's all that I ever did after so many years doing the same old thing day in and day out, never getting a real vacation because when I was supposed to take one, I would work just trying to make more money to pay bills."

"Honey, you are a good man and a very hard worker. You have over worked yourself for years. Now it seems to me that you are finally enjoying what you are doing, am I right?"

"Yes, you are right. I am very happy at this job. I know that I have only been there for a few months now, but if you could only understand what it feels like to me, it's something that I have always wanted—to own my own business."

"I'm so glad that it has all worked out for you, with Sam selling you the store the way he did. Not too many people that I know would have done something like that, especially to someone he really doesn't know."

James sat there quiet for a minute, then he spoke, "You're right. Not too many people would do something like that for someone that they hardly knew." James spoke just barely above a whisper; it was almost like he thought that if he spoke too loud, Priscilla might know what he had done to get him that store.

"I almost forgot to tell you that we are having company over tomorrow night for supper."

"Oh really, and who might that be? We haven't had anyone come over for supper in a very long time, ever since Heather and Mike moved out of town. And we haven't seen Pete or Barbara in a while, either."

"It's none of them, but how I wish that it were." Priscilla looked at him with disappointment. "My parents will be in town tomorrow, so I asked them to stop over and visit with us. That is okay with you, isn't it?" she asked.

"It's whatever you want to do, I'm fine with that," he said, remembering how her parents have never liked him.

"You are coming home from work tomorrow night, aren't you?" She knew how he would do anything to avoid her parents.

"Do I have to? You know how much your mother hates me, and your dad acts like I'm the very worst man in the world for his little girl. How much longer do I need to go through this with them? We have been married for how long—eight years—and they still haven't accepted me yet. I'm just getting to the point that when I know that they are coming by, I want to leave, so

I don't have to hear about how they think that you would have been better off with marrying Greg."

"It won't be like that anymore. We have a baby now, so I know that they won't treat you like that anymore."

"Do you really think that will make a difference?"

"Honey, if my parents say one thing against you this time when they come over, I will set the both of them straight. I am so sorry that I never put an end to it a long time ago. Will you ever forgive me for not saying something to them before?"

James put the baby down and walked over to Priscilla. "Come over here, you beautiful woman. I knew why I married you eight years ago, and now I know why I stayed married to you. Thank you for understanding how I feel about what they say to me. I have tried for years to just ignore them, but I have to be honest. It's getting very old, and I don't want my son to hear that kind of talk."

"No more, I promise it will never happen again—that is, if they say anything to you tomorrow, I will come right out and tell them if they can't accept you as my husband after all of these years, then they can leave our home."

James just stood there looking at her for a minute. "Honey, I would never want to come between you and your folks. All I have ever wanted was for them to accept me as your husband, and their son-in-law."

"James you are the most honest man that I know. You have been a great husband loyal and faithful in every way."

Priscilla was still going on with talking about how great James was when all he could think about was what a terrible thing he had done behind his wife's back. Would she hate him if the truth was ever to come out? Would she despise him the way he was doing to himself at this particular time? James began to wonder if her parents had seen something in him eight years ago, when he first married Priscilla, that he didn't even know about himself.

Did they see that he would do something later in years that was so rotten as to sell his own child?

"So you can trust me to tell them off if they talk against you," Priscilla carried on.

James was glad that he hadn't heard everything that she had to say about him; if he had heard what she said, he might have felt so terrible about himself that he might have opened up his mouth and confessed to what evil he had done.

After they ate, Priscilla handed him the baby to hold while she cleaned up the kitchen. As he held the baby, he thought about how it would be for him to have both kids at home with them, knowing that if they did have both babies at home, they could not afford much for them or for him and Priscilla. The longer he held his little boy, the more he was convinced that he had done the right thing, like now he knew that both of his children were set for money and a future.

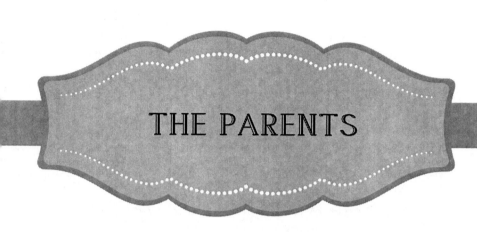

THE PARENTS

66 "HELLO, HONEY." BERNADINE Dell just about barged into James and Priscilla's home as if to own it. "Give your mother a hug. And where is that grandson of mine at? I have got to meet him to see if he takes after the Dell side of the family, which I sure hope for his sake, he does," she said under her breath, but just above a whisper so it would be enough for James to hear her if he was in reach of her, but trying to make it seem as though it was not done on purpose.

"Mother, please don't start. Every time you and Daddy come here, you act so mean to my husband. Mama, I don't want that any more. He is my husband, and if you two can't seem to try and get along with him, then I will not have you come back."

"Where is this all coming from? Why are you talking to me like that? I don't deserve this kind of talk from my own daughter. Has that man put you up to this?" She looked around at her daughter's new furniture. "I see you have finally gotten some new things around here. I should say it is about time. Your father and I were talking about buying it for you ourselves. Hmm, I wonder what he did to get all this for you—"

"Who put who up to what?" Zach Dell interrupted as he entered the home.

"Our daughter is having a bad attitude with me all because I said that I hope that our grandson takes after the Dell side of the family. Here we come all this way to meet our grandson, and I get treated like I'm some kind of a monster," Bernadine carried on.

Zach stood there with his large frame towering over everyone, his eyes sending darts into his daughter's very soul, then he shook his head. "Well, maybe we should just be on our way if you are going to be treated in such a way. I don't know what has happened to you since we talked yesterday, but to treat your own mother like this is just not like you. What has this man put you up to, Priscilla?"

"I don't think that you two even know who I am. Every time you come here, I hear you cut down my husband. And I have heard enough of it. Now I have the best man in all the world. He is a great husband and father to my son, and for you to come here and say what you do every time you see him, I will not stand for it anymore. Now I love the two of you very much, and I'd love for you to be part of my son's life, but if you cannot treat James like my husband, then you will just have to leave. I guess my son will not ever get to know who his grandparents are." Priscilla sighed.

"He did this to you, didn't he? I know that no daughter of mine would ever act like this to us. I have never liked the man. We wanted you to marry Greg. Do you even remember who he is? Now that is a man who is going places in his life. He knew what he wanted out of life, and I bet he got just what he wanted to," Zach ranted.

"Is that what you really think? Well then, let me tell you both something that will knock your socks right off of you. The man that you wanted me to marry, you know the one that had it all going on, well, it just so happens that he works for my husband now." Priscilla sat down at the kitchen table and put her head in her hands, shaking her head back and forth.

"What do you mean he works for your husband?" Bernadine looked liked she was going to a wedding or possibly a funeral.

Priscilla was already upset at the way the two have been acting since walking through the door, and they haven't even seen her son yet or her husband.

"It's just like I said—Greg works for my husband, you know the one that I married. Ever since, you have made him feel like he never belonged. Just for the record, I was really hoping that when you guys came here today, it wouldn't be the same as it was all the other times. Somehow, just for once, I was hoping that you could see in him what I have always seen in him."

"I wonder, do you really even know that man you married?" Bernadine stated.

Priscilla looked at her mother to answer the question when her father decided to talk.

"What are you talking about? How did James become a boss over anyone?" Zach asked.

"Well, Dad, he is the proud owner of the grocery store here in town, and Greg is the one who does his bookkeeping for him."

"Priscilla, I am so sorry for what your mother and I have put you through for all of these years." Zach opened his large arms, reaching out for his daughter right after being so cruel to her.

"Are you really sorry, Dad, for all of the years you hated a man that worked fourteen hours a day to take care of his wife, or are you just saying that you are because he now owns his own business?"

"You make it sound like your mother and I have been so rotten to James. When have I ever said anything mean to him?"

"Oh come on, Dad! Do we really need to do this? Can't you and Mom just admit you have never treated him right and have never accepted him as my husband."

"Okay, Priscilla!" Zach yelled. "What do you want me to say, that I was wrong? Okay, I will say it—*I was wrong*. Now can we please meet our grandson, or are you going to make us beg to see are only grandchild?"

"No, I'm not going to make you beg, but when you see James, treat him with respect, will you?"

"If I had known that it really bothered you all of these years, I would have taken that under consideration a long time ago, but yes when I see James, I will make sure that I am pleasant to him," Bernadine replied.

"Dad?"

"Yes, yes, I will talk with the man myself. Now can we meet our grandson?"

Priscilla knew that he was angry with her telling them how she feels, but she wasn't going to let it slip by this time for she knew that it was long overdue. "Come on, he's in his bedroom with James," she said, keeping her fingers crossed.

"Hello, James, how are you doing? It's good to see you. It's been awhile since we've last been here. So is this my little grandson?" Bernadine said as she bent over his crib to look at him for the first time and acted like she wasn't just out in the kitchen cutting down James like she always did.

James didn't have words to say; he acted like he was in shock. He just sat there, not knowing if he should get up out of the rocking chair he had bought Priscilla after David was born or if he should just sit there like he owned the place—because after all, he did.

"Good evening," Zach said, looking toward James.

"Good evening," James replied.

After that, he got out of the chair and walked out of the room, motioning for Priscilla to come in the other room with him.

"I take it you had that talk with your folks?" he asked.

"How did you know?" Priscilla looked at him apprehensively.

"Come on, honey. They might not have said a lot to me, but they did at least acknowledge me. That was the first time they did without giving me some bad vibes."

"I told them I never wanted them to mistreat you again. I told them that you are the proud owner of your own store."

"Well, at least now I know why they said something to me. I guess it's better than them talking against me all the time."

"It's a start, honey. Now maybe they will be able to see you for who you really are, and that is a good man and a very hard worker."

"Yeah, well, all I can say is I will do my best to try and overlook everything that they have done to me in the past and move on with the new," James replied, but at the back of his mind, he was hearing what his wife had said about her folks seeing him for who he really is.

What was he really? Would they see him as a man who saved his family from never having anything in life by staying with a job that didn't pay much, or would they see him as a man who did what he needed to do to get somewhere in life and to give his family a better way of living? No matter what way they would see him, James was doing everything that he could to convince himself that he did what he needed to do to save his family.

Zach and Bernadine were holding their little grandson now, making comments on who they thought he looked like.

Priscilla loved her parents very much, but for the first time, she was really seeing them for who they really were. She had always known that they never accepted James as her husband, but it was something that she would just put all of their insults as far out of her mind as fast as they came; she never would say much to them about the way they treated James before, but now she knew that she didn't want to hear the insults anymore, either. After all, for years, she has kept as much distance from them as possible.

"Honey, how long are your folks planning on staying?" James asked.

"They won't be here for too much longer. I don't think they want to be after the way I got upset at them. Why do you ask?"

"Because I have had a long day today, and I would like for us to spend some quiet time alone, if you wouldn't mind."

Priscilla looked at James, knowing that he was not acting like his usual self, but she just put that aside because she thought it was because her parents were there and she knew how James felt about them.

"I would like to spend some quiet time with you too, honey, but remember they are supposed to be eating with us tonight. I think we spend a lot of quiet time together now that you have your own store." She spoke softly so not to upset him for not wanting her parents there.

Not long after their talk, Zach and Bernadine ate supper as fast as they could; if they would have eaten any faster, they would have needed a shovel to help them. They left the home telling their daughter that she had a beautiful son; they forgot to mention that James was included in having a beautiful son. James was so happy when the kitchen door closed behind them. He hadn't cared much for them for several years. When he did all he could do to get them to like him, they never would give him a chance to get to know him.

"I'm sure glad they're gone," he spoke out loud without thinking that Priscilla was standing right there, ready to take him by his hand and lead him into the living room so they could spend time together while the baby slept. "I'm sorry, honey, I should never have said that."

"I know you don't mean to talk against them like that. I just don't know what took me so long to finally say something. It's not like they have been treating you good for all of these years. I know what they have been like, and I just wish that I should have said something a long time ago, and for that, I ask you to forgive me for not telling them off years ago."

James took his wife by her hand and led her over to a chair in the living room; sitting down in his big brown chair and placing her on his lap, he hugged her gently and spoke words of love to her.

THE OUTING

PRISCILLA LOOKED OUT the window after James had left for work. Seeing it to be a nice warm day out, she decided to take David and Moe for a walk. She figured the park would be a good place to go with David. Now turning five in just a few days, she would have him walk alongside of her.

After getting her household chores done then bathing David, she had him put a new outfit on that she had picked out for him. "Come on, honey," she would say. "Mama's going to take you and Moe to the park this afternoon." She took him by the hand and led him out the front door. "Wanna go to the park?"

"Yep, I want to go on the swings."

After getting to the park, she could see that she was just about the only mother there. She was enjoying watching him swing and laugh as she pushed him just a little at first, then heard him say, "Higher, higher." Then she noticed a woman she thought that she might have met before, now walking toward her.

"Hi, I was wondering when I was going to be seeing you and that beautiful daughter of yours again," Priscilla spoke.

At first, the woman looked at Priscilla, not sure if she knew her, then she realized that she did meet her a few years ago. "Yes, same here. It's been awhile since the last time I saw you. Marcia spoke.

"Yes, it has been."

"My husband works a lot, and I keep quite busy in my flower garden now, but it is such a beautiful day out today, and I hate to just stay home when I can enjoy this weather. And soon when school starts back up, Terri will be going into kindergarten."

"Oh, my gosh! Really? So will my David! I wonder if they will be in the same class together."

"Oh, I'm sure that they will be. I think there is only one kindergarten class." Marcia informed her.

The two women sat down to watch the children play, and they talked and talked like neither one had in a very long time.

"I think that it will be nice to have them in the same class. I've been watching the way the two of them play together, and they seem to get along quite well," Priscilla said as she watched the kids playing on the merry go round.

"Yes, they sure seem to be enjoying each other. Maybe your David will watch out for Terri at school." Marcia said, joking around.

Priscilla and Marcia sat together, trading stories about their child, then they talked about their husbands.

"I think that if Nick ever took a day off from work, it would be when he had gotten sick himself, instead of his patients getting sick. That man is so devoted to his work that he hasn't taken time off from work in months. I guess the hospital needs a good doctor, and when they call my husband to come to the hospital, they know that they are getting a good doctor."

"Your husband is doctor who?" Priscilla asked.

"His name is Dr. Nick O'Neil. If you ever need a good doctor, I can tell you that he is really something." Marcia spoke, laughing, watching the kids playing on the slides.

"Your daughter must look like her dad. I don't really see you in her."

"I have heard some people say that, but my husband and I adopted her." Marcia had a big smile across her face. "You have a very nice little boy. I see how he lets my little girl go down the slide before he goes. That is just so sweet. Not many little guys would do that. I have seen a lot where they'll push another child out of the way to get down it first, but not your little one. I've been watching him, and he's very nice with her."

"He must take after my husband. My husband is so gentle with me in every way. He would move mountains for me if he could."

"Oh, that is nice and a very good thing, I know a good man is hard to find now a days. I have a couple of friends who have been married to the wrong men, and they stayed with them because of the kids, but yet it has hurt the children to see them fighting all the time." All the while Marcia was talking about a good man, she was staring down at the ground.

Priscilla thought that it was normal for Marcia to be seemed happy when talking about the children, but when talking about a good man, she looked at the ground. "Oh, my James could never hurt me. He's the best man alive I think. We are fortunate to have such a great relationship. I don't think David had ever heard the two of us have a disagreement before. Whenever we have, we take it in our bedroom so he doesn't hear what we talk about. Maybe that's why he is being so kind to your little girl."

"My daughter is a very sweet gentle little girl, much like your son. If she sees a worm crawling on the ground or ants, she will walk way to the other side of the sidewalk so she doesn't walk on them. It's so funny to watch her at times because she doesn't realize how many times, when she's not paying any attention, that as she avoids some ants, she's walking all over the other ants."

"Aw. that is so sweet. I hope that when David gets to be older, he keeps his sweetness like his father. If he does, then he will make a very good husband also like his father."

"I'm not really sure who Terri takes after because I didn't know about her birth parents. I would like to think that they were good people. Maybe that's where she gets her kindness from." Marcia looked at how Priscilla was looking at her. Then she realized how she sounded. "Oh, I know that I teach her kindness, but I know that not every action she takes is coming from me. I know some of it is just her, but I also know that from her birth, there is something there that makes a child too."

"How old was she when she was adopted?"

"After I found out that I couldn't have any children, I waited twenty years before we adopted her at only one day old, and she was the greatest gift to us that I could have ever asked for. A prayer answered, that's for sure."

"I can understand that. My husband worked so hard for years, and I wanted a baby, but he said that we couldn't afford one. But I prayed for a baby, and one day, when I was least expecting it, I found out that I was pregnant and was going to have my prayers answered. And much like what you said, he is the best gift that I could have ever asked for."

The two women sat on the bench while watching their children play until they were plumb tuckered out. When they could see that they were slowing down and looking back at their moms, they knew that it was time to take their child home for a nap so they could prepare dinner for their husbands.

"I see David is ready for his nap, so I will be going home now, but please let's keep in touch before the years pass us by, like the last time I saw you," Priscilla stated, laughing.

"That is for sure. I really enjoyed our time of talking and watching our kids play together. We have to get together sometime other than the park. Do you and your husband like to play cards?"

"Yes, we sure do, and it's been a long time since we have with anyone other than ourselves. Why don't we plan on a time to get together and play some poker or cribs?"

"I think that would really be nice. We need to do that. I will talk with my husband tonight and ask him when he will have an evening off from work so we can get together. I think that our husbands will get along nicely. What do you think?" Marcia said.

"Oh, I do too for what you told me about him. So why don't I give you my phone number, and you can call me when it's a good time for the three of you to come over to our house?"

"Yes, that will be fine, and I will call you tomorrow, if not tonight, after I talk with my husband."

The women parted and went their own way to their home. Priscilla was feeling an excitement meeting the lady that she had met several years before. She thought back then that the two of them were going to be seeing each other from time to time at the park, but going to the park after their first encounter, she never saw her again until today. But it was different today; somehow, this time, she knew that she would be seeing a lot more of Marcia. She felt that the two of them had made a connection today that they never made before.

Priscilla went home and laid David down for a nap before James was due home from work. Opening up the kitchen window to let the fresh air in as she was about to start to cook her meal, she had a strong smell of lilac blowing through the window. Priscilla had planted two lilac trees next to her kitchen window when she and James first bought their home twelve years ago. When James came home from work, she told him all about her encounter with the woman she had met when David was just a baby. She told him about David being the perfect little gentlemen he possibly could be to Marcia's little girl, Terri. She talked and talked up a stream to James about her new friend, Marcia.

During their time of sitting down to eat their dinner, Priscilla heard the phone ringing and just knew that it was her friend Marcia. She answered the phone with excitement, but her excitement was quickly taken away from her when the person on the other end was not her friend after all, but it was her father with the news of her mother's death.

Priscilla could hardly believe her ears. "What are you telling me, dad? How can she be dead?"

James jumped up when he heard Priscilla say something about dead. He walked over to where Priscilla stood talking to her father.

"Your mother took very ill in the middle of the night. I wanted to take her to the hospital, but she said that she would be all right…so I trusted what she told me, and I didn't push her into going. She lay in bed all day and still said she just needed to rest, but when I went to the store to buy her something to drink, hoping that would make her feel better…by the time I came home…she was gone," Zach spoke crying on the phone.

Priscilla was all upset, and she started to cry. "Why didn't you make her go to the hospital, Dad? If you knew that she was that sick, why didn't you just make her go?"

"I tried to, honey, but she said that she just needed some rest."

James wrapped his arms around his wife's waist as she broke down crying.

"I'm going to be coming down to be with you, Dad."

"When will you be coming?"

"I'm going to be leaving tonight."

"Okay, honey, I'll see you when you get here. Be careful driving here. You probably won't be here until morning."

"Yes, I'm sure that's when it will be." She hung up the phone and looked at James in unbelief.

"Your mother passed away honey?" James asked, taking his wife into his arms and allowing her to cry on his shoulders.

"Daddy said that she got sick during the night, and she stayed in bed all day, and now she's gone."

"Why did he not take her to the hospital?"

"He said that she wouldn't go—he tried, but she just wouldn't go." Priscilla stood there shaking uncontrollably. "She hardly even got to know her grandson. I have to go be with my dad and help him make funeral arrangements."

"Honey, I don't want you to go tonight. It's late in the evening, and Tennessee is a long drive from here. Wait until you have rested and coped with what has happened."

"Maybe you're right. All I can do right now is cry. I want to go lie down. I can't clean up the dishes right now." She walked away, sobbing so hard that her tiny-framed body shook so bad that James figured it best not to leave her alone.

"I'll lie down with you, honey, then I will clean up the kitchen."

Priscilla didn't answer; she just walked over to her bed and flopped down and let out a loud cry. "I just can't believe that she's gone. I will never see her again never, and David will never really know his grandma."

James lay next to her and tried to comfort her while wrapping his arms around her. "I'm so sorry, honey. Would you like me to make you a hot tea?"

Priscilla didn't answer at first, then she nodded her head yes. James knew that whenever she was upset, she liked to have a hot tea, but whenever things were going good, she liked her coffee. So he made her up a hot cup of tea and took it in to her.

"Here, honey, sit up and try to drink some of this. I put honey in it just like you like it—not too sweet, but just a little honey to flavor it."

Priscilla sat up, taking the cup of tea and sipping it. "Thank you, honey. You made it just how I like it. I really should call Daddy and let him know that I won't be coming until tomorrow morning now."

"You drink your tea, and I will call him up," he stated.

"Okay," she answered, sipping her tea and shaking still with unbelief that her mother was gone.

While James was making his phone call, David woke up and went running into his parents' bedroom. Crawling up on the bed where his mother sat crying, he cuddled up next to her. "Why are you crying, Mama?"

"Because, honey, something terrible happened."

"What?"

"Your grandma died today, my mama, and I'm very sad that I won't be seeing her anymore."

"I'm sorry, Mama, that you won't see her anymore," David spoke in a soft little voice.

Priscilla put her arm around him to let him know that everything would be all right.

"Mama," David called out.

"Yes, honey, what is it?"

"Are you going to die too now?"

"No, honey, I'm not going to die. My mama was very sick, and I'm not, so you see, I'm not going anywhere, okay?"

"Okay, Mama. I love you."

"I love you to David, and your mama is not going anywhere," she reassured him.

"I called your dad and let him know that the three of us will be leaving in the morning," James said to her.

"What about your store?"

"I took care of that too. I called up Greg and ask him if he could open up for the next few days. I told him what happened, and he said for us not to worry because he will take care of everything at the store for me while I'm gone. Did you explain to David about your mom?"

"Yes, but I'm not really sure if he understands what really happened."

"Come on, David," James said as he picked him up. "Let's let Mama get some rest, while I take you into the kitchen and get you a snack to eat. Here, honey, hand me your cup."

James walked out of the bedroom to give Priscilla some time to sort through some of the feeling she was having after finding out about her mother dying. He knew that for several years, that the two of them have not been very close ever since she married James. And since having David, they have not seen her folks but just a few times, and even then, it was like they were almost not speaking much at all to each other. It seemed like ever since Bernadine disapproved of her marrying James so much, she never cared too much for her own daughter, and that had always hurt Priscilla in many ways.

"Oh, Mama, why did you have to go without us ever resolving this ugly thing that stood there in front of us?" Priscilla was talking out loud to herself. "Why couldn't you have ever given James a chance—the chance that he deserved? Why all these years have you hated him so?" She laid her head down on her pillow and wept.

James could hear her from the kitchen. When he was just about to walk back to the bedroom and check on her, he heard her start to talk again. So instead of walking to the bedroom, he stood in the kitchen and listened to what she was saying to no one.

"You never gave him a chance, Mama. Why? I want to know why you have never cared for him. You and Daddy both have been very cruel to my James, and I never really have known why." She continued to talk to her mother as if she was in the room with her.

James entered the room, "Honey, let it go. Don't do this to yourself. It doesn't matter why anymore."

"But you don't understand, James. She never told me why she and Daddy treated you like that for all of these years. I just want to know why they treated you like they did."

"Honey, maybe when the shock of your mother's passing is gone, you will be able to ask your dad. Maybe he will tell you everything you are looking answers for."

"Oh, I know that they have always said that they wanted me to marry someone who was going somewhere, and we proved to them that you were that someone, with the store and all, but yet they still treated you like dirt even after I told them that I would not have them over our home if they didn't stop. They must not

---

have loved me at all to not care how I felt." Priscilla began to weep all the harder.

"Honey, please stop doing this to yourself. Your parents loved you very much. It was me that they disliked, not you. Now come on, honey. You'll never be able to rest when you are thinking foolish thoughts. Now I want you to lie down and get some rest. Honey, think of all the good thoughts that you can remember about your mom, okay?"

Priscilla lay there not saying a word to what James was asking from her, but just as he was ready to exit the bedroom, he heard her say, "There isn't any."

"Now sure there is, honey. You're just focusing on all the bad right now. Come on, honey, I'm sure your mother wasn't always hateful." After he said the word *hateful*, he felt bad spilling it out like that.

"Why is that all I remember? I want to think of the good, but there isn't any, James, and I'm really trying to find some—I need to find some."

"Then why don't you think about when you were a little girl? That should make you happier. I remember some stories you told me about when you were little. Try thinking on these times, okay?"

"I'll try," Priscilla promised, sitting up sobbing at the edge of her bed.

After James walked out of the bedroom, she walked over to the window and looked out at the night closing in, opening up the window to feel the night breeze and to smell the night air, trying as she might to get her thoughts on when she was a young child, where her memories were filled with laughter and joy. She sat on the floor, looking out the window toward. the sky.

"Oh, Mama, how I wish we could have gotten a long much better. I'm sorry, Mama, I didn't try harder with you whenever you would come up to see me. Maybe I could have done better for you and Daddy. Maybe I should have shown you I loved you more, instead of finding fault with you every time I seen you.

Please forgive me, Mama. I'm so sorry for not ending our feuding a long time ago and holding on to -un-forgiveness."

James walked back into the room after putting David back to bed for the night. He knew that they had a long drive come morning, and it was time to go to bed so they could make the drive. "Honey are you ready to go to bed? I put David in his bed for the night. I'm quite tired myself, and I'd like to get some sleep. Why don't you come lie down with me and I'll hold you in my arms?"

"I guess you're right. I think I need to stop thinking for a while and rest my head. I've been trying to think about when I was a little girl, and all I can think about is how I treated my mom and dad like whenever they would come up for a visit."

"Now, honey, I want you to stop blaming yourself because you and your parents didn't see eye to eye. That is not your fault. You have tried for years, and you know that you did. Now I understand how you feel losing your mother. I lost both of my parents a long time ago, but you can't go blaming yourself for the two of you not getting along."

Priscilla never said anything after James talked to her; she lay down next to him and fell asleep with her head on his chest, and before she knew it, she was up getting dressed for their long ride to Tennessee.

James wrapped his arms around Priscilla. "How was your sleep last night?"

"I had a dream of Mama. She was very sad and all alone. I asked her what was the matter and why was she so sad, but she just sat there staring off at nothing important. When I woke up from that dream, I felt so sad for her. Do you believe in life after death?" she asked him.

"Well, I guess that I do, even though I haven't heard a lot of things about it, but there must be a god like I have heard of. Otherwise, where did we all come from? Let me ask you too. Do you believe in life after death?"

"I'm not really sure. We never went to church while I was growing up. There wasn't much talk about God or anything. In fact, my grandma told me when I was just a little girl that God was just a myth. Now I'm not saying I believe that because I do believe we just didn't appear here on earth—we had to have come from somewhere. Now I know some people think that we came from monkeys, but that is just stupid. In my sixth grade year of school, Mr. Sweet told the class that we came from monkeys. I got upset at what he had said because I had never believed in that junk. I told him that maybe he had a tail between his legs, but I sure didn't," Priscilla continued to say.

"I remember not liking him very much for a teacher. What did he say to you after that?" James asked.

"He told me to go sit in the hallway. I told him that I'd rather do that than be taught by a monkey anyway."

"Priscilla, I have never seen that side of you—wow, that really surprises me. You have always been so quiet and shy."

"When I hear something like that, I guess I just had to say something. I asked you if you believe in life after death because my friend Marcia, whom I was telling you about, well, she goes to church, and she talked to me about God."

"What did she say?"

"She said that she goes to church three times a week and she has been going for a couple of years when a friend of her husband led her to Jesus Christ. She said that she was never raised to go to church, either, but after going and finding out the truth about God, she has since asked him in her heart. She said that she is happier now since asking Jesus in her heart."

"Why does she feel that it made her more happy now after doing that?"

"I'm not real sure. She did say it gave her an inner peace she never had before. But when she was talking about God, it made me want to know more about him.] When Daddy called to tell me about my mother, I thought that it was going to be Marcia.

She had said that she wanted us to get together some time and play cards."

"Who? Just you and her?"

"No, she and her husband and us. I would really like to know more about what she was telling me about Jesus. She was telling me that he died on the cross so that we might be saved."

"What does that mean?"

"I'm not really sure, but she said that Jesus went to the cross and died there. Now when we do things that are sinful, all we have to do is ask him to forgive us for what we did, and he does."

"But that doesn't make any sense, does it?"

"You really need to hear how she told it to me because I can't remember how she said it. It made sense the way she told me." Priscilla glanced at the clock. "Wow, look at the time. We need to be getting David up and get going."

"Yep, you're right. We got so busy talking that we forgot to watch the time." James started to put some of his clothes in a suitcase. "So that dream you had about your mom made you sad, huh, honey?"

"Yes, it did. I don't know why she didn't look at me and why she sat there so still and sad. I wanted to talk to her very much, but she didn't see me standing there talking to her."

"I think that maybe you just went to bed thinking about the two of you and how you never got to talk much over the years. I'm sorry, honey, that you and she never had a good relationship with each other, like you wanted. I wish that things could have been better for the two of you."

"I know that you do, James, and I don't even want you to feel like any of this is your fault because it's not. You did nothing wrong. You have been a wonderful husband and father to David."

James never said anything after that, but his thoughts were deep, wondering what she would think of him if she was ever to find out the truth about their daughter he sold.

The ride was quiet for several hours, not much talking, but a whole lot of thinking was going on in James's head and in Priscilla's. Every once in a while, David would lean up to the front and say he was thirsty, so Priscilla would hand him some water she had brought with her. Then David would sit back to color again in his little coloring book.

THE FUNERAL

"DAD, I'M SO sorry that Mama's gone," Priscilla said as she put her arms around her father and cried with him. "Priscilla, you know that your mama loved you, don't you?"

"Yes, I know she did, Dad," Priscilla answered, but inside, she asked herself if she really did believe that. She felt she hadn't gotten any love from her mother in several years.

"Now I know that your mama and you haven't been close for a number of years, but I know that she loved you just the same as she always had. She'd tell me every once in a while that she missed having her talks with you. She'd tell me that she wanted to get to know our only grandchild better, but it just seemed that every time we'd plan to come up for a visit, something else would happen to keep us here. Now it's too late, and she'll never be able to come for that visit," Zach stated, breaking down.

"Dad, it doesn't have to be that way with us. We can make sure we get together more often than what we do. We don't have to let this sort of thing stop us from being father and daughter any longer."

Zach hugged his daughter. "I'd like that, honey, for us to be closer. That's the way it should be. Now where are James and that grandson of mine at?"

"He and David went to find us a motel to stay in, but he dropped me off first to come see you."

"Now why would he go to a motel? I have plenty of room here for the three of you. Please stay here with me, honey. I would like to spend as much time with you as I could."

"Dad, did you already make the funeral arrangements?" she asked, changing the subject, knowing that James might not feel welcome enough to stay at his home.

"No, I was hoping that you would help me with that today. Can you go with me into town to take care of it?"

"Yes, of course, I can. Maybe while James is gone, we should go and do that. Do you know who is doing the funeral?"

"Yes, his name is Pastor Timothy Button."

"Did Mama know him?"

"Yes, she went to his church."

"When did Mama start to go to church? I have never known her to go to church before."

"She started going with her friend Betty about three months ago."

"That's nice. Did you go with her?"

"No, I just thought that was something she liked to do with Betty, but she did tell me that she liked it. Maybe your mother and I should have brought you up in church. If we did, we all might have been better off."

"What do you mean by that, Dad?"

"Well, just maybe we could have all gotten along better. Maybe your mother and I could have treated James better than we have in the past."

"You still can do that, you know, Dad."

"Yes, honey, I can and I will. You'll see, it will be better between him and I."

"That's great, Dad. I know that he will really like that too, and that will make things so much easier for David too to see that his parents and grandparents"—right after she spoke the words *grandparents*, she felt terrible—"Sorry, Dad, I mean, better for you and us."

"I know what you meant, honey, and I know that it will take some getting used to not including your mother with everything now."

"Yes, it will take some time, but we will get through this." Priscilla felt like she was going to be fine now that she was with her dad; she felt that if she and her mother had been close in the past, then she would be taking her death a lot harder than she did now. "We better get going, Dad. Maybe we will be able to catch James trying to find a motel so we can ask him if he minds all of us staying here with you."

"Okay, let's get going then."

Priscilla and her father talked about the time she was young. She spent so much time trying to think about it the night before but was unable to remember, but now it was all coming back to her. They would laugh, then they would cry.

"Dad, James's car is right there in front of that motel." Priscilla pointed to the right of them.

"Run in there, honey, and try and catch him before he pays for a room."

"James! James!" Priscilla called out to him as she entered the building. "Daddy wants us to stay with him. You didn't already pay, did you?"

"No, I was just about to. Are you sure that would be the best thing to do?"

"Yes, honey, my dad wants to make everything right between you and him." Priscilla looked at him to see if he would walk away from the counter.

"Okay, honey, we can stay there with him. I'm sure, right now he really needs you."

"He really needs us."

James looked at her then at the man behind the counter. "Sorry, I guess we won't be staying after all. Come on, David, let's get going."

"Hey, why don't you and David go get a bite to eat, while I go with my dad to talk with Mama's pastor—"

Before she could finish her sentence James interrupted her. "Pastor? Since when did your mother ever go to church?"

"He said that she's been going for a few months now with her friend Betty." Priscilla saw the strange look of unbelief written all over James's face. "I know, weird, huh. It surprised me, that's for sure."

"David and I have already eaten, so we will just meet you back at your dad's when you are done doing what it is you have to do."

Priscilla walked out of the motel and got into her father's car and told him that James and David were going back to his house. After their talk with the pastor, they headed back to her father's house.

"Hello, Zach, how are you doing? I'm so sorry to hear about your wife," James said, holding out a hand to shake his.

"I'm still trying to get over the shock of her being gone forever. I want to thank you for coming down here and bringing my little girl and my grandson," Zach said as he rubbed the top of David's head. "It's been awhile since the last time I got to see any of you. It's so good to see my family." Tears rolled down his cheeks. "Priscilla, can you come with me just for a minute? I have something I have to give to you that was your mother's."

"Dad, we don't have to do this right now. We can wait," she said, as she could see the tears in her father's eyes.

"No, this is something your mother had told me you must have if anything was to happen to her. Please come."

Priscilla looked at James then followed behind her father as he had asked. "What is it, Dad, that Mama had wanted me to have?"

"I don't rightly know. She put it into our closet several months ago and told me that if anything was ever to happen to her, I must give it to you. Now when your mother told me that, I just thought she was being silly, but I've been wondering if she might have had a feeling she wasn't going to live long." Zach talked while getting whatever it was that her mother had wanted her to have out of the closet.

"That is really weird, Dad, that she would tell you to give something to me so many months ago. I think you're right. Maybe she did have a feeling of some kind that she was not going to live much longer."

Zach handed his daughter a shoe box from off the top of the self in the closet. "I don't know what's inside the box, honey, but she made sure that I knew you were to have it."

Priscilla walked over to the bed and was just about ready to take the lid off the box when Zach said he would go out.

"Okay, Dad, I'll be right out there."

"Okay, honey, I'll leave you to yourself right now."

Priscilla took the lid off the box, not knowing what to expect was inside that was of any importance when she saw what looked like letters.

"Letters," she spoke out loud to herself. She unfolded the top one that had her name on it and began to read.

> My dearest daughter Priscilla,
>
> I want you to know that I love you so very much, and I'm so very sorry for the way that I have treated you and James since your marriage. I know that you may never understand that it was not that I really disliked James, but it's that I have watched the two of you struggle for several years, and James seemed to be too proud of a man to let your father and I help you both out in any way. I watched you desire to be a mom

for several years before you became one, when your father and I still lived there in Michigan before moving to Tennessee.

One thing that you did not know is that when you had your baby, I was there. James didn't know that I was there, either, but I was watching from another room as you gave birth. I could see when the doctor gave you a shot to help ease the pain that you were having. Please forgive me, Priscilla, for not letting you know that I was there, but I want you to know that I love you and I understand why he did what he did.

I remember when I would have conversations with you about you wanting to be a mother so badly. It tore me up inside because James would always tell you that the two of you could not afford one and yet he refused to take any help from us. But that's okay now. It all worked out for the best of everyone.

Now I really need for you to focus on what I am about to tell you because this can strengthen you or it can hurt you in such a way that your life will forever be changed. Priscilla, I want you to know that I truly believe that James loves you far more than you or I have realized. I also know that him getting the store came at a great price, but he did whatever he could do to see that you were able to have the life you were always meant to have.

Someday, honey, you will come to understand what I am talking about, and I want you to remember what I have said *here in this letter. Choose today to forgive and understand.*

Priscilla sat there, not knowing what her mother was talking about in the letter—what she could possibly know that Priscilla herself didn't know. She began to read some more of the letter.

Honey, I had to forgive many things in my life, and I ask you to forgive me too for everything that had taken place between us. I want you to have all of my jewelry and anything else of mine that you would like to take. I know that your father will have no problem giving those things to you.

I never raised you in church or taught you the things of God, but one thing I have learned was to love God with my whole heart and love others. Find a good church to go to, where they'll teach you all about Jesus and his love. Raise David to know the things of God, and please tell him that I am sorry too for everything, and tell James that I understand why he did what he did and I don't hold it against him. Ask him to forgive me for the way I have treated him. I love you, my sweet girl. I'm in heaven now with Jesus, and I look forward to seeing you when your life on earth is over.

Your loving Mother.

Priscilla folded the letter back up, not knowing what it meant about James. She knew that she would be talking to him about the letter, but she knew that now was not the time to do that. She picked up another letter that had writing on it that stated, "To my grandson, David." Priscilla left that in the box for another time;

she figured that she would read it to David when her mother's funeral was all over with.

James watched Priscilla walk out to the living room carrying the box; he wondered what the box could possibly be holding. Did it have sentimental things in there from her mother? Did it contain jewelry, or things that her mother cherished.

"Are you okay honey?" he asked her, concerned at the way she was staring at him.

"Now's not the time, but I do want to talk with you about this later when we are alone."

"Okay." James was shocked by the way Priscilla was acting. It was like she was angry with him, and he couldn't understand what made her so upset. What could he have possibly done? He knew she was hurting about the death of her mother, so he would leave her well enough alone until she was ready to talk.

"When Dad and I went into town and talked with Mama's pastor and his wife, they said that the church folks would have a dinner after the funeral the day after tomorrow. I told them that would be very nice of them."

"What did your mother leave for you in the box?" he asked out of curiosity.

"A letter."

"A letter? What kind of a letter?"

"Yep, a letter, and she talked about you in it." Right after Priscilla said those words, she knew right then that she should have bitten her lip. But it was too late; she already opened up her mouth.

"Oh really, like what honey?"

She didn't want to talk about it, so the only answer he got was, "Not much."

"Okay." James knew that there was more to say, but he also knew that she wasn't ready to talk so he didn't question it anymore. He knew that when she was ready to talk that there would be nothing holding her back from doing so.

The funeral went as well as it could be expected. Priscilla thought that the pastor had done a great job describing her mother. The meal was very nicely prepared. The folks who came greeted her and her father were pleasant people. After spending four days away from her home, she was ready to go back. She missed her bed, and she knew she needed to get back to pick Moe up from the neighbor man, who was caring for him while they were gone. She hugged and gave her father a kiss good-bye, promising that they would get together soon.

On their way back home, after David had fallen to sleep in the back seat, Priscilla couldn't wait any longer to question James about the letter.

"James, Mama wrote something in this here letter of mine that I just don't understand."

"Like what, honey? I could see ever since you read the letter from her, you have been acting weird. What is this all about? Would you please tell me?"

"I'll read it to you, then you tell me what she means okay?"

"Okay." James couldn't possibly know what she could have written in the letter for Priscilla that had made her so upset. After hearing what the letter had said, he could barely breathe. *She was there at the hospital when Priscilla had the babies*, he thought. *So it was her I saw going around the corner, like I thought at first.*

"Well, could you shed some light on this please, James? It's driving me crazy what she said in this letter."

"I do know that I never wanted to borrow money from her or your dad, and she used to get upset with me about it. Now I know you would remember that, honey."

"I do, but what about the part that your store came at a great price? What does that mean?"

"Well I can't say for sure, but I do know that I worked for years trying to make ends meet without borrowing money, and I worked fourteen hours every day to try to pay our bills and keep our head above water. Maybe that's the high price that she was talking about."

"I have a feeling that there's more to it than that. Have you stolen anything or sold drugs to get where you're at?"

"Priscilla, I can't believe that you could ever think that of me! No, honey, I never did that."

I did a lot worse. The thoughts were ringing in his head. He wanted to tell her that he sold their daughter, but he kept his mouth shut. Then he got angry thinking about how Bernadine had known that Priscilla gave birth to twins and not mentioned anything to her daughter about it. Then he took a look at himself and thought how he could possibly be angry at her when it was indeed him who sold his little girl so he could have a better life.

James grew very quiet, and Priscilla was so caught up on trying to understand what her mother meant in her letter that she didn't even realize that James was upset too. After many long hours of driving, they were home and ready to unwind and go to bed.

Priscilla said, "I don't think that I have had that long of a drive before where you and I didn't talk. It had to be the quietest ride that you and I have ever had before."

James looked back at her. At first, he didn't know how to respond to her intuition, then he decided to show an act of love, walking up to her and putting his arms around her. "Honey, I don't like it when we fight. It makes me feel sad inside when I know that we are not acting as if we love each other because you and David are the best things that have ever happened to me. Will you please forgive me for raising my voice at you earlier?"

"Yes, if you will forgive me for questioning you like I did. I should have known that you would never have done any of those things. I don't know what got into me thinking that you could have stolen anything or sold drugs to buy a store."

"It was probably the letter that got you thinking crazy like that."

James wanted so much to tell his wife the truth, but how could he? Would she ever understand like her mother did? As much as he wanted to be mad at her mother for not telling Priscilla the terrible thing he did, he also understood why she never came out with the truth. It was for the same reason that he had not told her. It was plain that they never could have cared for the two babies the way they would have wanted to. They all would have been too poor for anything, but at least this way, they would all have a better chance at life, including his little girl being raised by a doctor and his wife who had plenty of money and love to take care of her.

THE VISIT

AFTER JAMES LEFT for work, Priscilla walked over to the neighbors to get Moe.

"Thank you, Pete, for caring for him while we were gone to Tennessee. Was he any trouble?"

"Not at all. How are you and your father doing?"

"It's going to be very hard for him at first getting used to being alone, but he's strong. I'm sure that he will be okay, and I am going to be fine. It will just take us awhile getting used to her being gone. This was really quite shocking for me, but I have the support of a good man, and I will be fine. Thanks for asking, and thanks for watching Moe."

"You have a good day." Pete waved bye as she was walking away with Moe.

Priscilla called up Marcia to ask her if she had tried to call her while she was gone for a week.

"Yes, I have tried to call several times, I was beginning to wonder if I might have had the wrong number, and when I didn't hear from you, I wondered if there could be something wrong," Marcia commented.

"My mother passed away last week, so James and I went to Tennessee to be with my father for a few days."

"Oh, I am so sorry to hear that. Why don't you and David come over today for a visit? I'd love to see you, and I'm sure that Terri would too."

"Okay, that does sound good. I feel like I could use a friend about now. What time would you like us to come over?" Priscilla asked.

"How about eleven o'clock?"

"Okay, we will be there."

After getting Marcia's address, the women hung up the phone.

Priscilla looked at the time and saw that she still had two hours before going over to see Marcia. "I'll make a coffee cake to take with me," she said to herself.

"What, Mama?" David asked.

Turning around, she found him standing at the entrance of the kitchen and rubbing his sleeping eyes. "Oh, I was just talking to myself, honey."

"I'm hungry, Mama."

"Okay, why don't you come up here in this seat?" Priscilla pulled out a chair for him to sit in. "Would you like a bowl of cereal?"

"Uh-huh." He was nodding his head up and down.

She got him a bowl of his favorite kind of cereal, and after giving it to him she went to work on making a coffee cake to take with her to Marcia's house.

After driving only for a couple of miles, they reached their destination. Priscilla was looking at all of Marcia's beautiful flowers she had outside of her home as she pulled into the driveway. The smell was very welcoming to her, even before she got out of the car. She sat there, taking in deep breaths of what smelled like lily of the valley flowers. If anything, what she liked during the months of summer was the smell of flowers.

Walking up to the door, she looked all around her to see what kinds of flowers had been planted in the little flower garden outside Marcia's home. Noticing that there were several kinds that she didn't even know the names of, she continued to the door.

"Come on in," Marcia said to Priscilla and then looked down at David. "Welcome, David. Terri has been waiting for you to show up." Marcia opened her door more to welcome her company.

As Priscilla walked through the doorway, she looked around at what she thought had to be the most beautiful home that she had ever seen before.

"You have a very lovely home. I would love to have a place that is so open and bright as your place is," she said as she was noticing the bright walls, and the pictures she had hanging on them. Not to mention all the vases were filled with so many kinds of flowers. "It seems to me, after seeing how light your walls are, that the walls at my place are just too dark."

"I painted them sometime ago. I went through a time in my life a few years back where I felt so out of place, and I was so sad everything around me seemed to be so dark and gloomy. I had to pick myself up for my daughter, so I went out and bought me several gallons of paint, and I went to work at brightening up this place."

"Well, you did a fine job, better than I could have done. I would never have guessed that you like to paint."

"If you must know, that was the first time I had ever done anything like this. I really didn't know that I could even do this until I did. I guess we can do anything we put our minds to when we want to. Come, we'll have some tea," Marcia said as she walked toward the kitchen.

"Oh, here, this is for you." Priscilla held out the coffee cake for her to take.

"Thank you." Marcia took the cake, placed it on the table, and prepared the tea. "What is it?"

"It's a cinnamon coffee cake."

"It sure smells good, thank you. The tea will be ready in just a minute. It didn't take the two long to play together," Marcia said, looking at the children playing in the living room. "What happened with your mother, if you don't mind me asking you?"

"My father said that she took ill in the middle of the night and she never got any better despite the whole time telling him that she was fine. I didn't even know that she was sick until she was already gone."

"Your father never called you to let you know that she was sick? Why would he not call? I'm sorry, I don't mean to pry."

"That's okay. I need someone to talk to. When I asked him why he didn't call me up and let me know that she was sick, he told me that my mother told him not to bother because she was going to be fine."

"I'm so sorry to hear that. So how are you dealing with this? I know what it's like to love someone then lose them."

"Yeah, it's not the easiest thing to go through, but what makes it worse for me, I think, is that for several years before my mother died, she and I never saw each other eye to eye. She never wanted me to marry James, and she always let me know just how she felt."

"Really! Why is that?"

"My folks never thought that he was good enough for me, and you can't find any better than my James. That man would move the skies for me if he could. Up until almost five years ago, he had worked fourteen hours every day in a nasty, old factory to make ends meet, but now he is the proud owner of the grocery store here in town." She was remembering the day he bought the store. "So you see, my parents had always wanted my husband to be an important man, and I think that being an owner of his own store would qualify him as an important man."

"It sure does."

"It's funny really, my parents have always wanted me to marry a guy whom I went to school with because they have always thought that he was going to be a big shot of some sort, but what happened was that man now works for my husband at the store."

"Now that is funny." Marcia chuckled. "Yep, one never really knows what life holds for them. I guess that could be a good thing because if we could see what our future was, maybe some of us could never handle it."

Priscilla didn't say anything to Marcia's way of thinking, but she tried to picture if she felt the same way about it.

"I believe God has our future all planned out for us. He knows just how everything is to be and how it will end up for each one of us," Marcia continued. "I just know that he created everyone, and if he did, then he must know our future. I told you that I've been going to church for about two years now, and I have learned so much about the things of God. What do you think?"

"Yes, I guess he would know it," Priscilla replied softly.

"So what are your plans for the future?"

Priscilla thought to herself while she sat there, sipping her tea and eating a slice of her cake, thinking about the question that Marcia had just asked. Then the tears began to come down her cheeks, and then the answer came. "I don't really know. I have been kind of numb since my mother passed away."

Marcia felt so sorry for the pain her new friend was having— at least she felt like she was a friend. She wished that there was something she could do to help her. "I'm sorry, Priscilla, for your pain. Is there anything I can do to help you?" She prayed silently for her.

"No, I'll be all right. I just wish that she and I could have made things right before she died."

"I can't imagine what you're going through, so I won't pretend that I do, but I want you to know that if you ever need anything, I am here for you."

"Thank you for that. That is very sweet of you. I'm glad that we ran into each other again at the park."

"Yes, I am too. I could always use a kind friend."

The two women sat there quietly for several minutes, then Priscilla said she was going to call her father up later when she returned home to check up on him.

"That probably is a good thing. After all they had been together a long time, haven't they?"

"Yes, and I'm sure it's got to be very lonely for him in that big house of theirs all alone now."

The two women seemed to connect with each other. Marcia asked Priscilla if she would like for them to get together that weekend and play some cards. "I think Nick can take some time off to enjoy some company, so what do you think? Are you ready to get together to get your mind off of sadness?"

"Yes, I will talk with James tonight, I'm sure that it will be fine with him. He's not on call like your husband is. The children are sure having fun, aren't they?" Priscilla said as she watched the children from the kitchen.

"Yes, I see that, and I am very glad to see that because Terri gets bored when there are no little kids around. She's forever asking me to have a tea party with her."

"I remember doing the same thing with my mom when I was little too. I think that there were times when she wished I had a sibling to play with."

The two women talked with each other in what seemed like hours. Then it was time for Priscilla and David to go back home. When Priscilla arrived home, she talked with James about the four of them getting together and playing some cards when the weekend comes.

"I haven't played in so long that I'm sure I'd be quite rusty at it," James said.

"It's like riding a bike. Once you sit down and see the cards in your hand, it will all come back to you," she replied.

"Oh really, you think so?" He took his wife in his arms and gave her a kiss. "Then I say yes, let's do it. It's been a long time since we got to hang out with some friends and play cards."

"I was hoping that you'd say that. I'll call her up then and let her know that we'll be coming over if she's still asking."

"And what makes you think that she'd change her mind? It seems to me that you found a good friend indeed. What you have told me about her, I don't think that she'll be changing her mind."

"I didn't mean it that way. I just meant that something might come up that would keep us from going over there is all. Like her husband not being able to get off from work."

"Well, let's just hope that he could. I see the look in your eyes when you talk about your friend—it's a look that I haven't see in you in a long time. You need a good friend. I know that it has to get boring being at home all the time, so I say, by all means, let's go over to their house and play some cards."

"I'll call her up and let her know that you said that we can go then." Priscilla walked away with a smile across her face; she had not had many friends come over for a while, but now she had a friend to share laughter with about her son and her friend's daughter.

Time went on, and the two women grew even closer, to where they would go to each others place at least two or three times a week. James never minded it; he knew that she needed a friend to hang out with. He and Nick seemed to get along quite well together, even though at times he would be talking with him when suddenly it would appear to him that Nick would lose focus on whatever they were talking about and would start getting angry about something that took place sometime ago with his daughter, Terri, not wanting to go to bed when asked to go. Although it seemed strange to him for Nick to act that way, he continued to be his friend and play cards with him.

The children were growing bigger and bigger. They had become best friends; it was no wonder the way the parents were together so much of the time. Whenever Marcia and her husband would go out for the night, Priscilla and James would have Terri come stay with them, and when James and Priscilla went out, Marcia and Nick would take care of David for them. They enjoyed watching each others kid. Terri was a real joy to have around; it seemed the more they watched her, the more they loved her like she was their own.

They all would gather at the church where they were all now attending for several years. Marcia and Nick got them going, and they found that they enjoyed going, so they just kept on going and learning the things of the Bible.

Priscilla mentioned to James one night while they lay in bed how Terri looked so much like her when she was a young girl. All she would get back from James was, "Now, honey, we know that can't really be true." Priscilla would shove it at the back of her mind that she was just being silly; there just was no way she could look anything like her because she knew they were not related in any way at all.

One day, while Terri was at school, she fell from the monkey bars and broke her arm. When the school called home to inform her mother what happened to her while playing at recess, Marcia called Priscilla up right away to ask her to come down to the hospital so she could be there for Terri too. After getting to the hospital, Priscilla went into the emergency room with Marcia and Terri to be there for them during this time. When Nick came into the room to take a look at Terri's arm, Priscilla was shocked by what she heard him say to her.

"Now why would you climb on something that you know darn well that you can fall from and get hurt? How many times do I have to tell you that in life, we must be aware of everything around us? Now because you didn't listen to me about being careful, like I've told you many times before, you will have to wear a cast on your arm for six weeks. I sure hope that this teaches you that life is not all fun and games."

"Nick, that is enough. She is just a child," Marcia said, embarrassed by Nick's actions.

Nick looked at Priscilla standing there; it was almost like he had forgotten all about her being there. "Please forgive me, Priscilla."

Not saying anything to him, she patted Terri on her knee as she was sitting on the edge of the bed, waiting to get a cast on her arm. She was so upset at what she had just witnessed that she couldn't even look at him in his eyes. She had never seen this side of Nick before, and it was quite shaking for her to see it now. She had always treated Terri like her own, and over the last seven years of knowing her, she had come to love her very much.

After Nick put the cast on Terri, the three walked out of the hospital, leaving Nick standing at the door, unsure of what to say.

"Mama," Terri said.

"Yes, honey, what can I do for you?" Marcia asked, feeling bad about the way she was treated by Nick.

"Why is Daddy always so mad at me? Doesn't he love me, mama?"

"Well, of course, he does, honey. He's just very tired right now. He's put in a lot of hours here at work last night and then again today. He just needs to rest."

Somehow, Priscilla thought that Marcia said all of that just to make up excuses on why he acted the way that he did to Terri. She knew that this was just not the normal way for a father to act toward his child, even if he was tired.

"Marcia, you know, if there is anything that you would like to talk about, I am always here for you if you need to talk."

"I know, and I thank you for that. I'm sorry that you had to see Nick act like that. You are a very dear friend to me. Thanks for coming up here to be here with us." Marcia started to walk toward her car.

Priscilla knew her well enough to know not to press the issue. "I'm glad that you called me up." Bending down to talk with

Terri, she said "You get better soon, kiddo. I love you, and I'll see you soon okay."

"Okay, Aunt Priscilla." Terri nodded, She had been calling Priscilla by that name for the last five years.

Time went by; winter, summer, fall, and spring came and went for several years since Marcia and Priscilla had become friends.

Priscilla and Marcia stayed very close over the thirteen years that they have known each other and watched the children grow to be loving young adults, much like their parents.

James was watching the two kids play. He watched as Terri ran up to David and jumped on his back. The more he watched the two of them, the more he became suspicious. James began to ask the kids questions about how they felt for each other.

David and Priscilla couldn't understand the concern that James was having all of a sudden about the two children being together; Priscilla knew that the two had basically grown up together and had always been very close since they were nearly five years old. Now James was acting like he was trying to keep the two apart, and Priscilla wanted to know why.

"Priscilla, it's not that I want to keep them apart, really. It's just that I don't want to see them falling in love with each other, like so many young kids do. Kids think that they know what love is, but the simple fact is, they don't really know what real love is all besides the kind you get from a parent."

"What makes you think that they are going to fall in love with each other?"

"Good lord, woman, haven't you been watching the two of them, the way they are with each other? Terri is always jumping up on his back, wanting a piggyback ride. And David is always tackling her down to the ground."

"She is just like I was when I was young, wanting a piggyback ride, and that makes them 'falling in love'? You do beat all, James. They are children just having a little fun, like brother and sister."

When James heard the words 'like brother and sister,' that struck a nerve in him, and he walked away from Priscilla, going into the living room to sit down. He sat there quietly, with his hands folded underneath his chin, as if to be in deep thought. Priscilla wasn't quite sure what was going on with him; after all, she had never seen him act this way before.

Why was he starting to let David and Terri's friendship bother him so much that he would start to question their every move? Was it because he agreed with what Priscilla said about Terri looking like her when she was a young girl? Could Terri be his daughter? But how could she be? *Nick is her adopted father, not Michael.* His thoughts were running like wild fire right now.

One night, Terri came over to visit with David when James asked to talk with the two of them.

"I see that the two of you have become quite close. Is there anything that you want to tell me about the two of you?" he asked.

Terri looked at David then looked back at James. "What do you mean?"

"What I mean is what I said. Is there anything going on with the two of you that I should know about?"

"Dad, why are you asking us this? I already told you the other day that Terri and I are just friends, and you act like we are about to run away together or something," David replied.

"That's all we are. Honest, David is like a brother to me," Terri said, punching David on his arm then laughing.

Priscilla walked in the room and told the kids to go outside and play; she wanted to have a talk with James and get this thing all sorted out once and for all.

"Now, James, I know you have told me before that it was nothing and for me not to worry, but I'm telling you right now—I know that something is going on, and we are going to get to the bottom of this right now."

"I don't care to talk about it, Priscilla," James snapped at her and tried to walk away.

"Please, James, if you have ever loved me at all, you will sit down and talk to me right now."

"Don't you understand, woman? I can't. I want to really, I do, but right now, I just can't."

Priscilla saw tears in James's eyes as he walked away. She was left standing there in the living room, wondering what was going on. One way or another, she was going to find out; she just wasn't sure of how to go about finding it. She thought that maybe she would call up her pastor to see if he could have a talk with James and try to get this issue resolved before it would tear up her relationship with Terri and Marcia. She was so afraid by the way James was acting that he just might tell David that he thought it best if Terri didn't come over as much as she did. And the very thought of that, she couldn't stand any longer. Not only did she love Terri as if she were her own, but she was best friends with Terri's mother and didn't want to lose her as a friend.

THE TRUTH COMES OUT

JAMES FELT BAD keeping the truth from Priscilla, and he wasn't sure how much longer he would be able to. Seeing the way Terri and David acted together all the time, he couldn't help but wonder if there was a way that she could be his daughter. He heard of how kids who grow up close together and still fall in love with each other once they reach adulthood. All he ever wanted was for his family to have what he felt they deserved and for his little girl, whom he gave away thirteen years ago, to have a better life than what he could have gave to her at the time. But now he was questioning everything. Watching the kids play close together had got him so afraid that it seemed to have consumed him in a way that it was stealing his peace and joy, which he should be having with the way things had been going for the store and his family being very blessed.

He wanted to come clean with Priscilla about everything that Michael and he had done so many years ago. He wanted to know if Marcia was ever married to Michael, but how could he find out? How would he begin his search for the truth? What would he say? Would he be hated by everyone he loves? Should he take the chance that the two would never fall in love with each other and just stay friends if they are brother and sister? Yes, that's what he would do. He would keep his secret and keep an eye on them without letting them know. He knew that in order to stop Priscilla from asking him any more questions, he would have to lie low and keep to himself how he felt about the kids.

Priscilla called up her pastor to ask him if he could have a talk with James. She told him that she felt like he was having too much pressure from work and it was making him act crazy when it came to David and his best friend, Terri.

Pastor Rod Somerville told her that he would have a talk with James about the two of them getting together and finding out what was going on with him to make him act this way about his son and Terri. He knew the two kids from church, and he knew that the both of them were very good children, well behaved, and he never thought anything wrong about the two of them hanging out together. After all, everyone knew Priscilla and Marcia were the very best of friends and David and Terri were practically raised together.

Priscilla was glad that he had agreed to meet with James. Now it was up to her to get James to agree to meet with the pastor and to get all of this that seemed to be out of order back to order.

"James, I would like for you to talk with Pastor Rod about what's going on with you lately," Priscilla asked.

"Oh come on, Priscilla, what do you want me to do that for? You know how I feel about letting others know our business."

"Because things haven't been going right lately with you, and I really think that it's best if you can talk out some of your problems with a man of God. Maybe he can help you in a way that I can't. Right now I feel that I'm at my wits end with you and what you are doing to the kids."

"Let me think about it, Priscilla. I just don't know how I feel to talk about my problems to someone outside of the family. It's different for you women. You ladies can talk to a perfect stranger about anything, but us men, we aren't like that."

Priscilla wrapped her arms around James's waist. "I know it's harder for you men to open up about what's going on in your life, but I thought that if it was the preacher, then that might make things easier for you."

"Give me a chance to at least think about it, and I will let you know."

"Okay I will. I just want things to be back to normal, where we are happy and not seeing things that are not there. Maybe you should take a few days off from work. Maybe that will help."

"I can't take time off right now. We are adding on to the store right now, and I need to be there."

"I'm sorry, James, I forgot about that. I haven't been there in a while. I have you bring home what we need."

"Honey, trust me, this has nothing to do with the store. I will be okay, and I just might meet with the pastor. But for now, I have to go to work. I'll see you when I get home, and I will take you and David out to eat tonight, so don't make any supper, okay?"

"Okay, I won't," Priscilla replied.

James went to work and tried to concentrate on what he was doing, but his mind kept thinking about what his wife was asking from him. The more he thought about it, the more he was thinking that maybe it was the best thing for him to do.

Maybe I will go and talk with the pastor and get all of what I have done behind my wife's back off of my chest once and for all.

James decided after much consideration to call up his pastor and ask him if he could come down to the church and speak with him. He told him that it was very important that they talk. Then Pastor Rod agreed to have him come down to the church that afternoon.

On the way to the church, James was trying to rehearse what he would be saying to his pastor; he didn't want to just come out with what he had done. He needed a plan to lead him into telling the truth.

"Dear God," he spoke out loud, "help me with telling the truth. I have done such a terrible thing to my wife so many years ago, when I didn't know you or serve you. How do I come out with what I have done to my family? I know that I've been coming to church for a long time now, but, God, I still wasn't living for you until the last few months. Now that I know you better, and know that you hate what I have done to my wife by deceiving her like I did, I just have to come clean, and I don't know how to do that. Lord, I don't want to lose her. She means so much to me."

He continued to talk, then the tears began to fall. "Please help me, God. I don't know if I can do this. I don't want to lose my family. I love them so much."

James drove to the church trying, to get over the fear that had taken a hold of him. He wanted to come clean with what he had done thirteen years before, but he was having a hard time with how he would explain his actions to his pastor. Then he had a thought come to mind.

"Yep, that's what I will do. I'll ask him what he would have done under the same circumstance. I'll see if he would have done the same thing or at least would he blame me for what I have done."

Pulling into the church parking lot, he sat there for a few minutes debating about going in, then he heard a tap on his window.

"Come on, brother. No time is better than right now. Whatever is eating you up on the inside, it's time that you let it go. So come on, let's talk okay," Pastor Rod urged.

James opened up his door, and taking one look into his pastor's eyes, he felt like he was going to break right there outside. "Yes, I guess you are right. I need to get this off of my chest. I can't keep going like this. Every day, it feels like I'm still doing this over and over again."

Pastor Rod put his hand on James shoulder as they walked into the church. "Let's go into my office so we can talk." He led

James the way down the hallway to his office. Motioning for James to take a seat, he closed the door behind them. "Please sit. I'm not sure of what you are talking about when you say that it feels like you are still doing this over and over."

James felt scared and very nervous. "I don't know where to begin. It's been so long ago, and I can't stop feeling so guilty, but if I don't tell the truth, I just might lose my family, but then if I tell the truth, I might lose them there too."

"Okay, then let's start by you telling me how long ago it was," Pastor Rod said. "I can see that you are having a hard time talking about it."

"It was thirteen years ago." James could barely get that out without tears forming his eyes. "I don't know if I can do this."

Pastor Rod sat there waiting to see if James was going to tell more before he said anything to him. But after waiting for a few minutes and James not saying anything else, he decided to try and help him out.

"Okay, thirteen years ago—well that was sometime ago. Why now is this starting to bother you? Isn't that how old your son David is?"

James sat there, nodding his head up and down while he was bent over, holding his hands underneath his chin.

"James, it's going to take you to do the talking, brother. I don't know what you could have possibly done way back then that is haunting you today. I mean, I can speculate, but that's all I can do." He waited for James to say something, but still no words was he hearing. "Did you have an affair on your wife, and now since you have come to the front of the church and accepted Jesus Christ as your Lord and Savior, it's eating you up on the inside?"

James shook his head no, then he said, "I didn't cheat on, Priscilla. I could never have done that. Can I ask you a question?"

"Sure, James, ask away."

"If you weren't a Christian, and you have worked your butt off for years trying to make ends meet working fourteen hours a day, and still it seemed like you could never do anything with the one you loved or you could never afford to take time off to spend any time with your family. What would you do?"

"Well, sometimes it feels much like that in my life now. I have to spend a considerable amount of time away from my wife and kids, and not always do they enjoy that."

"But do you ever get to take them out or buy something nice for them?"

"Yes, I do that from time to time. Why don't you try and tell me what you think that you have done so wrong that you think you can lose your family over it?"

"Okay, I'll tell you, but you must promise me that it won't go any farther than this room—you will not tell a soul what I am about to tell you."

"I will not speak a word of it. That is not for me to do. You make it seem so mysterious."

"First of all, I just want you to know that what I did at the time. I really believed that it was done out of love, and I hope that you won't hold it against me."

Just as the two men were to start there conversation of what took place in James life thirteen years ago, Mrs. Bittner just happened to be walking by the pastor's office when she heard voices. So being the nosy elderly lady that she was, she stopped dead in her tracks to listen on something that was meant to be kept a secret.

"I don't believe that there is anything that you could have done that will cause that, but just for the record whatever you say to me today stays in this room," Pastor Rod reassured him.

"What I'm about to tell you, no one knows about it, except the doctor who delivered David and his sister who was there in the delivery room when David was born. And from what I understand, they both are dead now." James looked away. He hesitated then continued. "This is really hard for me to talk about.

I tried for years to find a way to tell my wife, but I haven't been able to tell her about this terrible thing that I have done."

Mrs. Bittner was outside of the door with her ear pressed up against it so hard that it was likely that she would break the door down. The two men continued on talking not knowing about the snoopy woman who stood on the other side of the door.

"It's all right. You and I can talk, and I will try to help you in any way that I can," Pastor Rod reassured him.

"Thirteen years ago, when my wife went into labor, we didn't know what we were going to have. A boy or a girl, it didn't really matter. The fact is, I told Priscilla for years that we couldn't have a baby because we just couldn't afford one. But she got pregnant anyways. Whether we were prepared to have one or not, we were going to be having a baby. I really didn't know what we were going to do with another mouth to feed. I was working fourteen hours a day, trying to make ends meet as it was, and still not ever enjoying life."

Pastor Rod sat there listening to James, as he would carefully find the right words to speak, without going too fast to follow.

"I have always wanted to have my own business—you know, work for myself. Now I want you to know that I didn't plan this at all. It's just something that happened without seeing it coming right at me. That day when Priscilla went into labor…well…you see, Pastor, she…well…she," James stammered.

Pastor Rod could see that James was having a hard time finding his words now, so he tried to help him out. "James what happened that day when she was having the baby?"

"My wife…well…you see, she had two babies that day, not just the one."

As soon as the words fell out of his mouth, James began to flood with tears that have been bottled up for so long that he put his head down on his knees and wept until his whole body just shook.

When Mrs. Bittner heard about Priscilla having two babies instead of just the one, she was just about to run down the hallway of the church to go make some phone calls when she decided she better listen to all the story.

"Are you telling me that Priscilla had twins? What happened to the other baby, James? Did it die?" Pastor Rod asked softly.

James shook his head vigorously, then blurted out, "No, I sold her."

At that very moment Mrs. Bittner put her hand over her mouth so they couldn't hear her outside the door, ready to start her gossiping before ever reaching a phone.

Pastor Rod didn't know what to say. He sat there looking at James like he had just seen a ghost. He couldn't take his eyes off of him; it was like he was in shock. He couldn't believe his ears, then he found words that James knew was coming and wanted to avoid.

"You sold her! What do you mean you sold her? And how does Priscilla not know about this?"

James was trying to find his voice. "When Priscilla went into labor, we didn't know that she was carrying two babies. We only knew about the one. But she had many complications during labor and was telling the doctor that we were struggling with our finances and we didn't know what we were going to do with another mouth to feed. She was in a lot of pain, and the doctor had to give her a shot to help with the pain. That shot calmed her right down, and she fell asleep. Well during the time that she slept, the doctor had taken the babies because she couldn't deliver them."

"Are you telling me that she has never known that she gave birth to two children for all of these years?"

"Yes, that's what I am saying. I know that it was so wrong for me to never tell her about giving birth to two of them, but when the doctor told me that she was worried, and I was too, then he offered to give me money for my little girl. I took it while Priscilla was still sleeping."

"So you are telling me that the doctor wanted your baby girl, but why?"

"He told me that he and his wife have been married for twenty years and have always wanted a baby, but his wife has something wrong with her that prevented her from ever having a child. And then when he said that it would be better for me to take the money and be able to buy my own business and feed my son and have a real life without all the stress of never having anything. Well, he promised me that he would give my little girl a loving and a proper home, one that she would be very well provided for with a mom and a dad that would love her like their very own. After thinking about what he had said, and knowing that I could never take care of my family on what I earned, I took the money for the best of all of us."

"Do you even know where your little girl is now? Have you ever seen her since that day?"

"Yes, I think that I see her just about every day, and so does David and Priscilla. But they don't know she could belong to us."

"Please help me understand this. You say that the three of you see her just about every day, but yet they don't know who she really is?"

"Yes."

"How can that be?"

"Pastor, you know who my little girl is too—I mean, who I think that she is." James looked at him. "It's Terri."

The pastor sat there not knowing what to say. His hand went up to his forehead and wiped it like he was sweating. All of a sudden, he jumped up to his feet.

"Oh, my son, I can see why you have been in this amount of torment. That really is quite a story. Wow! Well, I can say that there is nothing too big for God. He has seen your heart back then, and he sees your heart now. Wow, this is going to need some deep prayer and thought before you come out with this one. So Terri's mom doesn't know about this, either?"

Mrs. Bittner wasn't about to let a story like this go quiet. She was hoping that they could just finish up already so she could run and make her calls to whoever wanted to know.

"No, she doesn't, but she told Priscilla that Terri was adopted.

"Yes, I knew that. Let me ask you something."

"Okay," James said as he looked at his pastor and quickly put his head back down as he was so ashamed for what he had just confessed to.

"Why, after all of this time, you now wanted to talk about this?"

"The truth is it has always bothered me, and another is because the older that Terri is getting, the more she looks like my wife, and even Priscilla had said that to me a few different times. She can't believe that her best friend's little girl can look so much like her when she was her age. She even brought out some pictures and showed me how much Terri looks like she did. Then I see how much she and David are so close and are hanging on each other. I would never want the two of them to decide that they like each other for more than friends if she is my daughter."

"Do you really think that it can be, the two of them liking each other in that way? I can see your concern."

"I don't know, but I had talked to them both, and they had told me that they are much like brother and sister. But I know that anything can happen between friends. It wouldn't be the first time that it did."

"No, it wouldn't. My wife and I were good friends for a long time before we started to date. In fact, she was going out with my best friend at the time. He used to talk about her all the time, but the more he would tell me things about her, the more I was liking her more than just a friend."

"How do I tell Priscilla what I have done, Pastor? If I would never have done that so long ago, my life would have been so different now."

"Like how do you mean 'so different'?"

"I probably would still be working at the factory fourteen hours a day, never being able to take my family out or put money aside for trips or buy my wife and kids the clothes that they need. I mean, I was dirt poor, and still she loved me through it all."

"Do you regret what you have done?"

"I do in many ways."

"Like what, James?"

"The biggest one is that I did this behind my wife's back and she never got a chance to make a decision if she felt like we should give one away. I deceived her, and I feel so sorry for what I have done because it will hurt so many people when this comes out. I just don't know if I can tell her—I don't know how to tell her."

"Why don't we have prayer right now and ask our heavenly Father to guide you in his way of doing things?"

"Okay."

As the two bowed their heads in prayer, Mrs. Bittner was standing outside of the pastor's office, overhearing every word that the two men have spoken in confidence. Although she was an elderly woman who worked at cleaning the church many times, she was known to be the town gossip. Had the two men known she was in the church, let alone outside of the office, they would never have continued their talk. They began to pray, not knowing anyone else was standing near.

"Heavenly Father, we come today in thanking you most of all that there is nothing that is too big for you to handle. Lord, you see, my brother here is hurting over past mistakes that he has made, and yes, Lord, we all have done them. I'm asking you right now to give him peace and wisdom on how to handle this situation. Lord, I ask that you give everyone involved in this the understanding to where he was coming from for all these years that had passed. Jesus, we give you the glory and the praise. Amen."

"Thank you, Pastor, for talking to me and praying with me. I'm going to pray tonight that I will not have fear when it comes time for me to confess to Priscilla what I have done. Because right now, I am scared to death that she will never forgive me and she and David will leave me."

"Somehow, I don't think that she will. I have never seen a woman so devoted to her husband as she is to you. I just believe that after you tell her everything, she will come around. It might take some time, and I think that just maybe you might want to do this with me, just in case she might want to hit you over the head with something." He was laughing just a little when saying that, trying to lighten things up.

"That's not really like her, but who knows, after I tell her about this, what she may be like. Thank you once again. I have taken up too much of your time already, so I will get out of here and be on my way. Good-bye and have a good afternoon."

When Mrs. Bittner heard James saying good-bye, she ran down the hall as fast as her short, chubby legs could run and hid so not to be seen. She was moving so fast to get around a corner that the bun she had in her hair was coming undone and her bobby pins were falling on the floor.

She talked quietly to herself while running. *I just can't believe that pastor can really believe that Priscilla will stay with him after what he has done. I just know that they will divorce, and that is what I will tell others. Who in their right mind would stay married after this? What an embarrassment this will be for the whole lot of them!*

She grabbed her belongings and headed out of the church to hurry home to make her many phone calls. She felt like she was on a mission, and it was up to her and her alone to accomplish spreading the word—the great new story of how it all began thirteen years ago. She was planning just how she would begin her telling of the story, in hopes to have many listeners. And then the listeners would begin to tell their own side of the story to others.

"Yes, you too, James, and you have a good evening," Pastor Rod said as he watched James leave his office.

When James walked out of the church, he noticed that it was starting to get dark out. *How long have I been there talking with Pastor?* Then he looked at his watch on his wrist, and it said six fifteen. *Wow, I can't believe I talked for that long. No wonder he said to me a good evening.*

James continued to talk to himself on his way home, trying to convince himself into confessing to Priscilla about the twins that she knew nothing about. Remembering that he told Priscilla not to make any supper because he was taking her and David out, he pressed his foot down on the pedal harder so he could get home faster.

THE CONFESSION

"I'M SORRY. HONEY. I'm home so late," James spoke as he entered the house.

"Oh, you're not that late." Priscilla replied, looking at the wall clock. "Where were you?"

"I went to see Pastor Rod, like you ask me to."

"Oh really, so how did that go? Did you talk about whatever it is that's been eating you?"

"Yes, honey, I did, and soon I will open up and talk to you about it too. Is that okay?"

"It sure is, and do you know when that might be?" Priscilla looked up at him.

"Not for sure, but I can tell you that it will be soon. Pastor asked me to pray about it first, then we will be able to talk."

Priscilla wondered what could be such a big secret, but she left it alone without going any further. "Are you hungry?"

"Yes I'm starving. It feels like I haven't eaten all day, I could eat a horse I think right about now." He laughed as he asked if she and David were ready to go out to eat.

"You seem to be in a good mood since talking with Pastor."

"I will say that it feels like a very heavy load has been lifted, so, yes, I am in a much better mood and I'm ready to take my family

to the best place in town to eat. So come on, let's get going."
James stood there thinking for a moment. "Now I know why I
feel so hungry. I haven't eaten a thing all day today. I was at work
thinking about calling up the pastor, while watching the men
work on the addition of the store, that I just plainly forgot to eat."

"Well then, we better get going." Priscilla called for David to
come out of his bedroom, "We are ready to leave to get something
to eat. Come on, buddy, let's go."

David come running out of his room. "What took you so long
to get home? I'm starving, and Ma wouldn't let me get anything
to eat because she said you were going to be taking us out to eat?"

"Well, that's what I am trying to do, if you could manage to
get your shoes on so we can leave."

"I'm working on it. Oh, and by the way, can Terri come with
us? She said that her ma was going away tonight and she didn't
want to stay at home and be bored."

James stood there watching David put his shoes on, thinking
if that would be such a good idea right now to have Terri
come along.

"I don't know, David, if that would be a good idea right now.
I thought that maybe it could be just us." Then the phone rang.
"Who can that be?" James said as he walked over to the phone.
"Hello, yeah sure, that would be fine. I'll be right there to pick
her up." James hung up the phone, looking toward David. "I guess
she is coming with us after all. That was Marcia, and she asked if
Terri could come over. She sounded like she was a little worried
about something." He was now looking at Priscilla. "Do you
know what could be going on with her right now?"

"I'll talk to you about it later. She shared something with
me. But right now, I think that we better go get Terri before she
thinks that we're not coming."

The three walked out of the house to go pick up Terri on
their way to the restaurant. As they were walking to their vehicle,

Priscilla told James to pray that everything would be all right with Marcia.

"I will, and when we get back home, I'd like us to discuss what is really going on," James requested.

After picking Terri up, it seemed like David was the only one talking.

"Why does everyone seem to be so down? What is wrong with everyone today? First, Dad comes home later than usual. Then I hear that he had a meeting with the pastor. Can someone please tell me what's this all about?"

"I don't know what you mean," Terri said, very irritated.

"Well, I'm usually a pretty good judge at knowing when something isn't right, and this is the one time I can just sense it, but if no one is going to tell me anything, then the heck with ya's."

"David, everything is fine. I don't know why you think anything otherwise, but trust me because it's all okay," Priscilla said.

"Yeah, you goof. What makes you think that you're the expert at what other people are thinking or even going through?" Terri said in a joking way, which was followed by a punch on David's arm.

"Man, you have quite the hit there. If you're not careful, I'm going to have to punch you back," David teased back at her.

"Oh yes, I hear you, master. I'll be more careful with you next time. I didn't know that I was so strong, or maybe it's just you are so weak."

"Yeah, I'll give you weak," David said as he grabbed her hand and gave it a light squeeze."

"Honey, what restaurant did you want to go too?" James asked Priscilla while looking at the rear view mirror at the kids teasing each other.

"How about at Sea Shore's? I really like that place?"

"Um, that sounds so good. I was hoping you would pick that place. I love seafood, and they have the best."

While they were eating, all seemed to be quiet; it was like all of them felt like they were starved. After the meal, the ride home was quiet too until James decided to break the ice.

"Are we to take you home, Terri, or does your mom want you to come back to our house?"

"I think that I should probably go home now. My mother should be back from the doctors. I want to know if she has found anything out."

Priscilla didn't say a word, but James wasn't prepared for what he had just heard.

"What do you mean 'the doctors'? Is that where she went? Why, what's wrong with her? Did you know anything about this, Priscilla?"

"Yes, James, I did. That's what I wanted us to talk about tonight when we get home. So can this wait until then? I promise to tell you everything I know, okay?"

James looked over at Priscilla but because of it being so dark in their car, he was unable to see the look on her face. But nonetheless, he agreed that they would talk after they got home.

James took Terri home, asking her to tell her mother that she was in their prayers. As Terri was getting out of the car, she assured him that she would let her mom know what he had said. James couldn't drive fast enough to get home. He wanted to find out everything that there was to know about Marcia. Once reaching his home, he almost jumped out of the car before he had it put in gear.

The two hadn't even got out of the car all the way when James began questioning Priscilla.

"Come on now, we are home. I need to know what this is all about with Marcia going to the doctors at night time."

"She thinks that she may have cancer in her breast," she said after making sure that David was out of ear shot.

"*Cancer!* You have got to be kidding me. Wow, I can hardly believe it. How old is she anyways? Fifty?"

"She is fifty-one years old."

"That is so young to have breast cancer, isn't it?"

"Yes, it is. I sure hope that she doesn't have it—I'd hate to have that happen to her. What would ever happen to Terri? If the truth be told, Nick and Terri aren't very close at all."

"What do you mean by that? Every time I see the two of them together, I never noticed that there was anything wrong with them."

"Yes, I know that, but Marcia told me that the two of them haven't been getting along very well lately. Not to mention, back when Terri broke her arm when she was only seven years old, he treated her so badly at the hospital right in front of me."

"He did? Why didn't you ever tell me about that?"

"I'm not really sure why I never said anything. Maybe because I didn't want anything to come between your friendship with him."

"What's wrong with the two of them?"

"I'm not sure, but if we ever get in the house, I'm going to call her up and talk to her." Priscilla had a lot on her mind, wondering what Marcia found out.

Priscilla walked over to the phone to place her call to Marcia when she entered the house. Pacing back and forth, waiting to hear her voice on the other end of the phone, James stood close by to find out for himself what was going on, but all he could do was hear what Priscilla was saying.

"So what did the doctor say?" Priscilla inquired.

James got a little closer as if he was going to hear Marcia's voice come through the phone.

"Oh, I am so sorry, Marcia. What can I do for you. Did he say what can be done?"

"What? What?" James interrupted, waiting to hear what Priscilla found out, just to see Priscilla hold her finger up to her lips to say, "Just wait a minute."

"Okay, I'll come over tomorrow after James leaves for work, and we can talk then. I'm praying for you, and I want you to be praying and not give up," Priscilla told her and hung up. She turned to James. "Before you say anything, can we go to our bedroom so we can talk in private? I don't want David to hear what I have to say."

"Okay," James replied, looking at her in a strange way, but followed close behind.

"Marcia just told me that they have found that she does have cancer."

"Oh my! How bad is it?" James asked.

"She asked if I would come over tomorrow while the kids are in school so we can talk. So at this point, I don't really know how bad it is. I think that she is in shock and just wants to think about it before talking to me."

"I hope she will be okay."

Priscilla sat there, listening to James as he talked, but she herself didn't feel much like talking. She had heard too many stories how women die because they get breast cancer, and she didn't want to even think that she could lose her friend to it.

"I think that I will go to bed now. I'm feeling pretty tired."

James gave her a good-night kiss and walked out of the bedroom to go see what David was doing.

"So, Dad, what's going on with Marcia?"

"Well, I don't know if she has said anything to Terri yet, so I don't want to say anything because I don't want you too at school tomorrow okay?"

"I won't," he promised.

"Marcia told your mother tonight over the phone that she found out she has breast cancer. I sure hope that it's treatable."

"You mean that she might die?"

James looked at David. "Yes, she could, but I don't want to hear any talk like that. We need to speak positive."

"Okay, Dad, I will."

"Tell me something, David."

"What?"

"Are you and Terri still keeping your relationship clearly as friends and nothing more?"

"Yes, Dad. Why do you always think that there's more to it than that? I have known her all my life. Just because we hang out together and like the same things, it doesn't mean that there's more to it than that. It's really weird. She and I would talk and think alike sometimes. And we are the same age and have the same birthdays. Pretty weird, huh. But no, Dad, we are just best friends—nothing more. In fact, she likes Jason Rogers, the kid who lives down the street."

She has just got to be my daughter. It all makes sense now, he thought to himself.

"What's the matter, Dad? You look like you've just seen a ghost."

"Nothing, son. I think that I'll join your mother and go to bed also. Good night, son. Don't stay up too late."

"I won't, Dad. Good night."

James lay in bed next to his wife. He wanted so much to wake her up and tell her that Terri was their daughter, but how dare he even think about confessing it right now? After all, he wasn't that sure that Terri was their child—and right when she found out that her best friend in all the world has breast cancer. Maybe he won't even have to confess—if Marcia was to die, then his secret would be safe with him forever. He lay there getting angry with himself for the wicked thoughts that were trying to take place in his mind.

The next morning, Priscilla got up to make James his breakfast. She knew that he would be headed down to the store, and she wanted to go see how Marcia was doing. "I'll be going over to see Marcia today to check on her. I'm worried about her."

"I know that you are. I can see it written all over your face. But, Priscilla, I want you to remember that worrying is not going to help anything. We need to be strong for her and pray and speak positive to her." James hugged his wife.

"I know that. You're right. I just don't know how strong I can be when I feel so helpless right now."

James sat down at the table without saying another word about it. After he ate, he gave Priscilla a kiss, then he headed out the door to go to work. But before leaving, he had some last words to give her.

"Priscilla, please do me one favor before heading over to see Marcia today?"

"What would that be?"

"Pray before going over there."

"Yes, James, I plan on it. I'll see you after work."

James looked at her. He could tell that she wasn't up to talking, so without saying another word, he closed the door behind him. After driving down the road, his thoughts were on Priscilla and Marcia.

"Lord, please help Priscilla today as she goes to see Marcia. Help her to be a comfort and give her words that bring healing to Marcia in this time in her life. And help me to be able to tell my wife the truth about our little girl that I gave up. In Jesus name, amen."

James couldn't go on before he began to cry when mentioning what he did several years ago. All he could think about was what if Terri was his daughter and what if Marcia wouldn't make it? What would this do to Priscilla? Would it be just too much for her? Would she not understand why he did what he did, and she and David would leave him and hate him for not telling her a long time ago what he did? He had his mind racing on with all the what ifs until he finally said to himself that he had to just talk with her and get this over with before it killed him thinking about it.

James didn't expect the looks he was getting once he arrived at work, nor did he understand why he was getting looks from folks when he just got to the store.

What is going on with everyone staring at me? Did I wear unmatched clothes? Did I forget to brush my hair? James walked over to the cashier. "Why is everyone looking at me like I just killed someone?"

"You don't know?" Malinda asked.

"Know what?"

"There is rumor going around that you and your wife had twins and you sold your little girl."

James couldn't believe what he was hearing. He stood there in shock until he felt as though he was going to fall flat on his face right there in the middle of the store.

How dare Pastor Rod tell others what I told him in secret? he thought to himself. James headed right back out the same door that just moments before he came into. He started driving down the road; he was very angry with his pastor for telling someone about their talk before he even had a chance to tell Priscilla. Why would he tell me to pray before talking to Priscilla if he was going to open up his mouth and tell others himself? He didn't know what to do at this time or where he should go. he knew that he needed to have a talk with his pastor, but he had no way of knowing where he was at.

Priscilla prayed before going to see her best friend. She wanted to be a comfort to Marcia at this time, even though her own heart felt like she was going to break as she knew that it had to be so much harder on her friend. When getting to Marcia's home, she rang the doorbell, hoping that Marcia was in good spirits.

"Come on in Priscilla" Nick said, answering the door.

"How is she doing today?"

"Not good at all. She's in the bedroom, lying down." Nick walked in front of her, leading her back to the bedroom. "I'll leave the two of you to talk," he said as he opened the door for Priscilla.

"Thank you," Priscilla said as she walked in the room.

Walking over to the bed and looking at her friend, Priscilla could hardly believe what she was seeing; it looked as though her friend had aged twenty years overnight. She felt so saddened for her. She spoke silently Jesus help me be strong for her. Leaning over the bed, she spoke, "How are you doing today?"

"I'm not so good today. I just can't understand why."

"Understand what?"

"I've never been a smoker. I've been a good person all my life. Well, I did some little thing's wrong, like I told lies before, but it was nothing that was really bad."

Priscilla wanted so much to help her friend. She could hear her talk, but it was almost like she was just rambling on with words. "What did the doctor say to you, Marcia?"

"He said that there is nothing that he can do. He said that the cancer has spread and there is no chance of me making it. I will never see my little girl graduate or get married." Marcia began to sob uncontrollably.

Priscilla bent down, hugging her friend. Then without saying a word to her, she began to pray. "Oh, God, help my best friend. Please heal her. Don't let this cancer have its way in her life. You can do anything, so please heal her in Jesus name, amen."

"Thank you, Priscilla," Marcia said. The sobs were still coming, then she finally found words to say. "Priscilla, I have a big favor I want to ask you and James."

"Okay, what is it?"

"This is very hard, but I need to just get it over with and ask. When I die, do you think that you and James could take my little girl in and adopt her as your own?'

Priscilla wasn't expecting her to ask this of her; it took her by surprise. "What about her father? I don't think Nick would allow something like that."

"I have already talked to Nick about my decision if you and James are willing to take her in and love her as if she is your very own daughter, which I think the two of you already do."

"You're not going to die, and if you did, I need to know why you would rather James and I take care of her and not her dad.

I'm not saying that we wouldn't want her because I love Terri so very much as if she were my daughter. I just don't know why you would rather choose us than her own father."

"Over the past few years, I have noticed that Nick and Terri haven't seen eye to eye on anything, and when I asked Nick how was it going to be between the two of them when I die, he couldn't give me an answer. I need to know that she will be loved and taken care of, and I just believe that the two of you will give that to her. Besides, Nick adopted her when she was almost five years old. It's not like he raised her from a baby. Oh, that must sound so selfish of me saying it like that."

"I didn't know. I just thought that you and he adopted her together. You have never told me this in all of these years."

"Nick has been there for both her and me and has been a very good husband in many ways. But he doesn't have the fatherly instincts like I thought he would have, if you know what I mean. I know that he has tried, but it has been like the two of them never have really accepted each other. Could you at least think about what I am asking from you?"

"Oh, Marcia, I would take her in my home as my very own in a minute, but this is big, what you are asking me. I will have to talk with James about this, of course. I could never make this decision on my own."

"Of course, you couldn't, but I had to ask. So I will wait for your answer, and if you two decide you really couldn't, then I will have to make other arraignments. You will talk about this soon, won't you?"

"Yes, of course, but I wish that you would not allow yourself to get so worked up about this. You're going to be just fine, and you will be here for her. She won't need a new mom or dad."

Marcia stretched out her hand and took a hold of her best friend's hand. "No, I won't be here for her. I just know I won't."

Priscilla couldn't take her mind off of Marcia all evening; she couldn't help but feel completely helpless for her friend and what she was going through at this time in her life. She could tell just by talking with Marcia that her friend had already given up and felt that there was no hope for her. Now she had to have a talk with James if they could take Terri in if her best friend was to die. Why wouldn't they? After all, she had known her since she was just a baby. And David and her have been best friends since they could even talk.

When James came home from work, Priscilla decided to talk with him about them adopting Terri, so she ask if they could go to their bedroom so as not to be interrupted by David.

"What's this all about that you would pull me into the bedroom as soon as I come home?" James asked, fearing that she might had already heard the news from another source. "Let me explain before getting all mad at me."

Priscilla wanted to talk with James so much that she didn't even hear what he was saying. "When I went to see Marcia today, it was a very sad time. It's like she has completely given up, and she has asked from you and I a big favor."

"What kind of favor are we talking about here?" James looked at Priscilla all puzzled.

"Well, I was not expecting this coming from her at all, but she would like for us to adopt Terri when she dies. It's like she has already planned on dying. She feels that she will not live. She said that she knows she's going to die."

"Maybe she does know that she is. People say that a lot of times, we know when we are going to die. You hear about things like this all the time. Wow, she really wants us to adopt Terri, huh? Did she say why when Terri has a father already?"

"I learned something today I never even knew in all of these years."

"What was that?"

"She told me today that Nick didn't adopt Terri until she was about five years old, and for the last several years, he and Terri have not been close at all. She said that Nick is not really the fatherly type. And she also said that she already had a talk with Nick about her decision on wanting us to adopt Terri as our very own. She seems to really want this, and she asked me to talk with you about this, and if we can't, then she will make other arrangements. So what do you think?"

"Wow, really adopt her huh?" James stood there, not saying much but staring at Priscilla, all the while rubbing his chin with his fingers. "What do you think about it?"

"I could never have her go somewhere else. We are just like family to her. I could never imagine her losing her mother then us on top of it. I say yes if you do too."

"I agree. It's our job to take her in if her mother dies. I think you need to give Marcia peace about this as soon as you can."

James was quiet for the most part; he looked as though he was in deep thought.

Priscilla told James that she would go see Marcia in the morning and let her know what they have decided. James thought it was a good idea if she did that first thing in the morning.

James walked out of the bedroom and into the kitchen to see what was for supper and if there were any even made. He knew that Priscilla was always very good at having it made each night, but this was different. He knew that she was going through some things about her friend. He looked around to see what he smelled and found she had made baked chicken and rice waiting for him in the oven.

Even though he heard what Priscilla had told him about Terri coming to live with them if Marcia was to die, and although thoughts were swirling around in his head, he still felt like he could eat a bear. He just was not sure if his appetite was coming because everything he had thought about Terri being his daughter could now really be happening. He knew he needed to have that talk with Priscilla, and he needed to fast, possibly before she was to go over to see Marcia the following day—or someone else might tell her what they heard or tell David at school. He dished up his food and sat down all by himself. Looking around for David to see if he was going to come join him, he called out to him.

"Yeah, Dad, what do you need?" David asked.

"Are you going to eat? I don't think that your mom is feeling up to it right now."

"Sorry, Dad, but I ate while you and mom were in the bedroom talking."

"Oh, okay. I guess I will sit here all by myself and eat then."

James turned back facing his plate of food and tried to reason in his head on what to say to Priscilla; he knew he just couldn't live with the lies anymore. He had to come clean, and it had to be tonight. After he ate, he walked into the living room and thanked Priscilla for a great supper, then he asked if the two of them could go have another talk alone. Priscilla looked at him, but without a word, she got up and walked toward their usual place they went to whenever they needed to be alone to talk.

"What's on your mind James? You're not changing it about Terri coming to live with us, are you?"

"No, not at all." James was beginning to break out with hot sweats, which he wiped out of his forehead. "Honey," he said as he knelt down on his knees in front of her as she was sitting on the bed, "what I am about to tell you is the most difficult thing that I ever have to say to you and the second most hardest thing I have ever did in my life." Sweat was now pouring from James.

"James, you are scaring me. What is this all about? You are sweating so badly all over. Please tell me right now what is going on."

"I'm trying to tell you. I have always wanted to tell you."

"Oh my gosh, you're in love with another woman?"

"No, don't be silly. I could never love anyone but you. Now will you please let me get this out before I lose my nerve?"

"Okay," Priscilla said as she sat there waiting to hear the big news that would make her husband sweat like someone had just poured water over him.

"Please hear me and try and understand what I am going to say to you. Thirteen years ago, I did something that every day since then, I have lied to you and felt like dying so many times because of the decision I made on that one day."

"So you did cheat on me then? What did you think, that I was just too fat and ugly being pregnant?"

"No, Priscilla, please let me just finish. It was nothing like that at all. Do you remember when you went into labor with David?"

"Yes, of course."

"That day changed everything for us in so many ways. Much was for the better so we could survive, but there—"

Before he could go on she interrupted him again. "You were selling drugs then and that's how you were able to get the store."

"Honey, no! Please, will you let me finish? Priscilla, honey, I was so wrong for what I had done. I really don't know why I did what I did. I guess, no matter what I say, it will never be a good-enough reason. I have tried to call it surviving all of these years to get us to be able to live a life with means than to always hurt and struggle the way we did for the first seven years that we were married. But I have always tried to tell you about the night that you gave birth to David."

James sat on the floor and put his head in his hands and began to cry, his entire body now shaking uncontrollably.

"Please forgive me, Priscilla, but that night you gave birth, it was to two babies, a boy and a girl. What I am trying to tell you is that you had twins."

It was out now, and he stayed on the floor weeping with guilt and shame of all the years keeping this from his wife. Afraid to look up at her, he kept his head down.

Priscilla sat there not saying a word, like it was all a big nasty joke, then, in a voice that James never expected, said, "Is Terri our daughter?"

James looked up at her with a tear stained face, in unbelief that she wasn't yelling and screaming at him. He answered, "I don't know, and I want to know."

Keeping her voice low and remaining calm, she began to speak. "It all makes sense now. Now I understand the money, the store, you getting so angry for nothing, and you watching David and Terri so closely. Why, James, why? Tell me what happened that day when I was drugged up because of complications giving birth. I want to hear it all, James. I want the truth now." She was now raising her voice. It was like it was beginning to sink in.

James could hear that the shock of the news was starting to become real now, and he needed to tell her everything from the beginning. He tried to get his voice steady enough to talk without all the crying.

"I'll tell you all of it, honey. You went in the room to have the baby, and after you had already given birth to both babies, the doctor told me to come in the room. He said that he would like to talk with me. When I got in there, he told me that you had just given birth to two babies, a boy and a girl."

"I knew it! I just knew it! Something inside of me was telling me that Terri was my daughter, but I couldn't understand how." Priscilla stood up and started pacing her bedroom floor.

"Honey, we don't know if she is our daughter."

"Yes, I know she is. I think I have always known it deep down inside. I have often had thoughts that maybe they got the two kids mixed up. I can't even explain it, but I knew that she was. Finish telling me what happened, James," she demanded.

"The doctor who was on call that day was a Dr. Freytag, and he told me that you told him about me working all the time and still never having enough money for us to ever do anything. He said that you also told him I never wanted us to have a baby because we couldn't afford it. He told me about how he and his wife have always wanted a baby, but because his wife had several complications, she could never give birth, and they had been married for twenty some years, and all they ever wanted was to have a baby to love and take care of. When he told me how scared you were and you never even told me that, it made me feel that much more scared about taking two babies home to raise and care for when I knew we couldn't really even afford one, let alone two. It was unlike you to be scared because that is just not you."

"So you sold our baby girl? What were you thinking, James? Why have you never told me about this before? And why tell me now?"

"I have always wanted to, but you know, when your mother left you that letter telling you that she was there when you gave birth, she must have known but never have said anything all of these years, either, because she knew we would never have been able to take care of two babies. They cost money that we didn't have."

"All of these years, I would look at Terri and see how she looked like me and wonder how that could possibly be, and you knew the whole time that she could be our daughter. I don't know what you want me to say to you right now. And my own mother, how could she have known something like this and have never said anything to me for all of these years? I don't know how to even react to this. Me, her daughter—I just can't believe it. I am in complete shock. Does Marcia know anything about this?"

"No, Michael told me that no one would know but his sister and me. She was the nurse in the room."

"Did he pay you for our daughter?"

"Yes," James answered, so ashamed that he couldn't even look at Priscilla.

"How much? How much was our daughter worth to you, James, or, should I say, to that doctor?" Priscilla was starting to get more angry.

"Please, Priscilla, please forgive me, honey. I am so sorry I didn't know what to do. How would we have lived, Priscilla, how? I worked so hard and never got anywhere. I could never take you out or treat you special. Heck, I couldn't even bring you home a little flower unless I stopped by the roadside and picked them for you. I didn't know what to do. I'm so sorry…please forgive me, Priscilla. Honey, you deserved so much better in life, and I could never get you anything."

"What I deserved was to know that I had a daughter! I want to know how much money, James!" Anger in her voice was coming out loud and clear.

James sat there trying to find the words to say; he had never heard her so upset before. Even though he could understand why, it still bothered him to hear her so angry at him.

"One hundred thousand dollars." He could barely get it to come out of his mouth; he was so ashamed.

"What! A hundred thousand dollars? Where would he get all that money from?"

"He told me that he invested and it paid off," he said, looking at her, raising his voice.

"All of these years, the man I thought I knew, I guess, I never knew after all. Boy, was I ever a fool. I would never have thought for a million years that you could have done something like this." Priscilla was looking at James in complete shock. "Maybe my parents were right about you. Maybe it was me who was blind for all of these years."

"Please don't say that, Priscilla. I've always loved you with all my heart, and I've always tried to do what was best for us as a family. Please forgive me, honey. I am so sorry—if I could take it all back, I would. I have lived with this for thirteen long years. And it feels like my heart is being ripped out of me every day since then for what I've done."

"I don't believe you really know what *love* is, James. You see, when someone says that they love you, they don't deceive and hurt you like this. They are honest and caring and look out for the one they love," Priscilla went on to say.

"What do you want me to do? I'll do anything that you ask me to do to make this right."

"Now you really have gone crazy, James? How can you make this right? My little girl was taken from me when she was first born, and I never even had a chance to hold her or say if I wanted to give her away. I don't know what to think right now. I need some time to know what to do. But right now, I need to be alone and pray about some things."

"I'm so sorry, honey. I'm going to go for a drive, and I'll be back later," James said as he headed out the bedroom door.

Priscilla was so upset with James right at the moment that she didn't care where he was going or if he was even coming back.

How dare he sell my daughter? What was he thinking of. And my mother knew he did this all along—how could she not even tell me what he did behind my back? Does my father know about this too? Lord, please help me with this, I don't know what to do. Do I go over to Marcia's and tell her that Terri is my daughter and I want my daughter to come home with me? But how do I do that? She doesn't even know anything about this.

Priscilla sat at the edge of her bed with her mind now running wild.

Maybe she does know the truth. Maybe now that she is dying, she feels that it's best that she give me back my daughter. No, I can't believe that. Even James said that she didn't know about this.

Priscilla felt weak and sick to her stomach; all she wanted to do was to close her eyes and shut out the rest of the world. She lay down, trying to forget the last twenty minutes of her life, but somehow, all she could do was remember every last bit of detail of the words James said to her. All of a sudden, she let out the loudest cry she had ever had before; they were louder and much more painful than when her mother had passed away.

David heard his mother crying and knew that something terrible must have taken place in order for her to cry like that. "Mom, can I come in?" He knocked on the bedroom door.

"Yes, come on in."

"I heard you crying, and Dad just left. What's going on? Are the two of you fighting?" David had never seen his parents fight and argue before; it was something that just didn't happen in their home.

"Your dad told me something I never knew. Now I don't know what to do or if I should do anything."

"Like what?"

"Oh, honey, this is between your dad and me. I just have to find out what to do about it all."

"Please tell me, Mom. Maybe I can help with whatever it is."

"I think that it's best if you let your dad explain this to you. I don't even know where to begin. I'm in total shock of what I had just found out."

"Does this have anything to do with Terri?"

Priscilla looked at David. "Were you listening to our conversation?"

"No, I just know that her mother isn't doing so good, and Terri told me that she and her dad don't get along real good."

Priscilla sat there looking at David and wondered if she might as well say something to him before someone else did. She hated the thought of David finding this out by another source besides her or James.

"This is a hard thing to hear, but you are right about Marcia not doing well. She would like for us to adopt Terri if she were to die."

"Is that why Dad is mad, because he doesn't want us to adopt Terri?"

"No, honey, that's not it at all. He loves Terri just as much as you and I do, maybe a little bit more." Right after she spoke those words, she wished she could have just bitten her tongue.

"Why would he love her more than we do? What is going on here, Mom? You're not telling me something?"

"When your dad gets home, ask him to explain all this to you. This is his mess, not mine. Now I'm sorry, David, but I would really like to be alone right now."

"Okay." David turned his back toward his mother as he headed to leave the bedroom. "If you know what's going on, I don't know why you just can't tell me," he spoke just above a whisper as he closed the door.

FACING THE WORLD

JAMES KNOCKED ON the reverend's door to his home after going to the church and not finding him there.

"Well, good evening, James. What can I do for you at this time of the hour?" Pastor Rod looked at his watch, being aware that it was half past nine in the evening.

James stood there, not knowing if he should get mad at the reverend for letting others know about their talk of the twins or should he be relieved that it was out in the open and he could now move past the mistake he made thirteen years before.

"I need to know why you told others of our conversation that was supposed to be said in private," James said as a matter-of-fact..

"I told no one, laddie, not even my wife of our meeting. Where is this all coming from? What happened that made you feel that I gave any information out?"

"I walked in my store today, only to find that everyone there already knew all about me selling my daughter. Imagine my surprise when the cashier told me that everyone heard all about it. I felt so terrible with people staring at me like I was some kind of an animal."

"I never told a single soul. I don't know how anyone found out about it. Did you tell Priscilla yet?"

"Not until everyone else already found out. If you never told anyone, then how did others find out?"

"The only other way I know that it could have gotten out other than from you or me would be that Mrs. Bittner must have been at the church and overheard us talking. Now I don't want to accuse her, but she is known to be the town gossip after all. I don't know how she does it, but she finds out news before the news people find it, if you know what I mean. I will get to the bottom of this and find out if she is the one who spread this around. I am sorry, James, but if you would like to come in, I'll make a phone call right now to Mrs. Bittner and see if she was at the church when we were talking."

"Yes, I think that I will come in, I'd like to know who she told about this, I just can't believe that sweet lady would have said anything," James commented.

"You have got to be the first person I have ever heard say 'sweet lady.' Forgive me, James, for what I just said. Now I sound like I'm the town gossip. Like I said, I don't want to pass any judgment on her as of yet. I will get to the bottom of this to see who could have been the one who heard us talking."

"You must know more about her than I know because I would never have guessed her to be like that. I have always thought that she was just a sweet old woman. Please call her so then I could go on and ask if she is the one that started all this craziness. Imagine my surprise hearing from another source that my wife and I were getting a divorce."

"What?" the pastor asked, looking at James incredulously.

"A man at my job told me that he heard Priscilla and I were getting a divorce. And that was before I even told her about everything."

Pastor Rod picked up the phone to make his call; when he picked it up from his end, he could hear two people on the other end talking. He had a party line that he shared with several other homes. After listening to them for a short while, he recognized one of the woman's voices. It was Mrs. Bittner, and she was telling the other women all about James selling his daughter at birth. He could hardly believe what he was hearing; she was telling the same story that he had gotten from James himself. He motioned for James to come and listen in on the conversation.

James took the phone, not sure why he was taking it from the reverend, but nonetheless, he put the phone to his ear, shocked at what he was hearing coming from the woman whom, just a few minutes before, he was defending from the reputation that the town had given her. Now he could see why she had it and very well deserving of it.

He couldn't keep his mouth shut any longer. "You old gossip Mrs. Bittner, how dare you call yourself a Christian woman when all you care about is hurting those who have never hurt you! You should be ashamed of yourself talking about others like this!"

Before he was to go on with more words to Mrs. Bittner, she was quick to hang up the phone.

"She hung up on me," he told the reverend. "I guess I need to apologize for accusing you of telling others. You were right when you said it had to be her. Why she would want to hurt others is beyond me. I never would have guessed her to be like that. I know if that was me having a church and I had people coming to me with problems, I would never use her after the first time she listened in on someone else conversation and told others about it."

"I know you are right, and I can assure you she will not be coming back to clean at my church. She cleans the church but then turns around and dirties it with her words, and if you ask me, the church being dirty with dust is not as bad as her nasty gossip is. I'm so sorry, James, for what she has done. I will be praying for you and your wife."

"Thank you, Pastor, we can use it. Priscilla is so mad at me right now. She can't even look at me without being so angry. I don't blame her. I wouldn't want to see me, either, after what I've

done. Well, I'll be going now. Thanks for clearing this up for me."
James walked away, with his head hanging low.

The reverend closed his door after James walked away. He stood inside his house, watching James walk back to his car, and just above a whisper, he prayed, "Dear Lord, you see that man's heart, and you know what took place several years ago. I ask that you give him and his wife love, peace, joy, and forgiveness with each other. Help Priscilla and David to love James through everything. In Jesus name, amen—oh, and, Jesus, if Terri is their daughter, then help her and everyone else who is involved to forgive him also. Amen."

James started to drive home, but he was driving a lot slower than usual. He was taking his time thinking about what he was going to do if Priscilla was to ask him to move out. He loved his family so very much and never wanted to lose them. He tried to picture what his life would be like if he never had sold his little girl. He thought about what he would tell her why he did what he did. No matter how he tried to picture what life would have been like, all he could do was see himself still working in the factory. That's all he ever knew before the babies were born. Then he stopped to take a good look at his life now, one without his daughter, and he began to cry.

"God, please help me to not lose my family. I really didn't want to give my baby away. I just didn't know what else to do anymore; I was so scared of not being able to support my family. Please help Priscilla and David to forgive me."

James drove home not knowing what it was going to be like for him when he got home. He wasn't sure if his clothes would be packed or if there would be blankets waiting for him on the couch. He prayed and believed that God was going to do a work in his life.

When he entered his home, Priscilla was up and waiting for him to come home. "Where have you been, all this time?" she asked.

"I went to see the reverend, and I was just driving and praying and trying to think what life would have been like for all of us if I would never have done what I did."

"I was trying to think about that also," Priscilla said while sitting down on the couch.

"Really, you were trying to think about that too? And what did you see when you thought about life with are daughter?"

"I was thinking about how it is now and how it has been for all of these years. Life has been good for us, and I know that what you did had to be the biggest decision you have ever made before, I'm trying to see it from your point of view."

"It was the biggest I had ever faced before, by far."

"Please, James, let me get this out. I have some things that need to be said, and if I don't say it now, I may not be able to later."

"Please, honey, don't tell me that you and David are leaving me."

"Just listen. I've been praying and thinking about what it was like before I got pregnant and how much I have always wanted a baby. In all the times I thought about having a baby, I never once thought about what it would be like if I had twins. Now I know how much we struggled to make ends meet. You have always been a very hard worker and a very good provider for us. And I even know there were times that all you ever wanted was to be able to take me out for the night or on a vacation but was never able too.

"What I am saying, James, is if I were the one who went to work all of those years and never did anything but pay bills, I don't know if I wouldn't have done the same thing that you have done for the family. Oh, I'm mad as I could be for what you did and all the lies that's been told over and over all of these years, but I want you to know that I forgive you. I also want you to know that it's going to take me some time to get used to the whole thing, not to mention the time that it will take to trust you again."

When James heard the words 'forgive you,' he fell down on his knees and began to weep uncontrollably. "Thank you, God, for answering my prayers." Then he looked up at Priscilla and took her hand, telling her how much he loved her and David with all of his heart and how sorry he was for deceiving her and causing her pain.

"James, we need to have a talk with Marcia about this. I need to know if Terri is our daughter, and if she is not, we need to find out where she is at. I want to know my daughter, James. I want her to know me—" she paused—"I want her to know us."

"It's has to be Terri. I just know that it has to be. How can a child we don't even know look so much like you did when you were young? How can she and David have the same birthday? It just has to be our little girl, and I want to find out for sure."

"Are you willing, come morning, that the two of us go see Marcia? We can ask her questions, and one way or another, we will find out."

"Yes, honey, I will call in at work and let them know I have something that needs to be attended to, and then we can go see Marcia. It's getting late, and we need to be able to get David up for school in the morning. What do you say if we go on to bed now?" James was thankful that she never packed his things or that she wasn't asking him to sleep on the couch."

"Yes, let's go to bed. I'm getting pretty tired too. I want you to know that David heard me crying and wondered what was going on with the two of us."

"What did you tell him?"

"I told him he needed to talk to you about it. I told him that something happened and it was up to you to explain it to him."

"I'll talk with him in the morning before he leaves for school. I just don't know how I'll ever explain this to him. I wonder if he will ever look at Terri the same again or will it be different for the two of them. If anything, I hope this will make them even closer. Maybe I should wait to talk to him after we talk to Marcia and find out more if Terri is our daughter."

"What are you hoping to find out when we talk with Marcia tomorrow?"

"I just want to know whom she was married to before. I know she told us that she and her first husband adopted Terri, but who was her first husband?"

"She told me he died in a car accident when Terri was a few years old, then she met Nick and the two of them got married when Terri was around five years old."

"I wonder why Terri and Nick don't get along when he adopted her at such a young age. You know it's hard for me to believe that a young girl like Terri would have problems with a grown man such as Nick. He has always seemed like he was a very pleasant man to me. I would never have guessed that he and Terri were having problems. There are a couple of times, now I remember, that he got upset and started to bring things up that happened in the past. But besides those times, I have always thought he was a nice guy."

"Do you really think he would have shown his bad side in front of us? I would think that is not something that he would let just anyone see. I know that something is going on in that home that we really don't even know about. Otherwise, why would Marcia ask us to adopt Terri she wants what's best for her, and she knows just how much we love her. When we go see her tomorrow I want us to get to the bottom of this whole thing. I want to know if Terri is our daughter—that is the most important thing, then I want to know why she wants us to adopt her. Oh, I know that it's because she and Nick don't get along, but that happens with parents, and you just don't adopt your children out. There is more to it. I just know there is, and I want to know what it is."

Priscilla didn't sleep well during the night; she tossed and turned all night. She got up and walked to the window, looking out at the stars that lit up the sky.

"Dear God," she prayed, "please help me know what to do and say to my dear friend, Marcia. I need to know if Terri is my daughter and how do I tell her and Marcia the horrible truth about James selling her."

She went back to bed in hopes of having some sort of peace of mind after talking to the Lord in prayer. Just about the time she had to get up with David to get him off to school, she fell asleep.

"Honey," James said, nudging Priscilla, "it's time to get up to get David up for school."

"Okay, I'm getting up." Hesitantly, she turned over, facing her side of the bed, trying to get herself off the bed. "I had just finally fallen to sleep after the worst night of sleeplessness I think that I have ever had before." She sat on the side of the bed, talking in a very low, sleepy voice.

"Never slept well, huh? What was wrong with you?" James asked.

"All I did was think about what we would say to Marcia today and wondered if Terri is our daughter and how would we tell her and Marcia the truth, not to mention tell David."

Priscilla got up and walked out of the room to go get David up for school, but to her surprise, he had already gone without a word to his parents. Finding it a little strange that he left earlier then usual, she just assumed it was to play some basketball with friends before school. So she and James got dressed to go over to Marcia's house.

GETTING ANSWERS

DAVID WAS GETTING his homework out of his locker when Sonny Bittner, a boy in his class, came up to him telling him things he never heard before.

"I heard that your dad sold your twin sister at birth, huh? Wow, I bet you and your mom must be really mad, huh. I heard that your parents are now going to get a divorce, but by the looks of it, you must have already known it, huh?"

David looked at Sonny, not knowing what he was talking about. "What are you trying to start now huh? I don't have a sister."

"Do you mean to tell me that your dad never told you about your twin sister he sold when you were born? How else do you think that a poor man like your dad got enough money to buy a store?"

David grabbed Sonny by his shirt, throwing him hard up against his locker. "Shut your lying mouth! Why are you saying things about my dad that's not true? Unless you want to lose your teeth, you will stop talking about my dad." David let him go and started to walk away when Sonny had more to say.

"If you don't believe what I said, then ask your dad yourself. My grandma told me all about it. She said that he told the preacher," Sonny yelled.

David ran out the school door and began to run down the sidewalk toward his home.

What is Sonny talking about? Can this be true? Is that why I heard my parents having a talk the other day, where they were yelling at each other? But how can that be true? Who would be my sister anyway? And how would Sonny's grandma know before my mom and me?

David ran all the way until he reached his house, but before going in, he stood outside the door all bent over, trying to catch his breath. *Could Sonny be telling the truth? But why would my dad do something like that?* Standing up straight, he opened the door to the kitchen, and walking in as quiet as a mouse, in hopes that his mom would not be startled to hear him, he peeked around the corner to the living room to see if his mom was in there. But to his surprise, she was nowhere in the house.

James and Priscilla sat down on the couch at Marcia's to talk about Terri. Not knowing where to begin, James said, "We need to talk about what it is that you want Priscilla and I to do about Terri."

Marcia was weak and had lost weight over the course of days after hearing that she had cancer.

"It's really quite simple. The two of you are my very best friends and have been for the last eight years or more. I would really like the two of you to care for Terri when I'm gone. If this is asking too much, then please let me know because I still have a chance of finding her a good home. I don't know how much longer I have, but I do know it's not going to be much longer." Marcia sat there looking at the two of them, trying to catch her breath; she seemed to run out of breath faster these days than before.

"Marcia, I'd like to ask you a few questions, if you feel like you can talk for a while longer?"

"I'm here for anything you want to ask me," she replied, putting a napkin up to her mouth and coughed.

"I know that we have never really discussed about you adopting Terri before. Priscilla told me that you mentioned it to her. What I want to know is if you know who her birth parents are."

"No, I have no idea who they are. Does that make a difference? My husband and my sister-in-law were the ones who found the mother to the baby."

James looked over at Priscilla before answering Marcia. "I was hoping to talk with you about something that took place thirteen years ago." The very thought of him possibly finding out the truth about Terri was making him feel scared, but everything was just way too much of a coincident.

"What is on your mind, James?" Marcia asked.

James began to feel very uncomfortable that he began to get fidgety.

"Wow, this is harder than I thought that it would be. What I am about to tell you may come as a big surprise, but I did something that I am so ashamed of doing thirteen years ago behind my wife's back." He looked over at Priscilla before going on. "You see, thirteen years ago, when my wife was ready to give birth to our baby"—he stopped again and began to rub his sweaty hands on his pants—"my wife didn't know about any of this until yesterday. When she gave birth to our son, she also gave birth to a little baby girl."

Priscilla started to cry and put her face in her hands, and James wrapped his arms around her.

"I'm so sorry for hurting you like this," he said, then looking back toward Marcia, he continued on. "You see, I think Terri might be the baby I gave away thirteen years ago."

"Sold!" Priscilla blurted out, raising her voice in anger again at James.

James looked down at Priscilla when she said that hurtful word he wanted so desperately to forget but was now coming back to haunt him once again.

Even in all of Marcia's weakness, she managed to speak loud and clear. "Are you telling me that Priscilla gave birth to twins, a boy and a girl, and you think that Terri is the baby you sold thirteen years ago?"

"I know it was so wrong of me to do something like that. I don't know what I was even thinking, selling my own child. How I could have done such a thing to my wife and son, not to mention my own little baby girl that I held in my arms before placing her in the doctor's hands? I just didn't know how my family was going to survive with two more mouths to feed and care for." James was picturing what he had done so many years beforehand.

"What was the name of the doctor whom you gave your baby to?" Marcia asked.

"That is a name that I will never forget. His name was Dr. Michael Freytag."

As soon as Marcia heard the name come out of James's mouth, she put her hand over her own mouth as she made a loud noise that shocked everyone in the room. "Oh my! He was my husband, but I swear I didn't know. He never told me where she came from. I was so happy to finally have a baby that I never bothered to ask questions."

"I knew it! I just knew that she had to be!" Priscilla exclaimed.

James jumped up from the couch. "We found our baby girl! Now where do we go from here?"

"I can hardly believe it, but God knew all along that I needed a sweet child before he was to take me home to be with him, and at the same time, he was taking care of you and your family in a way that none of us even knew about," Marcia said.

James and Priscilla sat there looking at Marcia as she went on talking about how God had his hand in the entire situation.

"You see, you didn't have to struggle to feed your family anymore and you got your own business. I'm sure it came from Michael paying you for our daughter. Oh, I know that you never got to raise Terri, but ever since she was almost five years of age, we became best friends. So really, throughout her whole life, you have been a big part of hers."

Priscilla stood up and walked over to Marcia, then sitting down next to her, she put her arms around her and began to cry. "I thank God that I met you at the park that one day, and then years later, we met up again, and that's where we became best friends. I need to know how you feel about us now." She was trying to keep her composer after finding out it was indeed her best friend who had raised her little girl.

Marcia looked at her, then taking her hands, she said, "You are one of the best people in the whole world to me, and I thank God that we met. I would like to be the one to tell Terri, if the two of you wouldn't mind. I think something like this might be better off if it comes from me. I just know that God is calling me home. Now I know why. It is time for the two of you to have your daughter back."

"I know you know what is best for her, and I trust you will do the right thing for all of us. Do you know when you are going to talk with her?" James asked.

"Tonight, when she comes in from school, which will be in a few hours from now," Marcia said while looking at the clock that hung above the fireplace.

"Wow, it's that time already. I didn't realize we have been here for nearly three hours," Priscilla said.

"I think Priscilla and I are going to get out of your way for now," James offered. "David will be home in a few hours too, and we will need to have a talk with him. I want you to know that it wasn't about the money I received from your husband—it was about surviving."

Marcia looked at James as he talked, then without saying anything back to him, she focused her attention on Priscilla. "I will call you after I have a talk with Terri, and let you know how it went with our talk."

Priscilla hugged Marcia. "Thank you, Marcia. I love you and will be praying that she will understand and not be angry with James and me."

The two walked away feeling anxious about the truth coming out and them knowing the truth about Terri.

"I just can't believe it. Until yesterday, I thought I had everything all figured out. I thought that life was good for all of us. Then I found out I had a baby girl and she was sold, then today I find out that my baby was raised by my best friend. Now I ask you, James, how do we tell David and get him to understand without him getting all upset? This is so overwhelming for me and hard to comprehend I can only imagine what it will be like for him," Priscilla stated.

"My biggest worry right now is not him getting upset, but about him and Terri hating me. Will they ever understand and forgive me for what I have done?" James looked at his wife as if she knew the answer.

"I found it to be so much easier to forgive you when you took the time to explain your reasoning for what you did. And when I see how Marcia took it and the way she looked at it, that too made me feel so much better about this whole thing. Although I can't say when I will completely trust you again."

James reached his hand out to take Priscilla's. "Did I ever tell you how much I love you? I am so glad that you forgave me for that terrible thing that I did. And if it takes me the rest of my life to make this up to you and to get you to trust me again, then that's what I will do. I really didn't do this for the money. I know that's the first thing that people will think it's about."

"Honey, I can't help but think how I might feel if we never got to know our daughter over the years. We may have missed out on raising her, but we were there and part of her life ever since she was five years old. We know her just as much as we know David. When you think about it, she and David have been together just about every day for the last three years. Now we must talk with David about this. And please don't let what others say or think come between us. It's something that has happened, and no matter what, we can't change the past. So we need to hold on to God and our faith, knowing that he forgave you when you asked him to."

"Thank you, honey. I love you so much, and I thank God that you have stood by me in this time of finding some very hurtful things out. I know that at any time, you could have kicked me to the curb, and I'm sure there will be people that will wonder why you haven't. But we will be strong and face whatever comes our way."

When the two of them entered the house, David hopped up off the couch. "Where have you guys been all this time?" he asked with anger in his voice.

"What is the matter with you? Why are you talking with so much anger? What is wrong with you?" Priscilla asked.

David looked at his dad then at his mom. "I heard something in school today that caused me to get in a fight with Sonny Bittner."

"No need to say anything else, son, Please sit down. We need to talk," James requested.

"Just tell me that it's not true." He knew just by the look on his dad's face that Sonny heard something of the truth.

"What is going on here? What am I missing?" Priscilla asked, looking at the both of them.

"Honey, when I went to see the pastor the other day, Mrs. Bittner was outside of the door listening in on our conversation."

"You mean to tell me she heard what you told the pastor?"

"Yes, and I heard her on the phone telling others."

"So what Sonny told me in school today was the truth? Are you kidding me? I have a sister out there somewhere that you sold for money?" David was yelling at his dad, and he had never even raised his voice to him before now.

"Now that must mean that the whole town knows before we even got to talk with the kids. Everyone knows what a gossip that old Bitty is," Priscilla commented.

"Mom, Dad, can we please talk?" David asked. "What is going on? Why would Sonny say that you sold your daughter to buy a store?" David's whole body began to shake and tremble at the very thought of his father doing something so terrible.

James and Priscilla both looked toward David then they sat down.

"Son, first of all, I don't ever want you to talk that way to me again. No matter what might have taken place thirteen years ago still doesn't give you any right to disrespect me. I am still your father. Do I make myself clear?"

Before answering his dad, he looked over at his mom to see if she might have something else to add. When seeing she had nothing to say, he looked back at his dad. "Yes, sir."

"Now Sonny's grandma overheard some of a conversation that the pastor and myself were having. Please give me a chance to explain everything to you before judging me too harshly," James requested.

"So it's true what he said. Do I have a sister somewhere out there?" David got up off the couch, rubbing his hands through his hair." I can't believe it. I just can't believe it."

"Please sit down and allow your father to explain himself. If I was willing to hear what happened, then you need to be open enough to listen to him," Priscilla scolded him, pointing to the chair for him to take a seat.

David reluctantly sat back down. "Okay, I'm listening."

"First of all, I want you to know if I could have done anything else, I would have. But what I did I really believed at the time was the only thing I do. Now that I am older and wiser, I'm sure that there were more choices out there I could have done. Yes, it's true. I did sell your sister,"

David hopped up once again from his chair. "Oh my gosh!"

James continued on. "But it was the hardest choice I have ever made in all my life."

"How does someone just sell their child?" David asked angrily.

"There wasn't a day that went by that I wish I could have done something different or would have done something different. You see, son, your mother and I were very poor. I worked from sun up to sun down, and never seemed to get anywhere. Your mother had always wanted a baby, but I told her we couldn't afford another mouth to feed. For seven years, she would cry because she longed to be a mother. To be honest, I wanted to be a father too, but I knew that times were tough, and it would be nearly impossible on what I made to feed another mouth."

"So you sold your very own baby?"

I couldn't support two of ya's, let alone buy clothes and toys for the both of you. I know that it's no excuse for this terrible thing that I have done behind your mother's back. I wish that things could have been different. I have made so many mistakes. Now I ask you to please forgive me, son, for not telling you and your mother what I have done."

David sat back down not knowing what to say, looking at his mother then his father. After the three sat there looking at each other, David decided to ask the big question. "Have you ever seen her since you sold her?"

James looked at his wife then his son. "Yes, I have seen her many times over the years."

"Where? Why would you get to see her and not us?"

"David, you have known her for several years too," Priscilla said.

"I have? Well, who is she and where did I see her at?" David was now confused.

Priscilla stood up and walked over to David. Sitting down next to him, she took a hold of his hand. She began to speak with caution, trying carefully to tell him what she and James had just found out an hour beforehand. "You are asking us to tell you what your dad and I have just found out an hour ago ourselves."

"So who is she then? Please, just tell me."

"Your sister is Terri. She is your twin."

David jumped up. "No way!" He was looking back and forth at both of his parents. "Are you sure? How do you know this to be sure?"

"We went to see Marcia today and had a long talk with her, and it was confirmed to us that Terri is your twin sister. So you see, we have known her all along. Through all of the pain that thirteen years ago had caused, we were still together in many ways. And when Marcia found out that she was dying of cancer, she asked us to take Terri in as our very own."

"Wait a minute. Are you telling me that Marcia knew all along Terri was my sister and said nothing?"

"No, it's not like that. She herself just found out when we did today," James explained.

"Then how do you know if it's true for sure?"

"When your mother was ready to give birth to what she thought was to one child, she told the doctor we couldn't afford it, and she didn't know what we were going to do. So when she had the two of you, I made the choice to give both of you a better life, so I sold my little girl to the doctor. I knew there was just no way I could take care of the both of you. It was Marcia's first husband, Michael, who took Terri home for him and her to raise. She never knew until today who the parents were. They both had wanted a baby for twenty years and were never able to have one. So that's why the doctor had asked your dad for one of his babies."

"How come you didn't know you had two babies, Mom?"

"I only went to the doctor's a couple of times before having you because we couldn't afford to go. When I went into labor, I was having a lot of problems giving birth to two babies, even though I didn't know it was to two of them. The doctor gave me a shot to put me to sleep, and he took the babies while I slept. When I came to, I only knew about you. I will not hold your dad at fault for this. I know it had to be so hard for him to make that kind of a decision behind my back. He worked so hard to make ends meet, then we still struggled to get by. That place he worked at never paid their men very well, and he worked so much that by the time he came home from work, we barely got to talk before going to bed every night. He was so tired. Not only that, your father was not a Christian back then, either. Now that everything is out in the open, we have got to learn to forgive and to love."

"Have you told Terri about this?"

"No, her mother will tonight."

"But you are her mother."

"Please understand, son, to her, Marcia is her mother. It is going to take time for all of us to get used to the idea that she is our daughter and your twin. Marcia is going to explain to her about us, and I pray that she will be able to understand it all and forgive your dad."

"You want to know something?" David said, staring off into space.

"What, honey?"

"Terri and I would talk many times. Well, we thought it was just silly about us being twins since we had the same birthdays, and we liked so many of the same things."

"I have told your father many times that I thought she looked like me when I was younger. We even went as far as to bring out some of my old pictures when I was a kid and compared them to her.

"Really!"

"Yes, really! I pray that she will understand after she hears what happened."

Just as Priscilla was talking, the phone rang.

"I'll get it," James said as he got up and walked over to the corner shelf where the phone sat.

David and his mother never spoke another word; they were too busy listening to what James had to say on his end of the phone.

"Really, I guess that's to be expected. Maybe she will let me and Priscilla talk with her. Yes, we both talked to him about everything. I think he can kind of understand, but I think that it's going to take time for all of us to get used to it. Okay, well, thanks for calling us and letting us know. I'll be sure to tell Priscilla."

"I heard," Priscilla quickly answered. "She's not taking this so well, huh?"

"No, she's not. Marcia said that Terri told her that she never wants to see me again as long as she lives. It will take some time, and I will be very patient with her."

"You really can't blame her for this, I don't really know what to think about it myself. I wonder if I can talk with her," David proposed.

James looked at his son, then he sat down on the couch, looking so heartbroken for what he did to his family. Placing his head into his hands, he began to weep so hard that even David was moved by his father's tears.

Priscilla looked at David, thinking what it must be like for Terri right now. "She just might let you talk to her. After all, the two of you are very close."

"I'll call her and ask if we can get together and talk. Maybe we can take a walk to the park."

"That's a very good idea. She has no reason to be upset with you. If anything, you would think as close as the two of you are, she would have a lot of things to talk about."

"We'll see." David walked over to the phone and began dialing the numbers. "Hi, Terri, it's me, David. I was wondering if I can come over and we take a walk to the park so we can talk?"

"I sure hope she doesn't take this out on him. After all, the two of them have been best friends for years. None of this is any of his doings or yours. I hope she will sit down and allow you to talk with her," James said, tears still lingering in his eyes.

"Okay, I'll be right there." David hung the phone up, giving his parents a big smile. "She said that she wants the two of us to talk. Does it matter how long I'm gone for?"

"No, not really as long as your home before dark, and please try to get her to understand where your father was coming from," Priscilla requested.

"I will, Mom. I'll do my best," he said as he was closing the door behind him, hopping on his bike for a two-mile ride.

TERRI COMES HOME

"HI. ARE YOU ready?" David asked, her giving her a weary look.

"Yep," Terri said, holding her head down, trying to avoid any eye contact.

"Terri, please look at me. We are the same people that we were in school today."

"How can you say that? Doesn't this bother you at all what your dad has done?"

"At first, when I heard it at school, I wanted to kill Sonny for what he said to me. I didn't even believe what he said. How could my dad do something like that? No way, not my dad. I freaked out when I heard that. I thought it was just another one of his stories that he was telling just to start trouble like he usually does. But this time, he was right about what he said, and I still am having a hard time at the whole thing."

"What are you talking about? What did he say to you?"

"He came up to me when I was at my locker, and he told me that my dad sold my twin sister. I thought that he was just making up junk to start a bunch of crap like he always does. It just so happened to be true this time."

"How did he even know about it?"

"My dad went to talk with the pastor about what he had done, and his nosy grandma was standing outside of the pastor's office door, listening in on whatever they were talking about."

"Wow, so she opened up her big mouth and told her rotten grandson just so he could go to school and tell the world that my father didn't want me, so he sold me and kept you." She began to cry at the mention of being sold.

"Please let me explain it to you. It wasn't like that at all. Really, it wasn't. My dad sat me down and told me everything, but before he did, I was so mad at him I didn't even want to see him or talk to him, either. I still am upset, even though I can understand why he did what he did."

"Really!" she said with anger written all over her face.

"Really, now can we sit here on the bench so I can tell you what our parents told me?"

"Yes, but just to let you know, they are your parents, not mine."

David at first didn't know how to respond to her anger, then he took her by the hand. "Well, technically they are. Remember I just found out about this today myself, and wow, what a big surprise it was, after all the times you and I have played around, saying we were twins because our birthdays being on the same day."

"I know this is a shock to you too, but please tell me everything your dad told you."

"I will try to remember everything like he told me."

David began telling her as he remembered it being told to him. Through the story of her being sold, he watched her cry and put her head down to her lap and shake so uncontrollably that he too would have to stop what he was saying and cry with her. Then like a brother talking with his sister, he would continue on.

"If you can try to understand why he did what he did, it does make perfect sense. I know you have never known them as your parents like I did, but I do know that if he could have in anyway afforded the two of us, he would have never even considered letting someone else raise you."

"I'm glad you told me about what took place back then. now at least I could kind of see that he did what he did to give us all a much better life. And my mother who raised me, she is my mother and is a very good mother to me. She has always been there for me," Terri said, wiping her tears from her eyes, trying to give David a smile. "I can't even imagine her not raising me like I was her own child. She told me a few years ago that I was adopted. I told you all about that when I found out. This whole thing is so weird for me to understand, but I'm glad that you're all right with it all."

"I wonder what would have happened to us if he didn't do what he did. Would we have been happy being poor? Would we have been hungry at times? I have thought of all these things since I heard what had happened. That is something I think I will think on now for a long time, and just for the record, I wouldn't say that I'm all right with it all. It's just something that no matter what can never be undone, it's something that happened and we all have to live with it, like it or not," David said.

"Maybe I should try to look at it from where he was coming from. I have known them both for all of my life, and what I have seen is that outside of my mom, you have the best parents ever. I wonder if he ever thought of me over all the years."

"Are you kidding me? He told me that there has not been one day that he has not thought of you. And he questioned if he did the right thing about giving you away. Trust me, this has him all torn up on the inside. He hates himself for what he did to all of us. He just talks about it, and he will cry."

"You're kidding me. He said that about me? Are you teasing me just to try and make me feel better about this whole thing? I guess I would hate myself too if I gave my child away. So he must of thought that one child was too many, huh." She was fidgeting with her fingers.

"Oh come on! Do I look like I'm teasing you? He just told me that when he was telling me what really happened and why it happened."

"I wonder if he wants to talk to me about why he did what he did."

"Are you telling me you are willing to talk with him? Because I know that he would love a chance to explain everything to you. He really isn't such a bad guy."

After David said "He wasn't a bad guy," Terri gave him a look that made him question what he had just said.

"Now come on, I know what he had done, and it doesn't make him look like he is any good, but if you can just remember who you have always thought he was before any of this came out, that's who he really is. He's not a monster who wanted to give you away. He just felt at the time that he was saving all of us as a family." After David said that to her, he felt guilty for the way he was thinking about his dad deep inside of his heart that he didn't want Terri to know about.

"I think I will talk to him. I mean, I will try and give him the chance to talk with me. I just don't want to get mad at him and walk away."

"I'm glad you are willing to listen to him because I know that if he could have done something different, then he would have had. When do you want to talk with him? And please, try not to walk away?"

"How about after school tomorrow? It's getting late, and my mom doesn't like me to stay out after dark. I better get going home, but after school tomorrow, I will come over and talk with your mom and your dad."

"Okay, I'll let them know that you will be coming over tomorrow. I'm sure that will make the both of them very happy. I'm sure that after you hear it come from my dad it will give you a better understanding to everything, and it will make better sense to you."

David walked Terri home.

"Until tomorrow, sis."

At first she gave him a funny look, hearing the words *sis* come out of his mouth, then she smiled. "Okay, I'll see you at school tomorrow," she said as she started to close the door to her house.

"Hi, how did it go for you and David?" Marcia asked when Terri came into her bedroom. "I hope that you listened with your heart and not in anger.

"He told me why his dad did what he did. And I tried to hear from my heart, Mom, but I just can't wrap my mind around it."

"Come here, honey, sit next to me. I want to try and explain something to you." Marcia slid over a tad to let Terri in next to her. "I really believe this all happened for the good," she said while wrapping her arm around Terri and playing with her hair. "You see, honey, had James never made that choice, then I would have never had a chance to be your mother. It would have killed me along time ago when your father who adopted you died. You see, it was you who had given me a reason to live when he died in that terrible car crash when you were only two. You see, honey, God knew I would need you in my life, and he gave you to me. Sure, I know that a lot of people have been hurt through this, but look at the good that came out of it. I have you, and the Cole's have always been a part of your life. And now when I go home to be with Jesus, they will have you as their daughter."

"Mama, please don't die. I need you here with me. I love you, Mama." Terri held on to her mother like never before. She felt like everything she had ever known was all a big lie. Now the very thought of her mother dying was just breaking her heart.

"Oh, honey, you are a very bright and intelligent young lady. I know with all of my heart that you will be okay with James and Priscilla. Now tell me, does anything that David and I had said to you make any sense?"

"Yes, it makes sense, I guess, but it still hurts me to know that he sold me for whatever reason he said that he did it for," she spoke with sobs still coming from her broken heart.

Marcia took Terri's hand and gave it a light squeeze. "If he did not do what he did, I never would have had the privilege to raise and love you. That may sound so selfish, but I thank God he did what he did. You have been such a blessing to me in so many ways. You are the daughter that I have spent many years praying for."

Terri leaned over to give her mother a hug, "I know, Mama, and I feel that my life could not have been any better without you being my mother. Please try and understand where I'm coming from, Mama. I have known them all of my life, only to find out that they are my birth parents. Do you have any idea what that feels like for me?" She stood up walking over to the bay window, looking out toward the woods. "I love you, Mama, I really do, but I don't know how I'm supposed to feel about them now. I mean, I just can't believe that he sold me for money. Who does that?"

"I understand, honey. I guess it's the same as who would pay that amount of money to have a child? Your father did because he and I have always wanted a child, and we would have done just about anything to have one."

"I'm glad that you raised me, Mama. I love you so much. I just can't imagine my life without you being my mom." She changed the subject before she was to break down and cry again. "Can I get you anything before I go do my homework?"

"If you wouldn't mind, please make me a cup of tea, while I get myself out of this bed and go out into the living room. I have been in bed just about all day. Now it's time for me to get up."

"Okay, I'll get you that tea." Terri walked out feeling sad about her mother's health, but she was glad that they had their talk; it helped her in many ways to understand a little better. She knew how much her mother had loved her and would never lead her in the wrong direction.

Marcia watched Terri as she entered the living room with her tea. She patted on the couch cushion, waiting for Terri to sit down so she could have a talk with her.

"What is it, Mama?" she asked seeing her mother patting the couch for her to come and sit down.

"I would really like to talk with you about something. You know that I've been very sick lately."

Terri knew that the two of them had just talked about this in the bedroom; now it was like her mother didn't even remember their talk. She wondered if it could be the pills her dad Nick had her mother on to help with the pain. But she would allow her mother to say whatever she felt she needed to say again.

"Yes, Mama, but you are going to get better."

"No, honey, I don't believe I will be. I don't think I will be able to stay strong for much longer."

"Mama, don't say that. Stop talking to me like that. You are going to get better. You just have to believe that you will, and you will."

"Terri, I want you to listen to me, and I mean, *listen*. I am not going to be here much longer, and I want you and your birth parents to get along and talk about whatever needs talking. After I go home to be with the Lord, you will be living with them. I want you to know that you will be in safe hands, and I have everything willed over to you and them. Nick will be moving back into his home when I'm gone. There will be no need for you to have to move any of your things out of this home."

"Mama, I hate you talking like this. You sound like you want to die."

"Honey, last night, I had a dream of me being in heaven. It was the most glorious place I have ever seen before. There was so much peace there that it was hard for me to take it all in. I never want to leave you, but God will be here watching over you, as well as your other family."

Terri leaned down next to her mother and lay on her chest, crying like a little baby. "I love you, Mama. I'm going to miss you."

Right when she was telling her mother how much she was going to miss her, her mother took her last breath.

"Mama! Mama!" she screamed. "No…not yet…Mama! Please don't die, Mama!"

Terri lay there next to her mom crying so hard until Nick came in the living room.

"Terri?" he called out.

"Mama's gone…she's gone!" She lay there crying out of control.

Nick walked out of the room and called up Priscilla. "This is Nick. I just wanted to let you know that Marcia's gone now, and Terri will need someone here for her."

"What…she died…when?" Priscilla was in complete shock.

"Just a moment ago, and Terri is taking her passing pretty hard. Someone might want to come get her, so I can call the coroners to come get Marcia's body."

"We will be right there." Priscilla hung the phone up and sat down. She couldn't believe her best friend was forever gone from her place on earth.

"Marcia just went home to be with the Lord. That was Nick, and he sounded so cold. He wants us to come get Terri right now so he can have the coroners come get Marcia. I just can't believe she's gone just like that, and we were just talking with her earlier."

"Wow, you're kidding me she went just like that, and Nick seems to be cold, huh? We better get over there for our daughter—wow, that sounded so nice to say that. We better call for David to come with us. She might not want to see us so soon after Marcia died."

"You may be right. David, come with us," she called out. It was beginning to sink in to Priscilla, and she began to cry. "I just can't believe she died this fast after finding out that she had cancer."

David ran into the house. "What's going on? Where are we going?"

"Nick just called and told us that Marcia died. He asked us to come get Terri."

"You're kidding me. Just like that, she's gone? I have to get over to Terri right now." He was so worried over his sister that he was in the car before either of his parents were even outside.

"We will all go right now. She's going to need each one of us." Priscilla spoke, looking at James with tears flowing from her sad eyes.

They gathered their composure and headed over to comfort Terri; their short ride was left with no words spoken between the three of them. David sat in the backseat, staring out the window while tapping his fingers on his knee. Priscilla sat in the passenger side of the car, humming an old hymn called "When the Roll is Called Up Yonder." And James sat in a silent thought of his daughter getting to know him as her father and not just a friend.

Once arriving at their destination, Priscilla was the first to walk into the place that she would soon call home. She walked down the hallway that led to the living room, which Marcia once painted to perfection but now held her lifeless body on the couch. Seeing Terri slumped over the only mother she had ever known brought tears to all of their eyes. She felt so much compassion it touched her very soul as she reached out and brought Terri up to her feet and held her close to her breast.

"I'm so sorry, honey, for your mother leaving you. She loved you so much that it was breaking her heart at the thought of her not being here for you."

Terri allowed her birth mother to hold on to her as long as she was willing to do so. That was until they were rudely interrupted by Nick and were asked to leave the home until the coroners removed Marcia's body. Taking Terri by her hand, Priscilla led her outside to the car. Without saying a word, James walked to the driver's side and started up the car and waited for the rest of them to get in so he could drive back home. He was so upset at the way Nick had just treated his little girl after losing the only mother she had ever known. He knew if he didn't leave quickly, it just might have been the coroners picking up Nick along with Marcia.

After getting alone so the children would not overhear anything that was said, Priscilla spoke with much anger to her husband about Nick.

"I just can't believe the very nerve of that man! How can he be so heartless about the passing of his own wife? How can he call himself a Christian and act the way that I have just witnessed? And how dare he do that to our little girl who had just lost the only mother she had ever known? It's no wonder Marcia asked us to care for her when she was gone. I thought I knew that man, but I guess he had me completely fooled. Maybe it was me being a fool. I knew something was wrong a long time ago. The way he acted when she was only seven and broke her arm, he was terrible to her back then."

James could see how upset Priscilla was, so he walked over to her. "Come now, honey, you're getting yourself all upset. Right now when Terri needs us to be there for her."

"I know. I'm going to miss her so much. She was my best friend for the last eight years. But I will be strong for Terri because she needs me right now. I'm going to see what she and David are doing, and you call up Nick to see if the coroners have come to take Marcia away."

James hugged his wife then walked out of the bedroom to make the phone call she had asked from him.

"Nick, this is James. How is everything going over there?"

With a nasty comment that took James by surprise, Nick showed himself in a way he would never have expected to come from a man who, just days before, considered him as a friend.

"Well, with the death of my wife and her leaving me nothing in her will, things couldn't be better."

James didn't know what to say; he stood at the other end of the phone speechless. Then without hearing anything else from Nick, he heard the phone hang up. He was talking to himself loud enough for Priscilla to hear some mumbling as she entered the door of the kitchen.

"What's the matter?" Priscilla inquired.

"It was the weirdest thing. I just got off the phone with Nick, and he clearly didn't even sound like himself at all."

"It's no wonder. He just lost his wife."

"No, honey, it's not like that at all. He was rude and very mean. He talked about Marcia not leaving him anything in her will. I just can't believe that at a time like this, this is what he was thinking about."

"You're kidding me he said that! It's no wonder she didn't want to leave Terri in his care. She told me months ago that he and Terri didn't get along at all. At the time she told me that I had only seen a bad side of him one time. I have to be honest—I thought that maybe Terri was just being a rebellious child and Marcia wasn't seeing it that way because Terri was her daughter. But now after what I have seen earlier and what you have just told me, it all makes sense why she wanted Terri with us."

"She must have left everything to Terri in her will, and she must have told Nick what she was doing. If I know anything at all about Marcia, she was a very sweet person. So in order for her to have done that to her husband, she must have known there was something unlikable about him. Maybe she felt he was never going to give anything to Terri. I'm sure she did what she felt that she needed to do."

"I'm ready to go back over to the house to see what Terri might need to get so we can come back here, and I will make funeral arrangements for Marcia. It's not like I can expect Nick to do anything about it."

"Honey, I don't want you to do anything of that sort. You let me take care of everything. Terri will need you and David right now. I want you three to be there for each other. I'll call into work and let them know I won't be coming into work for a few days."

"Thank you, honey. I'm going to have a talk with Terri and David." Priscilla walked away to find the kids sitting on the couch, talking. "Terri, I'd like to talk with you for a minute, if I may."

"Okay," Terri answered, looking at Priscilla with tears flooding her deep brown eyes and her beautiful face.

Priscilla noticed how she had the curls like her father James and the olive skin color like her. She sat next to Terri, putting her arms around her. "I know it hurts, honey, and it will take some time. James and I were wondering if there is anything at your home that you need."

"Yes," she spoke just above a whisper while wiping her hair and tears out of her eyes.

Priscilla knew that Terri was having a hard time with the death of the woman she called mother for the last thirteen years. She was trying to be strong and understanding at the same time for her; she knew that her calling Marcia mom for all of these years was none of her doing anything wrong. She was actually grateful of Marcia taking such wonderful care of the daughter she never knew and what a wonderful friend she was to her as well.

"Come with me, honey. I will take you back to your home, and you can get some of your things together and bring them back here."

Terri looked at David as if she wanted him to come with her. "I'm coming," she said as she stood up, looking at David once again. "But my mom told me I won't have to move any of my things."

David, reading the look in her eyes, said, "Mama, do you care if I come along with the two of you?"

"Not at all. I can see that Terri wants you to come." Priscilla put her hand on Terri's hand. "It's okay. I understand that finding out who we really are has got to be hard to comprehend. I know it will take all of us some time to get used to it. I just know that I will do whatever I have to do to give you and David the time both of you need to adjust to finding out that the two of you are twins. Please understand me when I say that it's going to take me time also at seeing you as my daughter and not just my best friend's daughter. I do want you to know that I love you, and I am glad to know that you are my child. I will do whatever it takes to make you feel part of this family, and I know that it will take time, especially after you just lost your mother. And as far as not bringing any of your things over here, we will get just enough for the night."

"Thank you for understanding. I will try and get used to seeing it that way too. My mama told me what happened when I was born." Tears began to flow at the mention of her being a baby, and the talk about her mom made her cry.

Priscilla could see that it would indeed take her time getting used to the idea of her being sold as a baby; she knew it must make her feel unwanted and unloved with David being chosen to keep over her. But now the question was what could she do to possibly make her feel that she was loved as well as David was loved. Would it be up to James to make things right? Would Terri receive from him as she would from David or her? She knew she must have a talk with James about him making things right for Terri to feel part of the family.

"Come on, honey, lets go get whatever it is that you will need for the night."

Getting in the car to go back to the only place Terri knew as her home for a number of years, Priscilla prayed silently, asking God to help Nick show some sort of kindness toward Terri when they got to the house. After getting there, they walked up to the home and entered, just to find that Nick had already removed his belongings from the premises. In some sort of way, that brought relief to Priscilla. She thought it was better for him to be gone than to see him take out on Terri the outcome of what Marcia had done not leaving him with anything. She knew that in order for Marcia to have not left him with anything, she must have had a very good reason to feel that way.

"It looks to me like Nick is already gone."

"I don't think he even cared at all that my mother died. He never said he was sorry or anything. I didn't even see him cry at all. I'm beginning to wonder if he ever loved her in the first place. I don't think he ever loved me, and if he did, he sure had a funny way of showing me that he did."

"I'm so sorry, honey, he acted that way toward you. Your mother never told me anything about the way he treated you until about a month ago." Priscilla never wanted to bring up the time that she witnessed what he did to her when she was so young.

"My mom was a very private person. She never liked to talk about it, even to me. But when she found out she had cancer, she began to talk a little more about things and the way Nick was treating her and me."

"What do you mean the way that he treated her?"

"I could hear him yelling at her all the time. I even heard when he'd throw some of her things and break them when she wouldn't do what he wanted her to do."

"Oh my, I really had no idea that this was even going on. Do you know why she wouldn't do what he asked from her?"

"He'd tell her to wash his feet when he'd come in from work," Terri said while keeping her head down.

"Why would he want her to wash his feet? Why wouldn't he wash his own feet?"

"I don't know why. My mother never talked about it to me."

Priscilla felt so bad for Terri's pain that all she could do was pray silently and put her arms around her. "Let's get what you need for tonight, then we can come back tomorrow for more if you need too."

"Okay, I'll get what I need."

David looked at his mother when Terri went to her bedroom. "Mom, I feel so bad for her. First, she's treated like crap by the man she called dad. Then she finds out that we are her true family.

Then the only mother she had ever known died right there in front of her. I don't know what to say or do. I feel so helpless."

"I know that you do, honey, but all we can do is listen to her when she's expressing herself, when she's crying, or even when she's angry. Right now, Terri has a lot on her plate. She is going through a lot of mixed feeling and emotions. Just be there for her in every way that you can. Remember to be praying for her. She may not let your dad or I get close to her after her just losing her mom."

That night, as Terri lay in bed, she cried most of the night. Priscilla came to her door and tried to comfort her, but it was like she didn't want to be comforted. She only wanted David to talk to. Although Terri pushing her away hurt Priscilla, she understood right now that the last thing she needed was another mother, when she had just lost her mother. Priscilla went into David's room to tell him to go see Terri and bring her as much comfort as she would allow him too. James stayed out of it; he lay next to Priscilla, and the two of them prayed together for Terri. He knew at this time she didn't really want anything from him, knowing he gave her up as a baby.

Morning came, and James decided to go to work after feeling he would not be wanted around for the day. Before walking out, he gave Terri a little hug, asking her to forgive him for what he did a long time ago.

"Maybe one day you will find it in your heart to forgive me and to love me because there is not a day that has went by that I have not thought of you and wished so many times that I never have done that terrible thing I did by giving you away." With that, James started to cry, so he made a fast dodge toward the door, and he was gone.

Terri stood there not knowing what to say to the rest of the family. If the truth be told, she felt kind of numb. All she wanted to do was feel safe once again like her mother had always tried to do for her, especially when her dad Nick was being so cruel.

The days seemed to slowly drift by after Marcia's funeral. It was hard for James and Priscilla to watch Terri as she seemed to slip into some sort of depression since her mother's death. She seemed to grow quiet, even when it came time for David trying to be there for her. David was taking it hard to watch his sister and best friend in all the world suddenly close up to where it was like she was becoming a walking zombie.

The phone rang, and David answered it. "Hello? Yes, just a minute, I'll get her. Mom, the phone is for you or Dad."

Priscilla took the phone just to find out it was Marcia's lawyer. "Yes, we can be there, and thank you." She hung up the phone, then called James at the store. "Honey, we have to go down to Marcia's lawyer's office at four o'clock today for the reading of the will. He just called asking us to be there, so can you meet us there?"

"You don't want me coming to get the rest of you?" he asked.

"No, that won't be necessary."

"Okay, honey, I'll see you then. How is Terri doing?"

"She cries a lot, but that is expected to happen for a while. These things take time to heal. Then there's you and me. That's got to be very hard for her to understand and get used to.

"After this is done, it just might help her. I pray that it does. Honey, I'll see you in a few hours."

"I'll see you there," Priscilla said.

THE READING

JAMES MET PRISCILLA at the lawyer's office, not looking at Terri in her eyes because he knew what he had done brought her so much hurt and pain. As he walked in behind the rest of them, he tried to keep himself at a certain distance so it wouldn't be like he was trying to force his way into her life as a father.

"Good afternoon, everyone," a tall elderly gentleman said as they entered the office. "Please have a seat as we read Marcia's will." Looking over to Terri's way, he said to her just how sorry he was that her mother passed away. "This will that she wrote out just a week before she died replaced the one she had written out before."

The man opened up an envelope and took out the will. "In this reading of her will, she leaves everything she owns, except the home, to Terri." He looked over his glasses, which was sitting low on his nose, at everyone in the room, then he continued on. "She asks that your family would kindly move into her home and make it your home. She is asking from the both of you, James and Priscilla, if you would be willing to make her home your home. She thinks it would make things easier for Terri and also make more room for your family. James and Priscilla, she asks that the two of you be an overseer of all that Terri is entitled to." Once again, he looked over his glasses at the two of them.

"But you just said that she left everything to Terri but the home. How are we to move there if she doesn't get the home?" Priscilla asked.

"She has asked that it be you and your husband's home."

The whole time, James just sat there not saying a word until now. "Overseer? Now what does that actually contain of?" James asked.

The man looked at him in disbelief and continued on. "The lump sum of three hundred and fifty four thousand dollars."

"Really, she had that much?" After those words fell out of James mouth, he felt so terrible. "Oh, please forgive me, I didn't mean anything by that."

"Terri, if you don't want to live at the home you were raised in, that's fine. We don't have to move there. Our home isn't as big or nice, but it's comfortable, and we will make room for you, of course." Priscilla said, trying to make Terri feel welcomed at their home.

"Thanks, but if you guys wouldn't mind, I'd like it if we can all live at my house as long as my dad won't be living there." As soon as she said that, she looked at James, "Oh, I wasn't meaning you. I meant Nick." She quickly turned her eyes away from looking at James. Ever since she found out about what happened thirteen years ago, she can't seem to look him in the face anymore. Looking back at Priscilla, she began to talk again. "My mom told me before she died that I wouldn't have to move anything out of my home." Then she looked at the lawyer. "Wait, you said my mom left everything to me except the house. Is that true?"

"Yes, that is what the will says. It was left to James and Priscilla."

"Well then, I guess it's up to you what you guys want to do," she said sarcastically.

"Honey if you want to live at your home, then that's what we will do, won't we James?" Priscilla said. "I think your mother's home is just a beautiful home. I'd love to call that my home," she said, looking at James.

"It sure is a nice place, and if you want us to move there, than that's where we will live," James answered.

After leaving the lawyer's office, the ride back home was quiet, leaving everyone in the car to their own thoughts. James was headed back to work, thinking about the beautiful big home that was left for him and Priscilla. And all the money that Marcia had willed over to his daughter was far more than he could ever think she would have had. *It must have come from her first husband after he died. He must have had good life insurance to leave her all that money. Or maybe he did more investments after he got Terri as a baby like he did before.* His mind began to think his and Priscilla's new home again. He had never thought that one day he would be living in a beautiful place such as Marcia's, let alone it being his place. He felt sad that it had to come with such a hard price. *Now why did Marcia not leave the only home that Terri knew to her? Why would she leave it to Priscilla and me?*

The rest of the day went by slow for Priscilla and her thoughts of moving into her best friend's home. It seemed like hours had went by, when in all reality, the time was slowly going by. She would look at the kitchen clock that hung on the wall just above the stove and see that time had hardly moved. She wanted to talk with James about when he felt that they should make their move; she could hardly wait until he would get home from work.

After dinner, Priscilla cleaned up the kitchen and put some coffee on so she and James could sit in the front room and talk about whats been going on with the store's addition. She never wanted to discuss the move to their new home when the kids were around; she felt that was something that just the two of them needed to talk about when they were alone.

James told her that it was going very good and better than he had expected it to go. "Soon I will be able to put all the shelves in and stack the food on them. I'm hoping it will bring more people to the store with all the new items that we will be carrying."

"When would you like us to start moving our things in our new home?" Priscilla asked James when the two of them lay down for bed.

"Maybe we should talk to Terri about some things before moving over there."

"Like what?" Priscilla asked.

"Well, like what room is hers and what room is for David and if we are supposed to move our things in Marcia's bedroom. Won't that make Terri feel bad with us staying in there?"

"Yeah, I guess you're right. There are things that we need to work out before moving. The last thing I want to do is see that she gets hurt again. I know everything will be okay in time, but I believe it will just take each of us time getting used to things and to each other."

"Maybe you can talk with her tomorrow while I'm at work and find out what she is expecting from us," James suggested.

"Yes I will, and then I can start to pack some boxes."

"Don't you need boxes to pack them?" James teased her.

"Haha, smarty pants! Of course, I will come down to the store in the morning after my talk with Terri and get lots of boxes. So make sure that the stacker doesn't break them down. Hey, I just thought, what are we going to do with our home and all of our furniture?"

"Maybe we can rent it out, and when David gets older, we can give it to him. Or we can sell it, but I would kind of like to keep it for David when he moves out."

"That's something we don't have to decide on right now. Maybe he won't want this place. Maybe he'll want one that he picks out."

"Well, that could be true too. Let's think on it and go from there."

James left for work, and shortly after, Priscilla went down to the store to pick up some boxes. As she was ready to enter the store, Marlon, one of the stock workers, came out carrying several boxes for her. "These are for you. Your husband told me that you guys are moving and you're coming to get them."

"Oh yes, thank you so much for bringing them out for me," Priscilla said as she was taking some out of his hands. She noticed that he was giving her a weird grin when handing her the boxes; at first, she thought nothing of it, then he gave her a light chuckle, followed by another grin. This bothered Priscilla, not knowing what he was thinking about. She had known him ever since he started to work for her husband, and he had never done anything like that before now.

"Oh, I have lots more for you if you need them," Marlon said.

"Yes, thank you. I can use quite a bit more than what I have here," she said as she was putting them in her station wagon, turning her back on him as she was shoving some boxes in the front seat.

Marlon turned and walked back into the store to get more boxes, then came out with another handful. "Here you go. I still have more in the store if you need them."

"I don't think that my car can fit anymore in here if I tried. But what you can do is give them to James and ask him to bring them back home with him after work."

"Okay, ma'am, I'll do that. Have a good day." He said as he headed back toward the store, looking at her with that same weird grin then shaking his head back and forth.

"You too, and thanks again." Priscilla got in her car, wondering why Marlon was acting so strange toward her. It bothered her that she decided when James got home from work, she would let him know about it. She went back home to start packing some boxes, but first, she wanted to have a talk with Terri.

"I see you're back and with boxes," David said, looking at his mother coming through the door with an armload of boxes tumbling out of her hands.

"Yes, I am, and would you mind giving me a little help? There are a lot more in the car you can go get. Where is Terri at?" she asked, looking around for her.

"She must still be sleeping. I haven't seen her yet this morning."

"I need to talk with her before we move over to her house."

"Wait a minute. I thought that was our house," he asked.

"Oh, I don't care what papers say. As far as I'm concerned, it's our entire family's house. She is my child just like you are, not to mention your twin." She sounded irritated.

"Oh, I know that, Mama. I didn't mean anything by that. I think it should still be hers. She lived there all of her life, and that's all she knows. I better go get some boxes now." He walked out the door, leaving Priscilla standing there with boxes all over the floor.

Priscilla picked up some boxes and headed to her bedroom to begin packing clothes.

"Wow I never noticed that I have so many clothes now," she spoke to herself while sitting on the floor in front of her dresser, going through a drawer.

"I think that we all have more than what we need," David said, walking in her room.

"That's probably true. Maybe we should only take with us what we will wear and leave the rest here."

"It will be better if we give what we don't wear to some poor people at our church. Like the English family, did you see how the kids all dress with rips on their clothes?"

"No, I guessed I never paid much attention. Why don't you give the boys Eric and Tommy your clothes? I must admit we do have a lot of things besides clothes. Maybe they could use some of the other things that we have and won't need now that we are moving."

"Like what?"

"Well, we have nice furniture and some kitchen things. I don't know, but what I do know if they need it, I will give it to them. We have been so blessed in so many ways, even though some things came at such a high price." After Priscilla spoke that, she bent her head down and spoke just above her breath, "Really, everything we have did."

"What, Mama? I didn't hear what you said."

"Oh, it's nothing, just talking to myself. Maybe you should go wake Terri up now. I have never heard of someone sleeping in this late unless they are either old or sick, and as far as I know, she's not either one of them."

"Okay, I'll go check on her." He went into another room just to find that Terri was nowhere in sight. "Mom, she's not in the bedroom anywhere!" David yelled, wondering where she could have gone too.

"What! She's not here?" she said, getting up off the floor as fast as she could.

"Maybe she went back to her house."

"That is a very long walk, especially if she left last night. Well, we better get over there and see if that's where she is at."

"Don't you think that you should call Dad up first and let him know that she's missing?"

"No I don't want to get him all worried for nothing if she is there. Let's go look first, then if she's not there, then I will call your dad."

The two started driving toward Terri's house; the whole time, they were looking out the windows in hopes of seeing her walking, but before they realized it, they were pulling into the driveway and getting out of the car. Priscilla jumped out so fast to get into the house in hopes of seeing Terri in there; David ran ahead of his mother, beating her to the door.

"Terri, are you here?" Priscilla yelled up the stairs, but after not hearing her reply, she sent David up there to look for her.

David walked to Terri's bedroom, and seeing her door was shut, he lightly tapped on the door to see if she might say come on in. After hearing no answer, he turned the doorknob slightly and began to push it open. To his amazement, he found her in her bed, lying very still as to be sleeping. He tapped on her shoulder to wake her. Jumping after feeling someone next to her, she sat up.

"How long have you been here?" David asked the sleepy girl.

"I woke up this morning around five o'clock, and everyone was still sleeping, so I decided to walk here," Terri answered.

"Mom, she's up here!" David shouted down the stairs. "You had Mom and me so worried about you. Would you do me a favor next time that you decide to do something like this?"

"And what is that?" she asked.

"No matter what time it is, will you please let me know when you are planning on leaving? I don't want Mom having a heart attack or something being worried about you." Right after David spoke like that to her, he felt bad. The whole time the two of them have known each other and been best of friends, he had never had bad words toward her until now.

Sitting the rest of the way up and looking down at her pants she was wearing, she came back with the same attitude that had just been given to her. "I wasn't the one who decided that I wasn't good enough to keep and gave my baby away."

"Wow, Terri, Mom didn't do that, either. I know that this is very hard for you finding out that you were sold as a baby and that you have me as a twin, but I wish that you'd try and understand where Dad was coming from."

She interrupted him with the harsh words, "He's not my dad. He's yours."

"Whatever way you want it to be, that is beside the point. What I am saying is, Mom is dealing with not only knowing that her husband has been lying to her for the past thirteen years, but finding out that her best friend raised a daughter she didn't even know that she had. She lies in bed at night crying because she feels so betrayed about what *my father* did to all of us." David made sure to mention *father* in a sarcastic voice, knowing that right now in Terri's life, she wasn't willing to understand why their dad did what he did.

"I'm sorry, David, for saying what I said about the whole giving me away as a baby. I just don't know who I am anymore ever since my mother told me about what happened to me as a baby. I don't know how you and your mom can forgive your dad for what he did to you guys, keeping a secret like that from you for all of these years."

"At times, I want to hate him for what he did. I mean, when I look at you and know that for all of these years, we could have been together as brother and sister and fight like brothers and sisters do." He started to laugh after saying that. "To tell you the truth, as much as I have always liked you and I being best friends, I wonder now how would it have been for us if we had been raised together, instead of you being raised by someone else, that is hard for all of us to comprehend."

"You do mean sold me right?" Terri quipped, looking down again.

"Yes, we know well enough that's what he did. I just don't like saying it that way."

"But that's the way it happened. You got to stay with the mother who had you. And I, on the other hand, was taken home by a man who wanted me, only for him to die when I was still a small child, so small I don't remember him."

"But you did have a loving mother to care for you all of these years. That's more than some people get. I'm sorry for saying it like that because I know that you miss her, and I wish that there was something that I could do for you to take away all your pain." David said to her as he put his arm around her shoulder. "Come on, we better get down stairs before Mom wonders what's going on."

What both the kids didn't know was that just outside the bedroom door was Priscilla, listening in on their conversation. After hearing David tell Terri they should go downstairs, she turned around and headed down before getting caught by the children.

"David, can I ask you a question about your dad?"

"You can ask me anything," he replied.

"I know that my mother tried to tell me why I was given away as a baby, but I guess I was in such a shock at the whole part about who I am that I really wasn't listening to her at the time. Since I will be living with all of you until I grow up, I need to try and understand what really took place back then. I mean, why was I given away?"

"I have already told you what I know."

"So he would give his own child away because he wanted new things and wanted to be able to go places?" Terri came back with anger in her voice.

"It wasn't like that," David shot back. "I know that this has got to be so hard for you to understand, not to mention you probably feel that he never even wanted you. But to tell you the truth, when all of this came out, I found out that for several years, he didn't want any children because he said they couldn't afford any."

"So why have us then if they didn't want any?" she asked.

"Mom had always wanted children, but she wasn't the one out there working and barely bringing anything home to show for it. It was all by accident that you and I are both here, unless you want to call it an act of God."

"God, why would you say that he would have caused this?"

"Maybe because God has control over our lives in ways that we don't see or even understand. I mean, my mom wanted a baby, your mom and dad wanted a baby and couldn't have any. So I think God took a bad thing like my dad giving you away to make two moms happy."

"I know what you're saying, but why did they choose to keep you and get rid of me?"

"That question, you will have to ask him yourself. I don't know why it happened like that."

"I don't think that is going to happen, I have a hard enough time just looking at him, let alone ask him why he kept you instead of me."

"Terri, he is still that same man you have known and talked to for years. The only thing that is different now is that you now know he is your birth father."

After going back home and finding that James was home from work, Priscilla called him into the bedroom to tell him about the incident that took place earlier at the store with Marlon. James couldn't hardly believe what he was hearing.

"Priscilla, are you sure that you're just not putting more into this than what really was going on? Marlon has always liked you. I have never heard him say a disrespectful word about anyone before."

"James, I know what I have seen. Now I'm not making this up. Something very strange is going on over there at your store, and I think you need to have a talk with your employees and set the record straight once and for all about what happened way back then."

"Okay, Priscilla, if that's what you think I should do, then that's what I'm going to do. You won't be getting any more looks like that from any of them again. Okay, honey?"

"All right, and thank you, James."

TERRI CONFRONTS HER FATHER

THE MOVE WAS a success as they all had hoped for, after taking only the things they knew they needed, like the clothes they wore the most, their pillows, toothbrushes, shavers, etc. Priscilla was glad to have Terri's approval about her and James being able to take Marcia's bedroom. When living at her home, oftentimes she would tell James that she would like to expand their bedroom because she felt like it was just too small for them. Now whenever she would walk into her new bedroom that was twice the size of her old one, she would have a warm feeling come all over her, never thinking that after losing her best friend, she would be given such a wonderful home.

Pulling back the burgundy drapes that hung from the large bay windows, she could see the pond that she and her family had swam in with Marcia oftentimes before. She had never expected it to be hers one day, but her wish for her to have one had come to pass for her. The pond was just beautiful and easier to care for than she thought it would be. When asking Marcia in the past how would one care for it and finding out all that was needed, she knew she and James could do what it took to keep it clean for them to swim in. Priscilla was talking to herself out loud about the pond and its beauty when James walked in on her.

"What's this I hear you saying is a beauty?" he asked, looking around the room to see if she was talking to someone. Then he gave her a funny look, seeing that there was no one else in the room. "So we're talking to ourselves these days, huh?" he said in a teasing manner.

"Haha, you're so funny, James. I was just looking out this bay window here at the beautiful pond. I guess I never realized before that we would be able to see it from our bedroom window. I was thinking about the day Marcia took time to show us how to keep it clean. Back when she did that, although I never said anything to you or her, I thought to myself, *Why would she show James and I how to care for her pond?* Not once did I think that one day we would need to know how to because it would be ours. Now I wish I could just have known it at that time."

"Honey, I don't think when she was showing us how to care for it that she even knew it would be ours one day. I think that she was just being herself, taking time to show us things. Look at how she showed us how to prune those trees over there. I have never done that sort of thing before, but she showed me how to do it, so when it's time to do that, I will know how to now."

"I guess you're right. Marcia was just like that. She always took time to show us things, even when we didn't know why she would show us. Oh, honey, come here and take a look at this how beautiful it is." She turned to face him while holding back a drape. "It looks so pretty right now with the sun shining down on it."

"Wow, that is beautiful looking, that's for sure."

"If I wasn't so busy unpacking right now, I'd go for a swim."

"So let's go," he said, looking at her.

"But I have to unpack all of these boxes," She looked down at them, then back up at James. "You think we should?"

"Sure, honey, why not? We have all the time in the world to unpack."

"Okay, I'm going to ask the kids if they want to go with us. You are going, aren't you?"

"Yes, I'll go. It looks too nice right now to pass up."

"Okay, then after that, I will have to make supper. Where are the kids at?" Priscilla asked.

"Terri is helping David unpack his things in his room. Did you see how much bigger the size of his bedroom is than his old room?"

"Yes, I did. This is going to be so nice living here. When you bought the store, we fixed up our place to be much nicer than what it was. But even after all of that, it was nothing compared to this house. James, I know this place came with the loss of Marcia, and I know it is going to take all of us getting used to a new place and having Terri with us as my best friend's daughter. But one day, I would sure love for her to call me mom and you dad."

James wrapped his arms around his wife's waist. "I know that's what you want, honey, and I do too. But the last thing we need to do is get pushy with her. I want her to see that we are not bad people. Well, she already knows you're not, but I want her to see that I'm not this monster that others have tried to make me look like when all of this came out about us being her birth parents. I want her to love us as well as we love her."

"And she will. I just know that after she gets over the loss of Marcia, she will start to get closer to us."

"Well, I wouldn't count on her ever getting over the loss of who she knew as her mother, honey. That is just something that we don't get over."

"I didn't mean it like that, James. I meant to say when the hurt of losing her mom isn't hurting her so much anymore. Lets go swimming now. I guess we will let the kids do what their doing, and if they want to join us, then they can."

James and Priscilla put their swimsuits on and walked out to the pond. At first, Priscilla stuck her toe in the water to check its warmth. "Oh, James, it feels so nice. I'm getting in it now."

Before James said anything back to her, he ran and dove right into it. "Oh wow, this feels so refreshing, honey. Hurry and get in here."

The two swam for about a half hour, not seeing neither kid come out to join them. Then Priscilla knew that she needed to get back into the house and unpack some more boxes. "Honey, go get me some more boxes, please."

James went out to his truck to bring more in for her. "I'm not sure where some of these go, not all of them have writing on them to show what room they belong too."

"Mom, I have all my boxes put away already," David said as he came in his parent's room. "Terri helped me with everything. Otherwise, I'd still be working on it."

"That's nice, honey. Where is she now?"

"She's still in my room."

"Will you go ask her if she will come in here so I can have a talk with her, please?"

"Yes, Mom, I'll go tell her that you want her. She might not want to come in here, though."

"David, I sure hope that you try and get her to understand that we are here for her and that we love her."

"Yes, Mom, I have been talking with her, but I can't make her want to talk to you guys."

"I know, honey. Will you please ask her to come in here?"

"I'm going," he said as he walked out of the bedroom, mumbling something that Priscilla wasn't quite sure what he was saying. He went back to his room to talk to his sister.

"Terri, my mom wants to know if you'd like to go to her bedroom and talk with her."

"Why?"

"I don't know. All I know is I was just in there, and she wants to know if you will go talk to her."

"I don't know what to say, and I really don't feel like going into that bedroom right now." She got up off the bed she was sitting on, waiting for David to come back in the room, he was just standing in the doorway. She walked to the door, looking down the stairs, as if to see through the walls, into Priscilla's bedroom. "Could you tell her that I'm not ready to go into my mom's bedroom yet?"

David stood there looking at her, then he walked over to the stairs. "I'll be right back." He felt like he was the messenger boy between his parents and his sister.

"Mom, she said that she doesn't think she can come in her mother's bedroom yet. Come on, Mom, if you want to talk to her, will you just come to my bedroom then?"

"Yes, let me finish with these two boxes then. I feel so stupid. I never even thought about the room being her mom's. Of course, she's not going to want to come in here yet and sit and talk with me so soon after just losing her mother. What was I even thinking?" Priscilla started getting upset with herself and began throwing some clothes on to the floor that was in a box.

David wasn't used to seeing his mom act like that, and he didn't know what to say, so he said nothing and walked back out of her room. Going back into his room, he found his sister sitting on the floor Indian style.

"When she's done putting away the rest of her boxes, she will come in here and talk with you, okay?"

"I guess"—she looked at David and saw him take in a deep breath—"that will be okay."

"Try not to look so sad when my mother gets in here, okay? Remember she had nothing to do with giving you away. All she wants is for all of us to get along and love each other, at least the way we did before it came out about you being my sister. I know that if you give her a chance at being there for you, you will love her for it."

"I do love your mom. I just don't know how to look at her like I used too. I'm trying to understand all of this—I'm trying to make sense out of it. But every time I try, I keep seeing me as a little baby being handed over to my dad who took me home from my birth dad. Does that make any sense to you what I'm talking about?" she asked.

"I guess it does a little."

"Boys never catch on like girls do. I guess that you'd have to be a girl to comprehend what I'm saying."

"Oh really, now you never used to say that about me before. We could always talk to each other and never have a problem. Now all of a sudden we find out that we are twins and I get accused of not understanding you."

"Oh, don't get mad at me. I'm only teasing you. Now look at it from my point of view. I used to be able to tease you, and you'd just laughed it off. Now all of a sudden you become so serious. What's with that, huh?" she said, poking her finger into his side, kidding around with him. She knew the two were allowing themselves to not play around anymore; they were becoming like strangers to each other.

"Yeah, I guess you're right. We are acting different toward each other now that we know who we are, and I liked it how we were before. You and I could talk to each other about anything before and could understand each other. I want us to be able to still do that again okay?" he asked.

"Agreed," she said as she punched him in his arm lightly.

Priscilla tapped on the door. "Can I come in?"

"Yes, Mom," David said with a sigh. "I told Terri that you want to have a talk with her already, so come on in."

"Terri, would you mind if we talk?" Priscilla asked.

"No not really, I don't mind. What did you want to talk about?"

"Do you mind if we go in another room and talk alone? I really would like to talk with you by yourself."

"Where do you want us to talk?"

"Why don't we go to the kitchen, and I will put some coffee on, then we can talk there."

"Okay."

The two walked out of David's room and downstairs to the kitchen. Terri sat down at the table, while Priscilla started a pot of coffee.

"You and I haven't really had much of a chance to talk since your mother's funeral the other day. I've wanted to talk with you, but at the same time I've wanted to give you some time to grieve the loss of your mom. How are you doing, honey?"

"I'm okay. I miss my mom. You know what I mean when I say 'my mom,' right?" she asked feeling a little silly talking to her birth mom about the woman that raised her.

"Yes, honey, I know what you mean, and just to let you know, it's okay that you call her you're mother when you talk to me. She raised you since you were born. I will say that I wish it had been me to raise my own child that I gave birth to, but I would never have picked a better mother to raise you since it wasn't me."

Terri sat there not knowing what to say, watching Priscilla pour two cups of coffee then bring one to her as she sat at the table across from her. "So you do wish that you could have raised me then, huh?"

"Yes, of course I do. I had cried so many times since I found out you are my daughter I wondered if I would ever have any tears left to cry again. I could never have given you up without a fight."

"Why do you think James gave me away? Do you think that it was for the money?"

"Oh heavens, no! Are you kidding me? Never for the money. When I first heard that I had another child, a baby girl, we didn't even know that it was you for sure. But James was beside himself wondering if it was you. He couldn't work a full day without feeling like he was just going to die for what he had done. It was eating at him for so long, the guilt and shame for going behind my back, and doing such a thing at selling his child, even though he knew that we were so poor we couldn't take care of two babies."

"If that is true, then why did he sell me and not David?"

"I asked him the same question, and he told me to carry on the family name. It wasn't because you were a girl that he didn't want you. He just wanted a child to carry on the last name."

Terri sat there looking down at what seemed to be her lap, but without another word coming from Priscilla, Terri looked at her and said the words that everyone had been waiting for. "I would like to talk with James if he will talk to me. I'm ready to hear what he has to say to me now."

"I'm so happy to hear that, honey. He has been wanting to talk with you ever since we found out that you are our daughter. Would you like for me to go get him now? I know he will come right in here."

"Yes, if you wouldn't mind, can I talk to him alone please?"

"Well, you sure can, honey," Priscilla said, tapping her on her shoulder. "I'll go tell him right now."

Terri sat there all nervous; she began to wiggle in her seat. *Come on stop being so afraid to talk to him*, she told herself.

"James, I have some really exciting news. Terri wants to talk with you. She just ask me if I'd come get you so the two of you can talk."

"Really? Wow! What brought this sudden change to take place?"

"She and I just had a nice long talk, and after we were done, she asked to talk with you. Honey, this is what we have been praying for. Now she's ready and waiting for you in the kitchen."

Priscilla was so excited that Terri was finally asking to talk with James; after all, the two used to talk before, and all she wanted was for everyone to be able to live together in peace and to love each other.

James looked excited in one hand than; in another, he looked scared of what he might say. He knew that he needed to be careful of how he would talk with her. He knew that at this time in her life, she was going through a lot of emotions and whatever she had to say to him, he was going to try and understand the way she feels.

"Hi, Terri, Priscilla said that you were asking to talk with me?"

"Yeah," she said, looking at him for just a moment, then quickly looking in another direction.

"Okay, honey, let's talk. I have been waiting for the right time. I'm very glad that you want us to talk."

"First, I want you to know that both David and Priscilla talked with me and told me that you gave me up because you couldn't afford to take care of me. Now I want to hear it from you what was going on in your mind when you sold me?"

James was shocked by the boldness of her asking him this way, he had never seen this side of her before. Although he could hear shaking in her voice as she talked to him, he knew that this was a beginning, and he was going to give to her the most honest answer that he possibly could ever give.

"Okay, I'll try and tell you everything that took place on that day that changed the lives of all of us." James sat down on a chair at the table and carefully began to tell her the whole story.

Without Terri interrupting once, he went on telling detail after detail. He could see when he was talking about a sensitive part of the story, her eyes would begin to tear up and she would lightly wipe them.

"That is everything that happened from the time that Priscilla and I married until now." He could see a half smile come across her face. "I hope and pray that one day you would understand I would never ever have given you away for all the money in the world, if I'd only had enough to support you in the first place.

I have always wanted you and have waited for the day that we would meet." James had tears coming down his rugged, unshaven cheeks, to where he turned aside, in hopes that she hadn't noticed them.

Terri walked over to the other side of the table, and standing behind James, she bent over and wrapped her arms around his neck and cried with him. "Thank you for sharing with me everything that you and my birth mama have gone through in life together. I'm sorry I've been so mean, not wanting to talk with you and hear anything you had to say."

"Oh, honey, you have nothing to be sorry for. It's me who is so sorry. I should have quit that job a long time ago and got me a different one. I was so stubborn trying to be the man that had all the answers. You never have to feel bad for not talking with me, but now that you have, how do you feel about me?"

"I understand so much more now that you and I have had this talk, and I believe you when you say you never did it for the money. I believe that if you just had money, you would have kept me too."

James turned around and stood up, wrapping his arms around his daughter. "I pray that one day you will be able to call me dad and Priscilla mom. It would truly be a prayer answered in every way."

"It's funny that you say that because just before my mom died, she told me that maybe one day I would be able to call you and Priscilla mom and dad."

"She really said that? You mean, she would have wanted you to."

"My mother was the kindest person I knew, and when she found out from you that I was your child, she never said an unkind word about you. She told me to forgive, understand, and listen to why it happened the way it did. Then she told me why she thought it happened."

"Please tell me why she felt like it happened."

"You know how my mother was. She was always finding the good in a bad situation. She told me that she believed it all happened the way that it did because I was what she prayed for, for twenty years. She said it was supposed to be this way, and that's why God put my two moms together at the park when David and I were only a few months old. She wanted me to be able to love you and Priscilla both as my parents. She told me to give you guys a chance to be my parents because she knew I would never forget her and what we were to each other."

"Wow, she was really some kind of a remarkable woman. I just can't believe Nick had treated her so badly when she was so wonderful. She did a swell job in raising you. I am proud to call you my daughter, and maybe one day you will be able to call me dad." He held her tight in his arms as if to never let her go.

"I believe that I will, and maybe sooner than you know. Thanks for talking with me. This is the best I have felt since my mom died. I can at least smile now, instead of holding my head in shame."

"Shame, honey, there is nothing you got to be ashamed of. And when you go back to school, be proud of who you are and hold your head high."

Terri did what she was asked to do when she went back to school; she held her head high despite what others said that could have brought hurt to her. Because of her talk with her dad, she knew that she was never to blame for what life had given to her. She knew that no matter what, she was loved by two parents and a brother who would move heaven and earth for her. Before long, she was calling James and Priscilla mom and dad, just like they and her mom had wanted her to do. The talk about James selling his child for money blew over as quickly as it came in; after people understood and got to know the family more, they came to never mention the shame that almost tore a family apart, although there were the very few who never let anything go, like Sonny Bittner. He was just too much like his grandma.

BACK TO SCHOOL

TERRI AND DAVID returned to school after summer vacation was over, like nothing had ever happened, after everyone seeing them as a family like they were meant to be.

"Hey, Terri!" a voice was yelling for her that came from down the school's hallway. "Wait up a minute," a guy's voice yelled out again.

Terri stopped and turned to see who was doing the yelling. "Are you doing all that yelling at me?" she asked Mark Clayborn as he caught up to her.

"Yes," he said, trying to catch his breath after running down a long hallway to catch up to her. "I was wondering if you would like to go out with me this Saturday."

Terri stood there looking at this tall, slim, and very nice-looking sixteen-year-old guy whom just one year ago she would have done just about anything to try and get him to notice her. She was looking at the way he stood a head taller than her, with the waves in his brown hair, and the way his green eyes looked like beautiful glass.

"Well, I'm waiting." He gave a smile that made her heart melt. "Please say you'll go out with me."

"I don't know if I can—what I mean is, I'm not sure if my parents will let me. I can ask them tonight after school and see if I can."

"I sure hope they'd let you. I've been trying to get up enough nerve for a while now to ask you out."

"Really, I never thought of you being a shy kind of guy," she said while laughing.

"Yeah, well, that's my cover. I really am quite shy. I've been trying to get over it so I could ask you out."

"It must have worked because you have now asked me to go out with you." Terri was giving him her adorable smile that so many have told her before that it would make any guy's heart melt. And if she ever wanted to make a heart melt, it would be Mark's.

"Some things are just not meant to keep being shy about. Now, on the other hand, reading in front of the whole class, that is okay to stay shy. So will you ask your folks tonight about going out with me?"

"Yes, I will ask them, but I'm not sure how they will feel about me dating a sixteen-year-old when I am only thirteen."

"You're only thirteen?"

Terri looked at him, not knowing what to say with him asking her that. *Oh shoot, maybe I should never have said anything about my age,* she was thinking, but she knew that he needed to know. "Yes, thirteen, I would have thought you already knew that before asking me out."

"I did know that. I was only teasing you," he said as he put his hand on her face and gave it a light rub.

"Oh, you looked so serious you would make a good actor."

"Thanks. I was thinking about when I graduate I'd like to go into acting. I wouldn't mind being on TV"

"I better go before the class starts. I don't want to be late. Otherwise, ole Mrs. Cooper just might make me stay after school." She started walking as fast as she could without calling it running in the hallways. "I'll let you know what my parents say about this weekend."

"Okay, bye. Maybe I'll see you again in the hallway or in the lunch room. If not, I'll see you tomorrow."

"Okay, bye,"Terri said as she opened the door to her classroom.

The teacher noticed that Terri came through the doors. "Well, you do beat all coming into the classroom after it's already started. Take your seat over there, and next time you decide to come into class late, you will be staying after school."

"Yes, Mrs. Cooper," she said as she looked at David, sitting on a seat next to where she was to sit.

"Man, is she ever a hag," David commented.

"Yes, she can be, but she's like that to everyone who's late. I try not to take it personally."

After school was out, Terri went to her locker to get her homework so she could take it home with her and have it done come morning, but her locker was stuck, and she couldn't get it opened. Seeing the buses were loading up everyone, she tried pulling on the lock, but she was still not getting it opened. Then hearing someone yell, "The buses are leaving," she took off out the door to catch hers before she would have to walk home. Pounding on the sides of the bus in hopes of it stopping and letting her on, she could hear kids yelling for the driver to stop.

"Young lady, you just about got left behind. You need to be here on time from now on," the bus driver stated, which was usually a grouch to everyone as her teacher was.

"Sorry I'll do better next time," she told the driver while finding a seat to sit in. She heard her brother, David, call for her to sit down with him.

"Man, she's such a grouch to everyone all the time," David mentioned when Terri sat next to him.

"Yeah, well, she just might have a lot on her mind, or maybe things aren't going so good for her at her home."

"You are one of a kind, Terri."

"What do you mean about that?" she asked.

"Oh, just how you will try and see the best in everyone, even when they were just mean to you."

"Yeah, I know. When God made me he broke the mold." She laughed.

"What took you so long to get on the bus?"

I couldn't get my locker open. Now I couldn't bring my homework home with me."

"Oh wow, I wonder what happened."

"I don't know, but Mark Clayborn asked me out today."

"Mark Clayborn asked you out?"

"Yes, you make that sound terrible. What's wrong with me?"

"Oh nothing, but Mark is sixteen, not to mention he can get any girl he wants too."

"He must have thought that I am nice looking or maybe just a nice person because he told me that he's wanted to ask me out for a long time but he was just too shy to ask."

"Mark shy? Yeah, right, I have never thought of him to be the shy type. I see him all the time hanging on girls, and trust me, he's not shy."

"Looks can be deceiving to the looker, maybe they're just friends. Do you think Mom and Dad will let me go out with him?"

"I don't know for sure. Maybe if you act like you're really sad if they say no, then maybe they will change their mind and let you."

"You're kidding me, aren't you?"

"I don't know what they will say. Maybe, under the circumstances, they might."

"What circumstances is that?"

"You know, now that they finally have you back with us after all of these years."

"Oh that." She looked sad when David said that to her. "I guess if they want to consider that, then that will be okay with me as long as they let me date," she stated after feeling sad for just a minute.

"They may let you go out with a boy your own age, and not Mark."

"But I don't want to go out with one my age. I want to go out with Mark. Do you remember me telling you about a year ago that I liked him but he never even noticed me?"

"I remember you telling me about a lot of guys."

"Now you're just being plain mean, David, now stop that," she said then added a punch to his arm.

"Wow, you hit so hard when I was only playing with you. Why do you have to hit me so hard?"

"Stop teasing me then if you don't want to get hurt."

"Come on, let's get off the bus, and you go ask Mom if you can go out with Mark."

"I'll race you into the house." She took off running before him.

David started to run after her while yelling at her, "You cheater, you got a running start."

When Terri entered the house all out of breath, her mother looked at her, wondering why she was so out of breath.

"What happened to you?" Right when she asked that, David come barging through the door. "What are you kids up to?"

Both of them gasping for air as if they had ran a mile.

"Terri asked me if I wanted to race her, then she cheated by running before me."

"She's a girl. We all catch on fast. Never let the guys get ahead of you." She gave Terri a wink.

"Mom, I was wondering if I could ask you a question?"

"Sure, what's on your mind, honey?"

Terri looked over at David before asking their mother, seeing him nudge his head, telling her to go ahead and ask. "I had a boy from my school ask me out today, and I was wondering if I could go out with him Saturday night."

"Do you mean like a date?" she asked.

Terri wasn't sure of what to say. David waved his hand behind their mother's back, saying, "Go ahead and ask," seeing that she wasn't sure of what to do.

"Yes, like a date." Terri hesitated.

"How is this boy going to pick you up, and where are you planning on going?"

"He has his driver's license, and I'm not sure where he is going to take me."

"Terri, how old is this guy anyway?" she asked, surprised by him driving already.

"He's sixteen years old, and I have liked him for a year now. Not that it makes any difference how long I liked him for, just saying I have for a long time now."

"What kind of a family does he come from? Is he a nice boy. I guess at sixteen one can hardly call him a boy, now can they. And for you to have liked him ever since last year, there must be something likeable about him. I'll have a talk with your father tonight and see what he thinks, okay?"

Terri nodded and started walking toward her room.

Terri," Priscilla called out to her, "how would your mother Marcia have handled about you dating at thirteen?"

"I'm not really sure," she said with a look on her face that said she really didn't know. Maybe because she had never asked to go out with a boy until now.

"Okay, I will talk with your dad tonight."

"Okay." Terri walked away feeling kind of disappointed. She had hoped that when she talked with her mom, she would say yes right away, but now her mother wanting to talk with her dad was making Terri feel nervous.

"Terri, what's wrong?" David asked as he started to go upstairs after her.

"It's nothing. I just wanted her to say it was okay for me to go out with him. Now she has to talk it over with dad, and what if he says no, then all my hopes and dreams of going out with Mark is all over with."

"I don't think that he will say no to you if Mark is a good guy. But when you think about it, none of us know him other than school. I know Mom and Dad—if they did say no, it's because they had already prayed about it and felt like God was telling them not to let you go out with him."

"So before they let me know if I can go out with him, they are going to pray about it first? Are you kidding me?"

"They always pray about the important things, but wouldn't you want to have God tell them ahead of time if he is a good guy? It's better to know ahead of time than to go out to find that you don't like him because he's a jerk."

Terri sat there not saying a word; she sat on her bed with her arms folded over the other. "I do trust that God knows what's best for each one of us. I just don't know if he is willing to give an answer to something like that."

"Of course, he is willing. He wants what's best for us, so he will tell them what they need to know. Don't think it is a bad thing. Look at it like you're asking something from God, and he is going to give you what you want."

"What I want is to be able to go out with Mark? Is he going to give me that?"

"Come on, Terri, I think you know what I mean. And I know that your mother taught you better than how you're acting right now."

"I know, and yes, she did. I'm just being silly because I want to go out with him. Okay, I will patiently wait to see what the answer is. No more talk about Mark until I know if I can go out with him."

"Good," David replied.

"I should go ask Mom if she needs any help making supper. Would you like to help us women in the kitchen?" She smiled an ear-to-ear smile while waiting for an answer.

"No, I think that I'll pass on that. I'm not into doing a woman's job."

"Oh, but you'll eat it?"

"Yep, that's what we men do. We eat what you cook," David stated as he headed out of the bedroom door and down the stairs laughing.

Must be nice to be a man when it comes time to never have to do any housework or cook, Terri told herself, then she went down stairs too offer her mother some help at preparing the meal. She knew her mother usually made big meals because her dad had a hearty appetite. . "Mom, would you like some help?" she asked.

"Sure, honey, if you wouldn't mind getting the cutting board out and chopping up all the things we put in a salad. That would save me time doing that."

"Can I ask you something, Mom?"

"Sure, honey, what's on your mind?"

"I'm wondering why men never have to cook any meals. Why is it always the women who do the cooking?"

"Well, from the beginning of time, it was a man's job to provide for his wife and kids. They were the ones who went to work, while the wife stayed home cooking, cleaning, and caring for the children. Your dad has always been the one to work outside of the home. He never wanted me or expected me to go to work outside of the home. We have always believed in the tradition of man, where a woman's place is taking care of the home while the man goes to work. It doesn't make a woman any lower than a man just because she stays home. She still has plenty of work at home. She cooks, she cleans, she irons, and she cans so the family will have food for the winter. The wife has many things to do for her family. And that's the way I want to raise David. I want him to know that he is the one to get a job to take care of his family. Now he's too young and in school to have an eight-hour job, but that's why I have him cut the lawn, empty the garbage, and also cut the neighbor's lawn so he can have a little responsibility."

"I think that my mother and dad were the same way. I don't think that she ever worked outside of the home. I will probably marry a man who doesn't want me to work in some dirty, old factory somewhere." Right after she said those words, she put her hand over her mouth. "I'm sorry, I didn't mean anything by it."

"I know you didn't, but when your dad worked there for all of those years it kept us alive. We may have had to go without a lot of things, but we survived. There is no shame in what he did. He did what he had to do to care for his family the best way he knew how."

"I'm really sorry. I need to keep my mouth shut before I say something that will hurt others," Terri stated.

"It's not that you hurt me. It's just I know he and I had a very hard life until"—she paused for a minute, looking at Terri—"well, you know the rest."

She put her head down before saying anything to what her mother implied. "Yes I know the rest."

"How are you coming on chopping up those veggies?" Priscilla asked.

"Good, how many would you like cut?"

Priscilla looked over at what Terri had cut up so far. "Wow, honey, you have a lot cut. That should be plenty for us. Where did you ever learn to cut up your veggies so fast? That's better than I can do."

"Oh, my mom taught me when I was just young. I liked to help her in the kitchen instead of being in the other room with Nick." After the name *Nick* fell off her lips, she stopped talking.

Priscilla knew that she had gone through some hard times with him, and she felt sad for Terri to have been hurt by him. "I'm glad that you don't have to let the past hurt you anymore. We can do all things through Christ Jesus who strengthens us. You don't have to let whatever Nick did to you hurt you now. You are an over comer, so you rise above what's happened to you."

"I know you're right. It's just whenever I think about it back then, which by the way wasn't that long ago, I feel kind of sad because I miss my mom"—she paused—"you know what I mean."

"Yes, honey, I do, and it's okay, I still miss her too, and I'm sure part of me always will. She was the sweetest, kindest person that I have ever known. And I will always be so grateful to have known her." She looked into Terri's eyes. "You know. honey. I know you're my daughter, but I can see in some of the things that you do, you remind me so much of Marcia. I know she did a fine job raising you. I could not have done better myself."

"Do you really believe that?" Terri asked.

"Yes, of course, I do. Your mother was a wonderful person, and she loved and cared for you as if you were her birth daughter. I could never have asked for more than that."

"Thank you for saying that. I miss her too very much a lot of times. Especially at night time, when I'm lying in bed, I think of her."

"I know that in your mind I have always been like an aunt to you, but I hope in time, with you getting to know me more as you're mother, that it will help you with your pain of losing her."

"I do too. I think it might help if I am able to go out with Mark."

Priscilla looked at her and gave her slight grin. "You do, do ya, funny, but nice try."

"I thought I'd give it a chance, never really believing you would fall for it." She smiled.

"How has school been for you and David since you two went back?"

"It's good. I don't really hear anyone making bad remarks anymore about Dad."

"I knew that in time the others kids would stop what they were doing if they'd see that you and David weren't going to let them bother you. Now what seems to be taking your father so long getting home? Everyone here is hungry, I'm sure of it."

"I know I am, but I'm not too sure about David. He just told me he'd eat whatever we make."

"That's my boy, a growing man who loves to eat. I'm just thankful he's not a picky eater, not wanting to eat his veggies like a lot of kids your age."

"My mom always told me to eat what is put before us. She said there are a lot of people that are homeless and cannot eat like we do every day. She always talked to me about the orphans, how they get big bellies because they lack eating."

"I've told David the same thing. Maybe that's why he has never complained about his food."

"You're probably right."

James came home with talk of his new addition to the store and how much more room they had to add things to the shelves and the different kinds of food they could carry now that they normally didn't carry before.

"Honey, I'd like to talk with you after we eat about a request that Terri has asked from us."

James looked at Terri. "Oh"

"Yes, but you and Mom can talk about it afterward, okay."

"Okay, that's fine."

Everyone was eating like there was no tomorrow. All was quiet until Terri talked about leaving the table; she was hoping that would give them time to decide whether to let her go out with Mark or not.

"May I be excused?" Terri asked.

With both of her parents looking down at her plate and seeing that it was all cleaned, they told her she was excused.

The next morning, Terri was wondering if her mother would mention if she could go out with Mark or not. She stood close to her mother in hopes of hearing that it would be all right.

"Oh, by the way, Terri, I had that talk with your father about you dating that one young man, and after he and I prayed about it, we felt it would be all right for you to go out with him this one time. But if there was to be a second date, we would like to see him come to church with us, unless he is already going to another."

"Really? Oh, thank you so much." She was so excited that she wrapped her arms around her mother, which she rarely ever did. "I am so happy. I can't wait to tell him at school today."

THE DATE

TERRI COULD HARDLY wait for the bus to pick her and David up for school; she wanted to see Mark very much and tell him the great news. She looked down the hallways in hopes of finding him walking down one of them, but she never did see him before the bell rang to tell the kids it was time for them to be in the classrooms. Finding someone to open up her locker, she hurried to her class.

She could hardly wait for her third hour because she knew Mark would be in her class, now that the new marking period begun, and she wanted to tell him the great news. Her first and second hour was not so good for her; she couldn't concentrate on her work at all. The teacher would catch her not paying attention in class, and raise his voice at her.

Third hour came, and Terri could hardly walk fast enough without calling it running in the hall. She knew that if she were to be seen by a teacher, she would get in trouble for running, not walking. As she entered her classroom, her eyes were looking for Mark when she noticed someone standing at the back of the classroom, with his back facing her, holding someone's hand. When he turned around with the girl he was with, it was not just anyone—it was Mark, her Mark, well at least that's what she thought that he was going to be. Mark turned around and noticed that Terri was standing there staring at him. Terri quickly turned her face, not wanting to give him the satisfaction of him knowing she was hurt by what she had just witnessed. Finding a seat, she made sure it was on the other side of the classroom. Once again, she found herself not being able to concentrate on her work, and all she wanted was to go home.

In the hallway, as she was headed to the lunchroom, Mark began to call her name. But again she walked so fast she might have been accused of running, but she didn't care. She wanted to get as far away from him as she could.

"Will you stop trying to run away from me? I know you heard me calling for you," he said as he tried to grab at her butt.

"So what if I did? I don't believe we have anything to talk about. And don't you ever touch me like that again. I was going to tell you today that my parents told me just before school that I could go out with you."

"Well, that's great, isn't it?" he said, hoping she would give him a chance.

"You know, I thought it was, but now, after you telling me yesterday that you have liked me for some time, it seems to me you've found another girl mighty quick. I don't think you are the guy I thought you were." She started to walk away when he had more to say.

"Oh that, that was nothing. To be honest, I really didn't believe that your folks would let you go out with me, being that they are so religious and all. So I thought that I might as well find another girl just in case. And I knew Tami has always had a thing for me, and I have never went out with her before. But if you'll go out with me, I'll tell Tami to take a hike and get lost."

"Wow, you really are not who I thought you were. How about I tell you to take a hike and get lost? I wouldn't go out with the likes of you if someone paid me to." She turned her back on him, only to find that the hallways had several people standing close enough to hear everything that was said. Some of the guys and girls all began to clap their hands when they heard how she put him in his place.

Mark looked at everyone clapping their hands when he was let down by a girl; he then turned his back and walked away. He wasn't used to any girl turning him down for any reason; he had always felt he could get any girl until now.

"Hey"—a guy in the tenth grade came up to her—"that was quite impressive. You put him in his place. Mark has thought for far too long now that he could get any girl he wants. I am just so glad to finally see that there is a real girl out here who don't fall down and worship him. If you ask me, the only man that should be worshiped is Jesus Christ and none other."

Before she could speak, she was thinking about what this guy was saying to her. "I agree. I would never go out with a man who thought that he was all that. And I like what you said about only Jesus is the man who should be worshiped. I completely agree. Are you a Christian?" she asked.

"I'm crushed." He put his hand over his heart. "Don't you remember me from the church? I'm Larry Perry, the drummer."

"Oh my gosh! I'm so sorry I didn't even recognize you. I feel so bad now." She placed her hand over her mouth as her face turned red of embarrassment.

"Oh, that's okay. I'm just glad to have finally met you in person and not just someone I see at church and in these hallways and never talk to. I know this is being straightforward, but would you ever consider going out with me? I know we have just met, but I promise you that I will never expect you to fall down and worship me." He laughed after saying that, and she joined him with laughter.

"Do you even know my name?"

"Well, of course, I do. I would never ask a girl out without knowing their name first."

"Then what is it?"

"Are you telling me you don't know your own name yet?" He laughed again, then seeing the look on her face, he decided to tell her that indeed he did know her name. "Your name is Terri."

"Okay, so you do know my name. I think my parents won't mind. If they were willing to let me go out with Mark, and he is nothing but a pig, so to speak, , then I'm sure they will let me go out with you."

"Your folks were really going to let you go out with him? Wow, that really surprises me. He is just not a good guy at all." he said with a smile. "Come on, I'll walk you to the lunchroom. I'll even sit with you if you don't mind."

"I don't mind at all. I'd like that," she said.

The two were sitting together and laughing over some silly things when Mark came up to her.

"So you would trade me for the likes of him, huh?" Mark asked rudely.

"You were never mine to trade. Now would you kindly leave us alone? We were having a good time."

"Come on, Terri, I know you want me."

Larry stood up, and when he did, everyone in the whole lunch room was watching what might take place. Terri looked up, noticing that Larry was just about a head taller than Mark, and she thought he was better looking too.

Larry looked down at Mark and said, "Now you will leave Terri and me alone, or you and I are going to have a problem."

Mark walked away after seeing Larry was much more built than he was. After he walked away, everyone in the room began to clap their hands again.

Before the day was done, Larry and Terri talked between classes, in the hallways, and everywhere they saw each other. By the end of the day, she had decided to go out with him and had wondered why she ever thought she wanted to date the likes of Mark.

After school was out and Terri arrived at home, she went to have a talk with her mom. "Can I ask you something?"

"Of course, honey, you can ask me anything."

"Why did you and dad decide to let me go out with Mark?"

"Well, the truth is, when you first asked me if you could, I wanted to say no right away. But I was a teenager once before myself, and I know that when you are told no, it would only want to make you rebel against your dad and me. So I told you we would pray about it, and that is what we did. We prayed that if God did not want you to go out with Mark, he would open your eyes to see Mark for who he really is, and then you would make the right choice if you still wanted to go out with him or not. Why did you ask me that? Did something happen in school that I should know about?"

"You're not kidding? Something did!"

David walked in the room and caught part of what they were talking about. "No wonder Mark said to me what he did about you," he said.

"What did he say about me?"

"He said you weren't the girl he thought you were. He said you traded him for Larry Perry."

"Larry Perry, where do I know that name from?" Priscilla asked.

"Larry plays the drums at our church. And no, I never traded Mark for anyone. He is a pig, and I will not go out with the likes of him in a million years. Larry is a good Christian guy whom I would date in a minute," Terri said with anger in her voice, looking toward David.

"You don't have to get mad at me. I only said what he did. I never wanted you to go out with him in the first place. He likes all the girls. It's like he's trying to see how many he can get."

"Why didn't you tell me that yesterday?" Terri asked.

"Trust me, I tried, but you didn't want to hear anything bad about Mark. You were so caught up in a fantasy about him."

"Mom, will you and Dad let me go out with Larry? He really is a good guy?"

"I know that he is, honey. Although he goes to our church faithfully, we still have to pray about it."

"That's okay. I don't mind at all. I'm glad you prayed about me going out with Mark. Because if you hadn't, who knows how bad he would have acted toward me if I did go out with him? Thank you for praying." She gave her mom a hug. "Would you like to help in making the supper tonight?"

"Sure, I do, and just for the record, I have a good feeling about you going out with Larry. I don't think he is anything like Mark. But I still have to pray, okay?"

"Okay," Terri said.

The next morning, James walked up to Terri in the kitchen.

"Your mother told me about what happened at school yesterday, and I want you to know that we don't mind if you go out with Larry. I have known that young man for a few years now, and I have never heard anything I didn't like. He not only is a hard worker in school and out of school, but he loves the Lord, and that is so important. He comes from a good Christian family that has been in a good church to learn the things of God. If he wants to date my daughter, then I can truly say he has my blessing."

"Really, that's good because I really think that he's a good guy too. I'll be sure to tell him what you said. I have to get going to school. Bye, I will see you tonight." Terri was gone out the door, with David following close behind her. It was like that although the two of them have come to know each other as brother and sister, they still were best friends and stayed very close together.

David, not wanting Terri to date anyone without him being close to her to make sure that she was being cared for in a proper way, decided that since she had their parents' permission to date, it was best he find someone fast to go out with too. He would ask if the two could double date. Now today he was on a mission at school to find the right girl to ask out.

Larry came walking up to Terri when she was at her locker before school started. "Hey, beautiful, how are you today?"

Terri, turning around to see for sure who was calling her beautiful, was surprised to know that it was Larry being open like that on the second day since they started talking to each other. "Hello, how are you today?"

"I'm good. Did you get a chance to ask you're folks if you can go out with me?"

"Yes, I did, and they said yes. My dad really likes you. Whatever you did, he thinks it was the right thing to do."

"That's awesome. I must have made quite an impression, even though I'm not sure what I've done to get your dad to notice me."

"He said something about you being a hard worker in school and out of school."

"Yeah, I do keep up on my grades, and I have a job after school. Since we can date with their blessing, how would you like to go out with me this weekend?"

"When this weekend?"

"How about we go out Saturday night?" Larry was looking at her with begging eyes.

"Sure, I'd love to."

"Really!"

"Yes, really, but for now, I have to get to class. We will talk later about it okay?" Terri started down the hallway half running and half walking.

"Yeah, sure, we'll talk later." Larry raised his voice just enough for her to hear him as she was halfway down the hallway by now.

Terri could hardly wait until Saturday. The more she thought about Larry, the less she liked Mark. She was happy that her parents agreed for her to date Larry; she knew just by talking with him that he was a nice guy. He had those trusting eyes that she could trust, almost like she could look right through them.

She sat in her class, trying to concentrate on her work, when she felt someone sitting behind her who was flicking her at the back of her neck. Getting frustrated that she wasn't able to do her work, she turned around to see the person who kept annoying her. To her surprise, Mark had switched seats with another classmate just so he could torment her.

"What are you doing?" Terri asked.

"You like it, don't you?" Mark said as he flicked her again.

"No, I don't. Leave me alone, and get back to your own seat." She was getting more upset at him bothering her.

"Oh, come on, Terri, quit playing hard to get. You know you want me. Look around here. Which girl here doesn't want to go out with me?"

Terri turned around angrier than she had ever felt toward any boy. Without thinking ahead of what she was about to yell out in front of the whole class, she just spoke what was on her mind. "Would you leave me alone? I don't want anything to do with you. I have a boyfriend, and he is by far more of a man than you will ever be."

"Terri, is there a problem that I'm not aware of?" the English teacher asked with a disgusted look on his face.

"Mr. Sam, Mark is flicking the back of my neck, and he's sitting in Martha's seat, when he should be over on that side of the room." She was pointing to the other side of the room.

"Mr. Clayborn, do you have a good reason to be out of your seat and into another?"

After Terri made him feel foolish for what she said about him, his answer came as no surprise. "No sir, no reason at all," he said as he looked at Terri with such disappointment in his eyes.

Terri felt bad after all was said and done, after seeing how he looked at her. She never liked to hurt anyone, not even the ones who seemed to get under her skin like Mark did. She had to stop thinking of how she hurt him or at least caused him to feel embarrassed. But then on the other hand, maybe this was just what was to be done to him to bring him to a place where he would stop thinking that he was God's gift to women. Maybe the next time she would talk to him, he would be more respectful toward her and other girls.

Saturday night finally came; Terri was looking forward for this night all week long. She had never dated any guy before, so this night, she wanted it to be perfect. She had no idea where Larry would take her or how she should dress for her date. So she decided to dress in a pantsuit and curl her long brown hair.

Larry was so excited to be taking Terri out that he wanted everything perfect. He borrowed some of his mother's perfume to spray in his car so it had the smell of lilac. He hoped that she liked the smell of flowers, at least the smell of lilacs.

"Mom, I'm leaving now to go pick up Terri. I won't stay out late," Larry promised.

"Okay, remember to show her how a good Christian boy acts," his mom reminded him.

"I will, Mom. Bye." And he was out the door, heading to pick up Terri.

Terri was waiting for Larry while she kept looking at the clock. Then she saw car lights shining through the window. Hopping off the couch, and getting her composure together, she walked over to the door to open it up. Just as she opened it, he had his hand in the air as he was ready to knock on the door.

"Hi," Terri said with an ear-to-ear smile.

"Hello, you sure do look beautiful tonight—oh that didn't come out right. You look very pretty every day, but exceptionally beautiful tonight," Larry said, looking up and down her.

"Larry, welcome," James said as he held out a hand to shake his.

"Hello, Mr. Cole, I want to thank you and your wife for allowing Terri to go out with me tonight. I want to let you know I won't be keeping her out to late. I know we have church come morning."

"I know I can trust that you will have her home no later than eleven o'clock. It's good seeing you again. How are your folks doing?"

"They are fine, sir." He was looking at Terri, holding out his hand so they could leave. "If we don't hurry, we won't catch the movie."

"I'm ready," she said as she took his hand, and they headed out the door. "Bye, Dad. Tell Mom I won't be late."

"Okay, you kids have a good time tonight. Oh, by the way, what movie are you going to see?" James asked.

"*Cinderella*, sir."

"Good very good," James said as he closed the door to the house with a smile written on his face.

"Did they leave already?" Priscilla asked, coming into the living room.

"Yes, Terri asked me to tell you she won't be out late. Where were you at?"

"I was just getting out of the bathtub. I needed to relax my back in some hot bathwater."

"Has your back been hurting you?"

"Yes, it has for the last couple of days," Priscilla said with a disappointed look on her face for missing Terri's first time going out with someone. She walked over to the window and looked out the curtain. "Did they say where they are going?"

"Yes, they're going to watch Cinderella, I told them not to be out past eleven."

"He's not taking her out to eat? She never ate any supper tonight because she just assumed that he would be taking her out to eat."

"Oh, I'm sure he will offer her something to eat. Isn't that what most of them always do?"

"I know that they used to. Who knows about kids now in the seventies? I watch how some of them act toward their girlfriend, and it's a darn shame they don't know how to treat the weaker vessel."

"Weaker vessel? I'd like to see them have a baby, let alone twins."

She spoke with a slight grin. "I know, honey, I was just playing around. Maybe their dad isn't treating their mother right, and they have no clue what a real man should treat a girl like."

"Do I treat you like a real woman?" he asked as he wrapped his arms around her, and pulled her close to him.

"You are a perfect gentleman, and I trust that David will learn how to treat a lady after watching you."

"And you are a perfect wife, and I trust that Terri will take after you."

"We can never forget everything that Marcia taught our girl. She raised her to be the girl that she is today, and she did a very good job at it too."

"Yes, I know that she has, but that's a part of my life that I wish I could forget. You know why I say that. It's nothing against Marcia. It's everything I have done, and I still feel terrible about it."

"So why don't we change the subject and think of the now what we can instill in our children to better them and us?" Priscilla said.

"Now that sounds like a plan. Let's look to the future and remember only the good things of the past. By the way, where is David at?"

"I think he's sulking in his bedroom. He was hoping to have a date tonight, so he could have double dated with Terri and Larry."

"Really, I never knew that he liked someone."

"He never said too much to me about it, just that he wanted to ask a girl out, but I think he might have chickened out," Priscilla said with a look of bewilderment.

"It's going on nine o'clock right now. I wonder if the movie is getting close to be over with yet. I gave them a lot of time to hang out with each other. If she is going to like any guys, then I'd rather it be Larry. I know he comes from a good home, one that not only go to church but love God with all of their hearts."

Both James and Priscilla waited for Terri to come home; they wanted to find out if Larry was the perfect gentleman that James had hoped he would be. After waiting for another hour, they saw car lights shining in their driveway. Running to the window like a couple of kids to see if it was them, they pulled back the curtain very slowly in hopes of them not getting noticed that they were watching the kids. It was them, and it was still an hour early.

"They're here an hour early, I wonder why. Maybe they didn't like each other's company," James stated.

"Maybe they don't have anything in common. Maybe after Larry spent some time with Terri, he noticed that she was just too immature for him. After all, he is sixteen years old versus her being thirteen."

"You have got to be kidding me! Him not like her? Look." James held the curtain open in full view, without thinking they would be seen. To both of their surprise, Larry was kissing Terri good night at the door, before opening it up.

"Wow, I don't remember you kissing me like that on our first date, and we were older than them," Priscilla stated, looking at her daughter being kissed on her first date.

Terri came through the door like she was floating on a cloud; she had an ear-to-ear smile that lit up the house when she entered. She didn't even notice that her parents were standing close by the front door, watching her every move. She was startled by a voice that she was sure that she had heard before. It was her dad standing right there as she was ready to go upstairs to bed.

"Did you have a good evening?"

It seemed to Terri like it was a cynical question. "Yes, I did. It was very nice," she answered.

"Have you had anything to eat?" Priscilla asked.

"Yes, he took me to a Chinese restaurant after the movie."

"Terri, let me ask you a question, if I may?"

"Okay." She looked at her like she was expecting twenty-one questions coming for her before she was to go to bed.

"Do you really think it's proper for a girl your age standing outside and kissing in the front yard? Not to mention it's your first time going out with him or the fact that it's your first date."

Terri was surprised by what she just heard her mother say. "Were you watching us?" she asked, trying to not sound so irritated.

"Yes, honey, your dad and I saw the lights of his car, so we went to the window to see who it was since you weren't due to be home for about another hour yet. Then when we could see that it was you, well, we saw the kiss as well."

"I'm sorry you had to see that, but that's what people do on dates—they kiss. Now can I go to bed? And thanks again for letting me go out with Larry. He was a perfect gentleman in every way. He even opened the door for me in the car and all the other places that we went to. I don't know any other guy who does that for their girlfriend, at least not the ones I go to school with."

"Girlfriend?" James asked.

"I think that's what I am now. He asked me out again. He said that he really likes me. I'm not like the other girls that he dated. Can I go to bed now? I'm a little tired."

"Yes, go ahead."

After Terri went to bed, James and Priscilla decided they needed to talk.

"What do you think about her having a boyfriend?" Priscilla asked.

"I guess if she is going to have a boyfriend, I'd want it to be Larry. These kids are both so young to get serious with each other. We will just have to keep a close eye on them to make sure it doesn't get to serious."

"And what are we supposed to do about it if they start to get that way?"

"No sense in worrying about it now. We will deal with it when and if it gets to that point. Let's go to bed and forget about what we have just seen our daughter do." James said, taking a hold of his wife's hand and leading her to their bedroom.

THE BIRTHDAY PARTY

"**D**O YOU REALIZE that Friday will be the first birthday that we will have with Terri as her parents?" Priscilla stated.

"I know. I've been thinking about that myself," James commented then turned his head away so Priscilla wouldn't see the expression on his face and the tears that were now forming in his eyes.

James didn't know that she had seen the tears fill his eyes before he turned away. Walking up behind him, she wrapped her arms around his waist. "James, I know what's wrong, honey, but I want you to remember that you are forgiven. Turn around and face me, honey."

James turned around to face the woman whom he betrayed almost fourteen years ago. He knew he had a good wife when all this came out about him selling their daughter at birth for reasons that no longer sounded like a good excuse. "Thank you, honey. You have forgiven me for something I did to you and David, and I am having a hard time forgiving myself."

"James, look at me, honey. I forgave you because I knew that if you had thought there was any way for you to support us as a family, then that's what you would have done. I have known you since we were in school. I know that you never wanted to do what you did. You have to let it go, honey. It's time to."

"I've tried to put it in the past, really I have. Ever since we got our daughter back, I tried to put it all behind me. But every time I see her, I think about what we missed in all of these years, and it feels like a knife cutting deep into my heart."

"But that's what is so great about the whole thing, God knew that you never wanted to give her away, so he sent us Marcia in our life when our children were just babies. So we never really did miss out on her because she was with us so much all of these years. We watched her grow, and we went to her kindergarten graduation along with David. We have been there for her all of these years, so now it's time to forgive yourself. We have a big party to plan. It's got to be a big one to let Terri know that her being with us means everything in the entire world to us. I want to invite all of our family and friends and her and David's friends too."

"Are we going to invite my aunt Judith?"

"Sure, why not? She's part of the family."

"I know, but she's so old she may not want to travel." James was remembering how his aunt always wanted to come visit whenever she could.

"If she doesn't think she can make it, then I leave it up to her to say she can't come."

It was weeks later, and everyone was coming through the door for the twins' party. Priscilla was setting out all the food with the help of her closest friends from the church. "I sure hope it doesn't rain today, and everything gets ruined outside. I want this day to go perfect for everyone here," she said anxiously.

"I watched the news today and didn't see where it was supposed to rain. It said sunshine all day," Berta stated, one of Priscilla's closest friends.

"Honey, did you see that Aunt Judith made it? She looks the same as she always did—white hair and cracks all over her face that shows her long life of laughter as well as hard times," James said.

"I'll go say hi to her in a minute. I just have to get the rest of the food outside." *Cracks all over her face, what next?* Priscilla thought to herself.

As she carried out the platter of ribs she held in her hand, she and aunt Judith bumped into each other. Spilling the entire platter of them onto the floor, she noticed that aunt Judith stood there with her mouth held wide open.

"I'm so sorry dear, you should have been paying a little closer attention to where you were walking."

Surprised by how she had just turned it all on to someone else fault, Priscilla was very polite with what she said back to her. "I'm sorry Aunt Judith, I wasn't paying attention to where I was going." she bent down to clean up the mess that was all over the walls and the floor, as aunt Judith kept on walking her own merry way.

"What happened in here?" Priscilla's friend Heather asked as she walked through the door.

"I was just about to bring these out for my guest, when aunt Judith came in, well the two of us bumped into each other. Now look at the mess, I sure hope that I have enough food out there for everyone."

"Let me help you get this cleaned up, I'm sure that you have plenty of food. I think that you worry to much, I know that there are a lot of folks out there, but you also have a lot of food too."

"Thank you Heather, you are a dear friend always trying to pick me up when I need it."

"What are friends for, your always right there for me too. Where is all your cleaning supplies at? I'll start to wash off the sauce from the walls right here." she said as she pointed to the walls that was about her height when Priscilla was down cleaning up ribs on the floor.

"Look under my kitchen sick, there should be something under there that you can use."

The two women worked hard at getting all the sauce scrubbed off the walls and the floor, until it looked like nothing had ever happened in the first place.

"What would I of ever done without you helping me in here? When I need to get out to my guest, thank you so much Heather for all your help."

"Come on lets get out there to your guest, you would have done the same thing for me." she told her as she took her friend by the hand and walked out side.

Priscilla let her guest know that the food was ready and for everyone to get a plate and start to eat. The celebration for the twins went great for everyone, and joy and laughter filled the air for hours of fun. Then when the people all left, Priscilla could hardly wait to get off her feet and go to bed.

"It was a great turn out today." James spoke as the two were getting ready for bed.

"Yes it was, I think the kids had a nice time with all of their friends and family."

"I thought that you had told me that you were going to make some ribs for everyone. Did you change your mind about that?" he asked.

"No, I didn't change my mind at all." she said in an irritated voice.

"Oh, I didn't see any out there, and I wondered why, because I new that you came down to the store and picked up quite a few packages of them."

"It was clearly an accident, but your aunt Judith and I kind of walked right into each other as I was carrying them out to our guest."

"Oh yike's, so what did you do with them?"

"Lets just say that the trash got them all." she looked at him while he was waiting for an answer. "They got spilled all over the floor, and Heather and I had to clean up a huge mess everywhere."

"Oh honey I'm so sorry for that happening, I know that must have made you very upset after cooking them all up."

"Yeah it did at first, mainly because I didn't think that I would have enough food for everyone. It just so happens that I had plenty of food to go around. I just feel bad because you still had to buy all of those ribs even though you own the store."

"Well honey, not always does things turn out the way that they are planned. I just thank God that everyone came and had a great time meeting our little girl, and to celebrate with us."

"Me too honey, after all is said and done, it was nice to see everyone again, even aunt Judith." she said with a smile. "Now I am going to bed and get me a good night sleep." she said as she rolled over facing her back towards her husband.

"Good night." he said without any more talk, he knew that she had worked hard at all the planning for the party, not to mention all the cooking she had to do. He turned over in bed as he got himself comfortable enough to fall asleep.

THE RING

"GOOD MORNING," PRISCILLA said to Terri after she came downstairs the day after her birthday party.

"Good morning, I want to thank you and Dad for the party last night. I met a lot of family I have never met before. Not to mention the nice gifts I received from some of them, especially the one that I got from Larry."

"I saw that he gave you a little box wrapped up, and I was wondering what that box held in it."

"Would you like to know what was in it?" Terri asked with much excitement in her voice.

"Yes, of course, I want to know what it was."

Terri held out her hand, showing her the beautiful ring that Larry got for her.

"Terri, don't you think that you're a little young for a ring from your boyfriend?"

"No, it's not like it's an engagement ring. It's just a promise ring. But it sure is beautiful, isn't it?" she exclaimed.

Priscilla didn't want to make her daughter feel bad after she was so excited to have the ring. "Yes, honey, it sure is a nice ring. I know Larry is very fond of you. He's real good to you. Your

----

dad said that he is a good man, and he's proved that to us a few months ago."

"I love him, Mom."

"I know that you do, and I believe that he loves you too. You kids are young, so I just want you to take things slowly."

"We are, Mom. We're just enjoy going out and watching movies and going bowling. We won't be doing what a lot of the other kids are doing?"

"What are the other kids doing?"

"Mom, some of them are getting so serious that they are sleeping together, some are smoking dope and drinking. Larry and I both don't want anything to do with that stuff, He's a good Christian man."

"Yes, he is. I've been watching him the way he is with you. I like to see how he opens up a door for you, instead of you opening it up or him walking in first. I know both of his parents well, and I know that they are very good people. They taught their son well."

"I really like his mom and dad. They are very nice to me too. They treat me like they would a daughter if they had one."

"Yes, they do like you. I was talking with his mother just yesterday at the party, and she told me how much her and her husband enjoy having you over at their house when Larry takes you over there."

"We play board games all the time when I'm over there. Have you ever heard of the game called Dreamopoly?"

"No, I haven't. What kind of game is that?"

"It's a board game a lot like monopoly, but better, I think. They have the game, and I'd like us to get it so we can play it at home. I think that you and Dad would really like it too, even David would like it."

"Why don't we go to the store and see if we can find one and buy it then? I haven't played games in a long time, and I'd love to play games with my family. If you would like, you can ask Larry if he wants to come over and play with us."

"Okay. I'll call him up, but after we see if we can find the game first."

Just as the two were talking about buying the game, David came into the kitchen. "What are you guys planning on buying so soon after the party? Didn't you get everything you wanted last night?"

"I was telling Mom about a game that Larry's parents have. It's a real fun game, and I'd like us to have it so we can all play."

"Oh, what kind of a game is it, a board game of some sort?"

"Yes, it is, but it is so much fun. I just love it."

"I'd like to go with you to the store. I need to pick up some things there."

"None of us have eaten yet this morning. Why don't we go out to a place to eat?" Priscilla asked.

"Okay, but I need to get out of my pajamas and get some clothes on," Terri said.

"Both of you get ready so we can go get a bite to eat and then find that game."

"Okay, I'll be right down," Terri yelled as she took off running up to her bedroom."

The morning was going good for Priscilla and her children until they were to have a run in with Mark Clayborn.

"Hi there, Terri," Mark said, standing close to her, while she was sitting down at a table in the restaurant.

Terri looked up, and without saying a word to him, she looked at her mom. "Mom, this is Mark."

Priscilla looked up from where she was sitting to see the young man who had tried to take advantage of her daughter. "So you are the young man that my daughter had better sense than to go out with you, huh."

No one said a word. They just all looked so surprised to hear her say that to a guy she had just met.

"Why is everyone just looking at me? It's true, isn't it? You were not so polite to my daughter now, were you?" she asked him, waiting for an answer.

"If a man can't have his way with a girl, then what would be the sense in going out with them?" Mark replied.

"Are you for real? I wonder what your folks would think about you saying that to me?"

"Who do you think taught me that but good ole dad? My dad raised me by himself and told me to take what I can get. So that is just what I aim to do—take what I can get."

"Then I feel sorry for you to have someone who is supposed to love you and teach you to do the right things, but have taught you to get what you can from life, even if these are things that don't belong to you." Priscilla was shaking her head back and forth.

"Whatever, I guess that you would rather see her with a loser like Larry than a man like me," Mark commented.

"Yes, a man like Larry is what her father and I want for our daughter. Mark, will you kindly leave my children and I alone now? We would like to eat in quietness."

"Oh, by the way give my best to your husband. I think that he was some great man when he chose to sell her off in the first place."

Before anyone could even respond to the nasty words that came out of his mouth, David jumped to his feet and punched Mark right in his face. Knocking him to the floor, the manager came running out from behind the counter to see what was going on.

"What is this?" he asked.

"Here is our money for our food. We will be going before things get worse," Priscilla replied, getting up from her seat.

As they were walking out of the restaurant, Mark got back up on his two feet, just to yell out some more insults before the door closed behind the trio. "I'm going to sue you for laying your hands on me."

"Mom, do you think that he can sue me?" David asked when walking to the car.

"No, of course not! Whoever heard of such a thing. That's the last thing I would be worried about. Terri, what I'd like to know is whatever did you see in him in the first place."

"I don't know…isn't it crazy to see good in people who aren't any good?" Terri said.

"No, that's not wrong to see good in people. It's wrong when the people we see good in don't live up to what we see."

"That's true. I never really liked him in the first place. I just liked the thought of going out with a guy every girl in school wanted to go out with. But Larry is altogether a different person than Mark. He is so sweet and handsome. He's a good Christian guy, and that means the world to me."

"Let's forget about Mark shall we? I don't want him to ruin our time out. We need to go to the store and look for that board game so we can go home and play it later on today."

After they had gotten everything from the store, including the game, they went back home. The car ride was nothing like it was on their ride into town. It was a ride of quietness; everyone seemed to be in a world all of their own. Their own space in the car, with their own thoughts, went uninterrupted until a tire went flat, which drove the car over to the side of the road. Taking a better hold of the steering wheel, Priscilla stopped the car and asked David if he knew how to change a tire.

"I've never had to change one before, and Dad never showed me how to. I'll go to the neighbors right over there and see if I can use their phone and call Dad to come and help us."

David was gone for a matter of minutes, then he came back with the news of his dad was on his way to change the tire.

After James had gotten to the car to change the tire, he noticed that Priscilla looked upset; he wasn't sure if it was because of what happened with the tire or if was something else.

"Honey I see a look of discouragement written all over you, is it the tire, or is there more to it?" he asked.

"I wanted to spend a little time with the kids going out to eat breakfast, but would you know who came along to ruin everything, to where we never even got to finish up with our breakfast?" Priscilla answered.

"Who?"

"You remember that boy Terri wanted to go out with before her and Larry got together?"

"Mark, wasn't it?"

"Yes, he is not a very nice kid at all. He came over to our table and started to talk nothing but junk. He even went as far as to say that you sold our daughter because she wasn't worth keeping."

James didn't know what to say at first; he finished changing the tire in silence. Priscilla watched him and wondered if she should have just kept what had happened at the restaurant to herself. She knew that when she spoke about selling their daughter, she had said too much. James was still trying to forget what he had done so long ago. Now some kid who didn't have a clue about his life back then would say something so mean and hateful, he just wasn't going to stand for it.

"I'll see you at home tonight after work. I'll stop in at Jeffery's first and pick you up another tire, then I'll be home." James walked away without waiting for her to reply. He got back into his truck like he was out to get someone. He had the look of anger written all over his face, and now he was leaving Priscilla standing next to her car without another word spoken to her.

James didn't go right back to work; he went to go see Mark and his dad. He was so upset at what Priscilla had told him that he needed to know why Mark would ever make a remark to Priscilla about selling their daughter. Pulling into the driveway, the first thing that he noticed was a 1977 Trans Am car sitting right there. He knew that had to be Mark's car. Terri had mentioned before that Mr. Clayborn had bought Mark a new car. Parking behind the car in case the boy would want to leave when he'd see James show up, he began to walk up the driveway to the sidewalk that led to the house, getting madder by the moment at what he had heard he said to his family. Without thinking about how loud he was going to be hitting the door, he began to pound on it, causing both Mr. Clayborn and his son to jump up to their feet and run to the door to see what all the pounding was about.

When the two men opened the door to the house, before James even thought about what he was going to do, he grabbed the son out of the house by his shirt and began to shake him, yelling things at him that the father of the boy couldn't understand. Mr. Clayborn grabbed ahold of the back of James's shirt and threw him to the ground. The two men began to yell and scream at each other, and neither one of them was hearing what the other was saying. The neighbor on the right side of the house came running over when he saw that the two men were punching each other. What James didn't know at the time was that the neighbor was a cop. He showed them his badge and told them that if they didn't stop their fighting, someone would be going to jail.

"Hey, hey, break it up! What's this all about?" he yelled, standing in between both of the men after James got back on his two feet. "Now what is going on with the two of you that would bring you to act like children?"

James stood there, trying to calm down; he was so upset at the statement his wife told him that Mark had made. Catching his breath so he could talk to the police officer, he allowed Mr. Clayborn to talk first.

"I don't know who this man even is, but my son and I were sitting into our home when we heard this terrible pounding on the door. It just about gave me a heart attack when he pounded like he did. We both jumped to our feet and ran to the door when this man grabbed ahold of my son and began to shake him all over."

"What do you have to say about this?" the officer asked James.

"I did grab his son, but it was after his son walked up to my wife and kids when they were having breakfast in town, and he said to my wife that I sold my daughter because she wasn't worth keeping."

The officer looked at Mr. Clayborn, wondering what kind of statement that was for him to say, then he looked at the son. "Did you make this kind of a remark to this man's family?"

"What difference does it make? It's true he sold his daughter for money, just so he can buy the grocery store."

"That's not what happened at all, and you have no right to ever talk to my wife and my children like you did." James looked over at the officer and told more of what this boy had done. "He wanted to go out with my daughter, and when she wouldn't go out with him, he began to grab her butt and talk dirty to her. He began to bother her all during school. When she walks in the hallway trying to get to her classroom, he will call her names, and he told her that his father told him that when he wants something in life, don't take no for an answer but take what you want."

"Is that how you have taught your son to behave himself? If that is, sir, then you have failed your child. Unless you want this man who loves his family bring charges up against your son for harassment, then I suggest that you better begin to teach your son how to behave like a proper young man."

"You are going to let him come over to my home and grab my son and shake him like he did, and you talk to me about my son?"

"Sir, if your son hadn't done what he did to this man's family, then he wouldn't have a reason to come here in the first place." The officer told him with a very stern look on his face. "And as for you young man, if I ever hear of you bothering this man's daughter again or any of his family members, I will come and pick you up myself and bring you downtown. Do I make myself clear?"

"Yes," Mark answered.

As James started to walk back to his car, he looked down at the dirt that was all over him. He had grass stains on his pants and his shirt elbows from being thrown to the ground. He began to brush off as much dirt as he could. He didn't want anyone from his store seeing him look like he was just playing a game of football. All the while why he stood by his car cleaning himself, he could hear Mr. Clayborn complaining about his son getting yelled at by the cop.

James was happy that the officer understood where he was coming from and told Mark that he had to leave his family alone. But how was he going to explain the grass stains to Priscilla? What would he say when she would see them when she did the laundry? Would he tell her a lie? No, he couldn't do that again— look where a lie got him before. He knew he needed to tell her the truth about everything, even if it meant her getting mad at him for going over to the Clayborns in the first place. He went to get his wife's tire fixed, then he headed home to go face the music.

Upon entering his home, Priscilla was standing in the kitchen, making her and Terri some coffee, when she saw James come through the door. By the look that was on her face as he was entering the house, James wasn't sure if he should walk right back out the door or if he should close the door behind him.

Before he could make a decision on what to do, Priscilla opened her mouth. "What on God's green earth happened to you?"

"I did something I never thought I would do."

"And what was that? Did you play hooky from work and go play some football instead?"

"No, not quite. I went over to the Clayborns to have a talk with that Mark kid. But after I got there, I got even the madder than I was when you first told me what happened. I began to bang on their door real hard, and when he and his dad came to the door and swung it open like they were such tough guys, I went kind of crazy."

"What do you mean you went kind of crazy? What did you do, James?" Priscilla asked.

"I grabbed the kid and pulled him out of his home. I began to yell and shake him like he was a little rag doll."

"So how did your clothes get grass stains all over them? I just can't believe you did that in the first place." She was shaking her head back and forth.

"I know. I can't believe I did that, either, but as far as the stains on my clothes, they came from his dad." He stopped for just a minute when he saw the way that his wife was looking at him. "His dad grabbed me away from Mark and threw me to the ground. Then before I even realized what was happening to me, I jumped back up, then he and I started fighting with each other, when the neighbor who is a cop came over and broke us up."

"A cop! You have got to be kidding me! Whatever came over you to cause you to act like you're still in school fighting like you're still a child, James? Really…wow, honey. So what did the police officer do?"

"The funny thing is I didn't get into any trouble at all. He told Mark that he better never hear of him bothering my family ever again. Mark's dad was so upset, but after meeting him, I can see why Mark is the way he is. He is a replica of his father. I sure hope the boy wises up before it's too late. I sure hope that he realizes his father is not a very nice person and he doesn't want to be like him.

"Honey, you were out of line going there in the first place. You could have gone to jail for what you did. I know that your heart was in the right place, but if something like this ever happens, will you please go to the police yourself before doing something crazy like that again?"

"Yes, honey, I promise I will never do something like that again. I'll let the law take care of it for me."

"Why don't you go and change your clothes so I can put some spray on your pants to get the stains out of them?"

"Yes, honey." James started to chuckle some at what he did, acting like a teenager again.

After he was out of the room, it gave the two ladies of the house room to talk without him being in the room.

"Wow, can you believe Dad going over there and fighting like that?" Terri commented.

The two got so caught up into their talking that they never noticed when James came down right in front of them and walked out the door without saying a word because he didn't want to interrupt their conversation. He was headed back to work.

"The last time I have known that your dad had a fight was way back in school, and it was with his best friend now."

"Are you telling me that he and Greg fought in school? Why?" Terri asked.

"Because I was Greg's girlfriend at the time, and I wanted to break up with him to go out with your dad. So when Greg knew I wanted to dump him for your dad, he thought that it was because your dad did something to encourage me."

"Well, did he?"

"No, not at all. I was friends with your dad, but after we spent time hanging out and talking, I realized that I liked him and not Greg in a romantic way. So I broke up with Greg so I could go out with your dad."

"Wow, after all the time that Greg and Penny come over here, this is the first time I'm hearing about this."

"When you were young, I thought you might want to date their son, Matt, when you grow up."

"Matt Martin? No, he's cute and all, but he's younger than me. I would never go out with someone younger than me."

"What, he can't be that much younger than you and David are. You act like he's a few years younger."

"No, I'm just not interested in anyone but Larry, and I know that Matt is only a few months younger than I am."

"Here's your coffee with just the right amount of cream and sugar in it." Priscilla said as she handed her daughter the cup.

"Thanks, Mom. I love it when the weekend gets here so we can sit down and have our coffee together. My mom and I used to do that to, and it was some of the best talks we ever had."

"I used to have coffee with my mother when I was a young girl too. It too was some of the best memories I have of her and me together. Mentioning my mom brings me to the thought of my dad. I haven't heard anything from him in a long time."

"Why didn't Grandpa come to our birthday party?"

"Julie's daughter has been very sick for the last few months, and they take care of her, so they were unable to come. Maybe I'll give him a call today and see when he plans on coming to see us."

"I miss seeing him. I never got to know him very well as my grandpa."

"I'll call him today and ask if he and Julie would like to come for a visit if her daughter is feeling better. I'll tell him that his granddaughter would like to get to know him more."

"Thanks, Mom. Do you think he will come for a visit?"

"Yes, honey, I'm sure he will. Now I don't know about if Julie will be coming with him. I'm going to call him here in a little while."

"Why would you think Julie might not want to come with him? Is she his wife?" Terri asked.

"Ever since she and my dad married, she hasn't cared to come visit us that much. I think that she likes to stick close to home where her daughter is at."

"Well, I think that's not fair for Grandpa not being able to see you, his only daughter. Mom, if Julie doesn't want to come, are you going to ask Grandpa to come anyway?"

"Yes, honey, I am. He has not come here in over a year because she hasn't wanted to. But like you said, I am his only daughter, and I want to see my dad. We went to see him the last time. Now it's his turn to come and see us," Priscilla said as she walked over to pick up the phone. "I'm going to call him right now and let him know we are missing them."

Terri sat at the table, drinking her coffee, waiting to find out what her grandpa had to say to her mom. She listened as her mother was speaking to him.

"Oh no, Dad, that is terrible! I'm so sorry to hear that. Is there anything that I can do to help?" Priscilla looked at Terri, concern reflected in her eyes.

"Yes, there is something, honey. You can keep us in your prayers. Julie is trying so hard to do everything right, in hopes that it will keep her daughter alive."

"We sure will be praying. I will let James know why we haven't got to see the two of you in a while. Tell Julie we are praying for her."

"Okay, honey, tell the family I love them and hope to see them soon."

After Priscilla and her father hung up, she felt terrible for the bad thoughts that she felt toward Julie not wanting to come and see them when all along, the poor woman was going through so much pain of trying to keep her only child alive. There must be something that she could do to help out.

I just have to help, but what can I do, Priscilla thought as she sat again at the table with Terri, not saying a word.

"Mom, what is it? Who's sick? Is it Julie?" Terri asked.

"No, it's her daughter, Becky. The doctor's say she has cancer, and she isn't expected to live for much longer."

Terri's eyes opened wide—that was what killed her mom Marcia.

Priscilla saw the look on her face then felt terrible for telling her about the cancer; she knew that it was a touchy situation for Terri. But now that it was out there, she had to try and get Terri to understand that some people just get cancer and die.

"Is she going to die like my mom did?" Terri asked softly.

"I don't now, honey, if she will. I pray that God heals her. Right now, my dad and Julie are going through a lot of pain with taking care of her day and night without getting a break from their work. There must be something I can do for them."

"Mom, what about if you were to go to them and let them have some time away from their duties of caring for her? Maybe you can go and help Becky get better."

"You know, honey, I think you're right. I can go to them and help. Your dad is here to see you and David get up for school, and he will be here shortly after you get home. That is, if I could convince him into not getting into any more fights and staying out of the grass, I would be able to go then." She chuckled after saying that comment about the fights and the grass.

"So when Dad comes back home from work, are you going to talk with him about it?"

"Yes, I sure am. I think he will have no problem with me going. And by what you said, I don't think that you will, either."

"No, Mom, I don't have a problem. It's not like David and I are little children anymore. We can clean and cook while you're gone."

"I know you can, but I still want to talk with David about this before I go running off. I don't think he will care, either, but I still want him to know my plan."

"When you have talked with him and Dad, when do you think you are going?"

"Probably tomorrow."

THE ROAD TRIP

PRISCILLA WAS PACKING up enough clothes and personal belongings to stay two weeks with her dad and his wife. She never told them ahead of time that she was coming down to Tennessee. She knew that with the travel time on the road, she had plenty of time to think about a good plan on getting them out of the house were they could relax with each other and she would care for her stepsister.

"Honey, I want you to call me as soon as you reach your dad's, and be very careful on traveling the roads. I love you, and I don't want you to worry about us here. We are all going to be fine," James said as he pulled his wife close to him and gave her a big bear hug and a kiss.

"I'll call you just as soon as I get there. I love you too, honey. Come on, kids, give your mom a hug." She gave her kids and James a hug, then she was headed down the road, waving good-bye to her family. Although she wanted to go and help her dad and his wife, her heart felt all broken as she was driving down the road, leaving her family behind.

"Come on, kids, it's time to be off for school. The bus will be here any minute from now," James said as he stood close by the road, still watching as his wife's car slowly disappeared out of sight. Looking toward the kids, he could see sadness in their eyes, just as he was feeling, with his wife leaving for a couple of weeks. He knew she was doing what she felt that she needed to do, and he was there to support her decision.

"Dad, are you going to miss, Mom?" David asked, while Terri stood close enough to hear his answer.

"Yes, of course. One day away from your mother is a day too much. But she will be back in a couple of weeks. So for now, we will have to all help each other with housework and cooking."

"I told Mom that David and I would do the housework and the cooking. My mom taught me how to take care of a house before she passed away."

"Oh well, thanks for offering me." David gave Terri a sly look as he walked toward the house to grab his things before the bus come to pick them up.

"I know you're not used to doing any housework or cooking, but by the time I'm done teaching you everything you need to know, you'll never have to wait on Mom or any other woman to cook for you."

"Oh gee, thanks! I like Mom cooking for me," David replied sarcastically.

"And she still can, but just maybe one day you and I will want to surprise her and Dad and make them a nice meal. After all that the two of them do for us, I think that is the least we can do for them."

"I agree. Mom and Dad both take good care of us, and we never have to go without. I'll help you and not give you any trouble, either."

"Thanks, David, I can use the help in this place. It's quite a bit larger than what you lived in before. My mom taught me when I was quite young how to pick up after myself, and I loved to help her cook all the time. I even know how to can too, even though we never did a lot of that because Nick would get mad at my mom whenever she canned."

The two were waiting for their bus as they continued to talk.

"Why would he get mad at her whenever she would can?" David asked.

"Because he said it took too much time away from him when he came home from work."

"Wow, really, that sounds a little selfish to me."

"It was selfish! He wasn't a very nice person to my mom or to me."

"I'm sorry you had to go through all of that. I liked your mom. She was always very nice to me. And my mom loved her, well, our mom loved her," David corrected himself.

"I know what you meant. Does it bother you when you hear me call Marcia my mom? Because she really was my mom to me."

"No, I know that she raised you, and this is all new to you. Well, to be honest, it's new to all of us, and at times, when you call our mother mom, it sounds funny to me. But then I just have to remember that we are brother and sister, so that makes her your mother just as much as she is mine. Does that make any sense to you?"

"Perfect sense," she answered him, giving him a warm smile.

While on the bus, the two overheard someone saying that the two of them had a crush on each other. Looking at each other and then around to see who was making such a stupid remark, they found it to be a little fifth grader not knowing that they were brother and sister. Not letting it go for the sake of others thinking like that, David looked at the kid and told him that the two of them are brother and sister.

"Then how come she didn't always ride the bus with you before?" the boy asked.

Not wanting to bring up an old can of worms again and wanting to just forget what he was asked, he replied, "She did. We just picked her up at another place."

Surprised by that answer, the boy never questioned him again. David was happy he never had any more to say to him. He hated it whenever he was questioned about him and Terri being brother and sister and not being raised together. He loved his dad and hated it whenever someone would say something against him.

"Don't you hate it when someone asks you questions about us?" Terri asked.

"Yes, I do, as if we had anything to do with what happened." David was sounding very irritated. "I'm just glad he didn't bother to say anything else to us, like people have done in the past."

"Me too. I feel so bad whenever people question me about it. I hate answering their questions. I just thank God that not too many people will say anything about it anymore. But there is always going to be that one person who crawls out of the woodwork to act like they know it all and try to tell you the way it was."

"I know, but if the same people keep asking me the same questions, I think I'm just going to punch them right in the mouth."

"If you do that, then you will be acting like Dad did the other day with Mark. Just tell them to mind their own business."

"Terri, either you're just too nice sometimes or you just feel you need to say that because you're a girl, and girls don't act like guys. Well, at least for the most part, they don't."

"Here we are at school. I hope that I see Larry. I didn't talk with him too much yesterday, and I miss him."

"I have to admit he seems to be a swell guy. I don't mind if my little sister goes out with him," David said laughingly.

"Oh yeah, your little sister, yeah right."

"I was born first."

"Oh what, by a few minutes? Who cares?" She chuckled.

Terri got her wish when she walked in the school—Larry was standing by the door, waiting for her as she entered. "Hey, beautiful, how are you doing this fine day?"

"I'm okay. My mom left to go to Tennessee for two weeks to go see my grandpa."

"Really, for two weeks, huh?"

"Yep, so David and I are going to be doing all the cooking and cleaning ourselves."

"That will be all new for him then, won't it?" Larry asked.

"It sure will. By the time my mother gets back home, he will know how to do his own cooking and cleaning."

"Oh yeah, so what's he think about that?"

"He said he's all for it. I better get to class before I get yelled at again by the teacher. I'll see you at lunch."

Priscilla was driving along singing when she heard what sounded like someone locking up their brakes. She looked at her rear mirror to see if that someone was coming up behind her, and when not seeing anyone, the next thing she heard was a loud crash. Looking over on the other side of the road, she could see that a car had smashed into the back end of another car. Seeing that everyone was coming to a quick stop, she herself stopped to see if anyone was hurt, not being able to see who was involved whether it was a woman with children or a man. She parked her car on the side of the road to see if she could be of some service.

Walking up to the smashed cars and peeking into the window, she yelled, "Is anyone hurt?" She saw what seemed to be an older man as the one driving the car that hit the one in front of him. "Sir, are you all right?"

"I'm all right. What about the people in front of me, are they all right?"

Priscilla looked in front of her while still standing next to the older man's car. She could see that there were already several other folks gathered around that car. "I'll go and see," she told the man.

Walking up to the other car and trying to get close enough to see who was inside the vehicle, she lightly pushed her way to the front and looked inside. Seeing it was a young woman, who was sitting up with the look of shock on her face, she asked her if she was all right.

"I think so. My dad's going to kill me for wrecking his car."

"Oh, I don't think that he will be mad. After all, it wasn't your fault, and I think he will be so happy just to know you're alive when this could have been much worse. Do you think you can move?" she asked her, seeing how tight she had her fingers gripping around the steering wheel.

"Yes, I think so." The girl tried to move her hands off of the wheel. "Is the person behind me okay?"

"He said that he is, but I'm going back there now to see if he is okay."

Walking away from the young girl, Priscilla felt sorry for her. She was blessed to be alive, but her worse fear was what her father would do to her when he'd find out about his car. Did this girl get love in her home, or was it a home without a father telling his daughter that he loved her no matter what happened in life?

Approaching the elderly man's car to see if he was okay, she overheard someone standing next to his car say that he was dead. Her heart sank way down to the pit of her stomach. *What? How can that be?* she thought. He had just told her that he was fine and had wanted to know if the person in front of him was okay. Priscilla got closer, and looking in at the man now slumped over the steering wheel, she reached her hand on the inside to check for his pulse, but when she didn't find one, she began to cry. Did this man whom she had just talked to a few minutes ago know Jesus as his Lord and Savior, or did he leave this world to a place called hell, where he will never know peace or love again? Hearing that an ambulance was coming closer to them, she looked up to see if she could get back to her car and out of their way.

Priscilla stayed on the side of the road for more than an hour, watching them put a cloth over the man's body and cover his face, then placing him at the back of an ambulance to take his dead body to the morgue. She watched as they put the frightened young girl at the back of another ambulance to take her to a hospital. Priscilla, being the loving mother that she was, prayed that the father of this girl would embrace her with love that she had only hoped for. She wanted to stop somewhere and use a payphone to call James to tell him what she had witnessed in the six hours that she was on the road.

Fear began to grip a hold of her when she started down the road again. She had never traveled by herself for a long period of time before. *Maybe I should have kept Terri out of school and brought her down here with me.* She had her mind racing on all the things that she thought she should have done. Remembering the words of God saying he gives his children peace, she began to think on the promises of God to get rid of the fear that she was feeling.

"Lord," she prayed, "I thank you for keeping that young girl safe, and I ask you that whomever is family to that man who just died, you speak to their heart and bring comfort to them. In your mighty name, I pray, amen."

As she was driving along, she noticed that there was a payphone outside of a party store, so she pulled her car over and parked right in front of the phone so she could call James up. She told him what had happened and how it had made her feel not knowing if the man had known Jesus as his Lord and Savior. Her heart sank at the very thought of her not knowing that he was going to die and not being able to share the love of Jesus with him. She felt guilt deep down inside of her, one that she couldn't even explain.

"Honey, now I want you to stop blaming yourself for that man's death. I know you wish you could have known, but you must remember that God knew this was going to take place ahead of time. Honey, I want you to pray and listen to some peaceful music the rest of the way down there. And then call me when you get there. I want to know you made it there okay."

After they hung up, she went over in her head the things that he told her to do. She put in an eight-track tape with soothing music that she loved to listen to. She knew it would help her to relax and not be so tensed about the accident.

"God, please save the girl if she doesn't know you, and I thank you for it," she prayed.

The rest of her ride down to see her dad was peaceful; she traveled several hours listening to her music and talking to God about the young girl in the car accident and about what she could do that would bring help to her dad and his wife and her stepsister. She was about ten miles from her father's house when her car began to swerve all over the road. Trying to get her car under control, she pulled over to the side of the road to see if it was a flat tire. She managed to pull over to the side, then got out and found the tire that went flat was the same one that James had just put on.

"How can this be? James just put this tire on. And I'm so close to Dad's. Now I will have to call him to come and help me," she talked to herself. She did not want to call her father up, as she so wanted it to be a surprise to both her dad and his wife. As she was looking around to see where the closest place was to go use a phone, she noticed that a truck had pulled over behind her car.

"Howdy!" came a deep southern voice from a short, round, robust man. "You having car trouble?"

"I have a flat on my front passenger side. My husband had just put it on a couple of days ago."

"Do you have a spare?"

"Yes, I believe he put one in my trunk."

The man walked to the back of her car as she popped open her trunk. He began to take everything out that he needed to fix her tire.

"Where ya'll comin from? Don't sound like ya from around these parts," the man commented.

"No, I'm not. I'm from up North."

"Where's about?" he asked while taking her tire off.

"I'm from Port Sanilac, Michigan. It's right by Lake Huron. Do you know where that is?" Priscilla asked the round man, who looked just as round as the tire that he had taken off her car.

"Can't say that I have. I lived in these parts pert near all of my life. What brings you to this neck of the woods?"

"I'm going to see my dad and his wife."

"It's all fixed now, ma'am. I wish you luck with your travel."

"I thank you so much for all your kind help. God bless you, sir."

"Oh, that's quite all right there. Glad that I was a comin down the road right when it took place. Bye," the man stated as he walked back to his truck.

Priscilla watched him as he walked back and got into his truck. *What a nice man he was. Thank you Lord for sending him my way to fix my tire for me.* She got back into her car and started down the road toward her father's once again.

After pulling into her father's driveway and shutting off her car, she started up the long walk to the front door. She stood there fixing her hair the best that she could before ringing the doorbell. Her hair was blown to the side of her face from the wind blowing; every time she straightened it out, it would just blow back to her side. After it did the same thing, no matter how she had tried to fix it, she finally decided to ring the doorbell.

Opening the door, her father stood there in shock. "Priscilla, what a nice surprise! What brings you here?"

"Hi, Dad, I have missed you! After our talk the other day, well, I just decided to come and see you guys. I would like to be of some kind of help to you two."

"Come on in here, Priscilla. I'll go get Julie." She watched as her father walked away to go and get his wife. Within a moment, he was back without her. "Where's Julie?"

"She's getting herself cleaned up. She'll be here in a minute. Becky seemed to take a turn for the worse overnight, and neither of us had any chance of sleep. I worry about Julie. She's trying to be so strong for Becky, and she's not willing to let her go."

Julie came out of the bedroom looking as best that she could after her not having any sleep the night before. "Hello, Priscilla, it's so good to see you. Your father and I have wanted to come and see ya'll, but with my daughter being ill, it's been just too hard to get away. You understand, don't you?"

"Yes, I understand. I came down to give you and my dad some help."

"I appreciate you coming this far for nothing. I don't need anyone's help. She is my daughter, and I will be the one to help her," she snapped at Priscilla.

"Now, honey, Priscilla knows that she's your daughter, and she isn't here to take over. But, honey, she knows that neither you or I have had any sleep, and if we are going to be some kind of help for Becky, then we must stay strong for her before something happens to one of us and no one will be here to care for her. All she wants to do is allow us to get a little rest so we will be here for Becky. Come on, honey, let's show her what must be done so you and I can have a little rest."

Julie looked over at Priscilla with sorrowful eyes. "I'm so sorry, honey, for what I said to you. It's just I'm so tired and I am so afraid of losing my daughter."

"I know you are. Why don't you show me what to do, and then you can sleep for a while? And don't you worry, I'll come get you just the minute something happens."

"What about you, my dear? You came all the way here with the long drive and all. We haven't even asked you if you are hungry or tired or in need of anything," Robert said.

"I would like a cup of coffee or some tea, and at this time, that's all I need. I want the two of you to get some sleep. And don't worry, I'll wake you in just a few hours."

Priscilla went into Becky's bedroom; as soon as she took her first step into the room, it had the smell of death. It was a smell that seemed to have never left her after the loss of her best friend, Marcia. It was a smell that she knew all too well from the loss of her mother and friends over the years. Now to smell it again, all she could do was pray. She knelt down at the bedside of her stepsister and began to talk to God.

"Father God, I come before you with thanksgiving for who you are and to ask you for a miracle."

She remembered that same prayer she asked for her best friend, Marcia, and yet she still died. But she knew that prayer was all they had left, and she knew that God does answer prayer.

"God, please, if for any reason you can find to let Becky live and not die, I ask you to breathe health into her body once again. Let her enjoy life on earth again and show her that you are truly the healer."

She wiped Becky's face down with a cool cloth that was on the end table next to the bed. She began to sing a song of praise to light up the gloomy feeling that was all over the room.

"I find joy, when I know that God is standing here with me. I find peace, when he is always near. His stripes has healed me, and I am made whole again."

As she continued to sing the song that was sung in the little country church to where she has been a member of for nine years, she could feel that darkness and death leaving the room. All of a sudden, after singing and praising God for about an hour, the smell of death was not lingering in the air anymore. She felt excitement hit her insides, like God was doing a miracle on Becky. She looked down at her lying there silent and so still, hoping to see her open her eyes and ask, "Why am I lying down in the middle of the day? I should be up doing something."

Looking at her lifeless body and still believing, she sensed that God was doing something. She let her dad and Julie sleep for six straight hours; she knew that she was in need of sleep before she was to drop right where she was standing. She drove for many hours without sleep, not to mention the hunger pains that she was now having. She knew that she would be no good to anyone if she too was to take ill. She decided it was time to wake her father up.

Walking to his bedroom door, she tapped lightly on it so she wouldn't startle them. "Dad, can I come in?"

"Yes," he answered in a low voice.

"Dad, maybe you or Julie should come and sit with Becky now. I am so very tired. If I don't get a little bite to eat and some sleep, I will just drop."

"Oh sure, honey. I'm getting up right now." He looked over at his wife lying next to him, and she didn't even flinch. "I'll let her sleep for a while longer, then I will get her up. She has been so tired lately. How does Becky seem to you?"

"I was singing and praying, and I felt the gloomy feeling I had when I first walked in there leave. I just believe God is doing something for her," Priscilla stated confidently.

"Wouldn't that be wonderful for God to bring a complete healing to her? Oh, how my wife would rejoice with laughter and thanksgiving."

"Dad, if I don't get a little bite to eat, I will be sick myself," she reminded him.

"Come on in here, honey." He began to walk toward the kitchen. "What are you craving for?"

"I'm not really craving for any one thing. I just know that if I don't get something in me, then I will be sick. I came down here to help you and Julie with Becky, so I need my strength so I will be able to help more."

Robert brought out a plate of leftover roast beef so she could make herself a sandwich. "Here, honey, I hope you still like roast beef."

"I love roast beef! This is fine, Dad. Thank you. Do you mind if I take a little nap after I eat? I feel so tired."

"By all means. You eat, then you go to the bedroom at the end of the hall and get yourself some sleep. I'll wake you in a few hours. We will take turns with Becky, if you don't mind."

"No, of course not. The one big reason that I came down here is to help out. I thought since you couldn't come to me because you were so busy caring for her, I would come and lend a helping hand."

Robert walked over to his daughter and gave her a warm hug. "Thank you for coming all this way to help us. As much as I hate to admit it, we needed you to come and give us a hand. Sometimes, we as parents think we can handle everything without asking someone else for help. Now I know that you must know what I'm talking about, you being a mother yourself."

"Yes, I do. Oftentimes I could use some help, but I would try to get it done all by myself, instead of asking others for help. This roast beef is really good. Is this what you made, or did Julie make this?"

"It's mine. These days I do most all of the cooking. And I'm fine with that. She likes to spend every waking moment with Becky. As you can tell by how long she is sleeping, she has worn herself out."

"Thanks, Dad, for the food. I think I will go take that nap now."

"You go ahead, honey, get yourself some sleep. I'm going to check in on Becky now."

As Robert walked into the room where Becky lay in her bed, he approached it slowly as he began praying. He could feel peace as he entered the room. Looking down at her as her eyes were closed shut, as they had been for several months now, he noticed that her fingers were tapping the bed as if she was hearing some kind of music. He couldn't believe what he was seeing. She was moving! That was something she had not done for a long time. He could hardly keep his composure; he began to yell almost at the top of his voice.

"Julie, Priscilla, come here! Hurry, come here." He waited for a few minutes, watching her very close, waiting for the ladies to come running into the bedroom to see what all the yelling was for. But when no one seemed to care nor hear, he went to Julie with the exciting news. "Julie, wake up. Becky is moving."

"What do you mean she's moving?"

Robert watched as his wife jumped out of bed so frantically, grabbing her clothes that lay on the floor next to the bed. "Honey, slow down."

"Why should I slow down? Didn't you just tell me that she is moving?"

"Yes, but I don't mean that she's up and running. It was her fingers," he said as he looked at his wife now standing listening to him.

"Her fingers? What about her fingers? Is she moving or not?" she asked, a little annoyed.

"Honey, I walked into her bedroom, and as I walked up to the bed, she was tapping her fingers on the bed. It was like she was tapping to some music. But that's the first time she even moved in months. Isn't that worth getting excited over it?"

"If she is tapping her fingers like you say that she is, then you are darn right it's worth getting excited. If you don't mind, I will go take a look at her for myself." She started to go out the bedroom door when she realized how she must have sounded. "Oh, honey, I don't mean to sound like you don't know what you're talking about. It's just I want to see my daughter move after all of this time."

"Come on, you will see she is tapping her fingers on the bed."

As the two walked into Becky's bedroom, Julie approached the hospital bed she was lying in. "Oh dear God! My baby is tapping her fingers." She stood as if she was frozen in place, with her hand over her mouth and tears now flowing on her cheeks. "What can this mean?"

"Maybe we should try and wake her? Maybe she's trying to wake up and needs our help. I'm going to go get Priscilla up and see what she thinks."

"Becky, Becky," Julie called, patting the side of her face lightly. She stood there hoping to see her daughter wake up, but after she stood there for what seemed to her like hours, Priscilla joined her in talking to Becky.

"Becky, it's me Priscilla. Your mom and my dad are here with you. Becky, can you hear me?"

The three stood there hoping to see a change in her movement, but still there was no change.

"Honey, I'm sorry I woke you up. I just thought that she was trying to wake up and that you could help her get up," Robert told Priscilla, knowing she had just lain down not long ago.

"Dad, I think it was brought on by my singing to her. Maybe you and Julie will want to sing to her and see if it helps wake her up.

Priscilla went to lie back down. She felt so tired, yet she wanted to know if Becky was trying to come out of her coma that she slipped into a few months ago. She knew that if she didn't get some kind of sleep, which usually required more than fifteen minutes, she wouldn't be any good to her dad, Julie, or Becky.

Julie and Robert began to sing to Becky about Jesus; the two refused to give up on her. All Julie wanted was to see her daughter healed and walking and talking again.

THE WAKE

PRISCILLA HAD SPENT her two weeks with her dad and his wife, and there was no more change in Becky than when she began tapping her fingers on the bed. She knew it was time for her to return home to her family. She had done all that she came to do; now her family needed her at home.

"Dad, Julie, keep singing to her. It was after I sang to her that she began this tapping, and that is more than where she was at before the singing. Don't give up. I believe she will come out of the coma soon. I have to go home to my James and kids. They need me, and I need them."

Priscilla was in her car and backing out of the driveway when her father came running out of the home screaming.

"Stop! Stop!"

Priscilla slammed on her brakes, not knowing why her father was screaming and waving his hand, motioning for her to come back into the house.

"Dad, what's wrong?"

"It's Becky."

"What about Becky?" she asked worriedly, seeing his facial expressions.

"She's awake! Becky's awake!"

Priscilla, without a thought, slammed the door to her car and ran into the house right behind her father.

"I really believed that God was going to touch her," she said as she headed down the hallway that led to Becky's bedroom. Opening up the door to her room and seeing Julie leaning over her daughter with tears and laughter all mixed up in one, Priscilla knew that it was all for joy. "Well hello, stranger," she said as Becky looked at her. "How do you feel?"

"I'm not sure how I should feel," Becky said as she sat with the look of shock written all over her face. "Mom, I'm not sure what's going on here? Can you help me to understand?"

"Well, sure, honey. Can you remember anything?" Julie asked.

"No not really." Becky sat there in thought, and then it was like she remembered something. "I remember Tim walking out on me because I got sick and the doctors said I would die."

"Yes, honey, he did leave you. You came to live with Robert and me a few months ago when you took real sick and couldn't care for yourself anymore."

"How long have I been asleep for?"

Julie looked at Robert. "What, it's been about two or three months now?"

"Yes, honey, it's been at least that long," Robert answered her bending down to give Becky a hug and a kiss on her forehead. "It's so good to see that you have woke up. How do you feel?" He asked the question that was once asked and never really answered.

"I feel good, maybe a little dazed, but good. I actually feel hungry."

Everyone started to laugh that one of the first things she felt after sleeping for so long was hunger.

"I will go right now and fix you something to eat," Julie said as she was ready to head out the bedroom door.

"You stay here with her and get caught up with life things. I will go and make something for her," Priscilla offered, but with a demand that Julie must stay with her daughter.

"Oh, thank you, Priscilla! I trust you know where everything is by now?" Julie asked.

"Yes, I do. I'll be back in a jiffy."

And she was gone to make something special for the long sleeper. *I better call James to let him know I might be staying and extra day or two just to help out a little more*, she told herself, picking up the phone and walking over to the fridge to find something for Becky to eat.

"Hello, honey," she said as James answered the phone. She told him of how she was leaving and ready to come back home when Becky woke up. After getting off the phone and preparing a light food for Becky to eat, she walked back to Becky's room just to find that she was out of her bed and was walking toward the kitchen.

"Oh you're up," she said as she saw how her father and Julie were walking on each side of her to stablilize her. "Well, come sit down here and try and eat." Placing the bowl of vegetable soup on the table for her, she sat down on a chair on the other side of the table. "I made this just today. It's very good. I didn't want to give you anything to heavy after you not eating solids for quite some time."

"Thank you so much for everything you have done for me and your dad and my mother. They told me how you came all the way down here to help them out with me and how you began singing to me when I moved for the first time in months."

"What are sisters for if it's not to help each other out?"

It was the beginning of many blessings for Priscilla. Not only did she get her child back after her being taken from her as a baby, but she also gained the love of her father and stepmother, along with gaining a sister. She felt that her life had found more purpose and meaning than ever before. Priscilla returned home to her husband and kids after a three-week stay with her father. She was welcomed home with love and warmth and promised that next trip she took would be with those she loved the most.